In Death's Shadow

Siobhan Muir

ISBN: 1-947221-00-0
ISBN-13: 978-1-947221-00-0

DEDICATION

Dedicated to Cara Michaels, for planting the seed.

ACKNOWLEDGMENTS

This story has been brewing a long time. It started with just an idea from a flashfiction challenge. Then it morphed into a whole world where TAKE THE REINS and A CENTAUR'S SOLSTICE WISH came into play. I have to thank Cara Michaels for all her brainstorming and messaging story building. I think we spent hours coming up with this idea and now it finally has a full form. Thanks to Silver James for taking the time to catch my typos and inconsistencies, and to my ARCtic Circle review crew who read the tale. Thanks also to model Philippe Lemire and photographer Paul Henry Serres for producing such a magnificent image for the hero, Quinn Tarlen. Great thanks to Kris Norris for creating this amazing new cover with Philippe's image and the beautiful woman in the fur coat, capturing the hero and heroine perfectly.

CHAPTER ONE

Quinn charged through the snow, each booted foot landing precisely with a muted thud. The breath puffed out before him with each stride, leaving a tell-tale sign of his passing as much as his tracks in the snow. His forward motion remained unhindered by the bow strung across his chest or small crossbow at his hip.

He'd been running a long time and his lungs burned from the frigid air sawing in his chest. He left an easy trail, but it couldn't be helped and the snow fell thick enough his prints would disappear. *Eventually.* Hopefully soon enough to evade capture by the army of ragged misfits on his tail. He'd taken out their captain per his contract, but the small page boy who'd cared for the captain's dogs returned early from their evening walk, and caught him leaving.

Quinn might be an assassin, but he didn't kill innocent children.

Unfortunately, it had set the camp all astir and they'd mobilized to come after him. His damn horse had fallen in with the regiment's mounts and he'd been unable to return to it. So he bolted, hurtling straight into a blinding snowstorm, hoping to make it to the

Centaur domain before his pursuers caught up to him.

The open land seemed to stretch on forever and he scanned the white drifts ahead for shelter, or anything to disguise his trail. A dark smudge on the horizon flashed through the swirling flecks filling the air and he pushed back his hood to see better. Cliffs? Trees? Army? All were possibilities, but the wrong choice could have him meeting his dark patron—death. They hadn't made a date yet, and Quinn hoped the encounter hadn't been added to his current schedule.

Slowing his strides, he pushed on, dragging the tails of his coat behind him to obscure his tracks. The wind had stopped and silence followed the crunch of his feet in the snow. He paused and held his breath, listening over the thunder of his own heartbeat.

Soft, cotton silence met his ears and nothing moved on the land except the falling flakes. He waited a few moments longer, but nothing came to his straining senses, and he resumed his trek toward the hint of structure on the horizon.

Time passed in increments of breaths and heartbeats, but the smudge resolved into a forest. *Shit.* That meant he'd miscalculated and hadn't made it to the Centaur lands. They had some forest forts, but the trees grew widely spaced there, and this forest sat choked with thick undergrowth. *Dryads. Fuck.*

The dryads had no love of humans after some fiasco, the details of which only they remembered. *And I'm as human as they come.* He knew the basics of the story. Twelve princesses had been charged with espionage and collusion, and had paid dearly for it. The dryads had turned them into brightly colored lamps gracing some of their creeks in response. *Served them right.* He had no sympathy, not when their father had put his own brother to death over their disappearance.

Another world, another time.

The past couldn't change his present. The dryads remained unforgiving and he was out of time. Voices echoed across the snow and he pulled out his spyglass to scan the snowy valley behind him. Riders and dogs forged through the drifts, heading his way.

No hope for it. He'd have to brave the forest. Quinn cursed under his breath and picked his way into the undergrowth. The bushes within held no snow, but slowed his passage. He resisted the urge to climb. If he wanted any friendliness from the dryads he had to respect their homes. He pushed his way deeper among the trees and pulled off his bow as he searched for a good place to hide and wait.

Settling behind some thick rhododendrons, he pushed his white hood off and grimaced at the cold biting his ears. He notched an arrow and held it loosely as he scanned the tree line. Black trunks and shrubs obscured most of his view, but sound carried well as his trackers approached.

"Cripes, it's the feckin' dryad forest, it is. I ain't goin' in there!" The rough voice barely made it over the yelps and barks of the hounds.

"Don't be such a ninny, Garlic. You know he went in there and he killed the Cap'n. He couldn't have made it far. Go on, now." Quinn recognized the captain's second-in-command.

"No one comes outta there alive, y'hear? I ain't goin' in." Garlic stood his ground.

The Second sighed. "Then send in the hounds. That's what they're for, right?"

But the dogs only milled around in the snow and whined, picking up the fear of their handler. Quinn's neck prickled with the dryads' magic, but he held his silence and waited.

"Oh for fuck's sake!" A whip cracked and the hounds yelped, but none entered the trees. "Fine. I'll

3

show you cowards how it's done."

The Second spurred his horse toward the break in the undergrowth, but the animal reared and squealed in protest. He cursed and yanked the reins, forcing his mount between the trunks. When the understory proved too thick to pass, he hacked at it with his sword, scoring the bark and bushes with his blade.

Whispers and a subsonic rumbling spread through the woods, raising the hair on the back of Quinn's neck. A breeze rattled the bare branches, but he saw no other movement beyond the man slashing his way into the forest. Quinn held his bow in a tight grip and breathed shallowly to keep the white plumes steaming from his nose small.

Suddenly the horse screamed as vines wrapped around its legs with thorns large enough to see from a distance. The animal struggled, jerking and lurching regardless of the man's grip on its mouth. Bloody foam sprinkled the trunks and bushes around it and the man shouted in frustration and fear.

The horse broke free and reared again, tossing the man from its back before plunging out of the forest toward its herdmates. The Second hit the ground with a grunt and slowly turned over. He muttered balefully and pushed up, only to be pinned to the ground with two great spears. He shrieked as he writhed around the one through his gut, but the second in his shoulder held him still.

"Akers?" The men outside sounded scared.

"I told yous." Garlic pulled the hounds back from the trees. "I told yous no one goes in that comes out."

Akers's cries settled down to whimpers and he tried to reach for his sword, but the thorny vines curled around the hilt and dragged the blade into the underbrush. Tall men appeared in the forest as if pine boughs had learned to walk. Intricate tattoos covered the exposed portions of their skin, giving the appearance of fine-grained wood. Only three stood around the pegged man, but Quinn suspected the trees hid others.

"Men are not welcome here, human. The message has been made clear."

"Please, please, I meant no harm," Akers wheezed.

"You hacked at our trees, scarred them, broke our brother shrubs' branches." The dryad's voice remained implacable. "For that there is a price."

Akers struggled again, but the spears held him fast. "We were chasing an assassin who killed our friend. I had to get through. He came in first…"

"But he did no damage and he will be dealt with."

Quinn's gut sank, but he held still. No need to draw attention to himself quite yet.

"Please…"

The lead dryad stared for a long time then nodded. "Very well, I shall grant you relief."

"Thank you." Akers relaxed just before a vine snaked around his throat. He inhaled to protest, but the vine tightened and he squeaked his panic.

"I relieve you of your ignorant life and you may take your lack of respect with you. Begone." The dryad turned away as the vine choked Akers into silence, his body kicking and shaking. An eerie crunch filled the forest followed by a wet tearing and the head rolled free of the twitching body.

"Take the body and bury it. It shall offer nourishment for the saplings." The dryad leader nudged the head with his boot toe. "Toss this out to his compatriots to renew the warnings."

Two dryads grasped the body and tore it from its spear moorings before dragging it away. A third grasped the head and hurled it out of the trees to land among the men and dogs still waiting to see if Akers would return.

Not today.

Panic ensued and they scrambled away from the forest back the way they'd come.

Quinn had seen his fair share of death—had dealt most of it—but beheading by vine topped his list of things to avoid at the moment. He remained crouched, weighing his options of escape. While they hadn't attacked him outright, he suspected the dryads knew where he hid. Quinn returned the arrow to his quiver and hung his bow across his chest. While he could probably take down several of them, he stood on their home turf and they could easily call in reinforcements.

No hope for it. He'd have to beg forgiveness and asylum. He tugged the hood back onto his head and stood. No point in hiding. They knew where he was. He latched the restraints on his visible knives and hatchet, and crossed his arms over his chest as he waited.

Quinn heard them before they appeared, but the space between sound and arrival couldn't be measured. Faced with the same dryad leader as Akers, Quinn raised his hands from his chest, opening his fingers wide.

"I seek asylum with the dryads of the Arborium and wish to speak with the Keeper of the Grove."

CHAPTER TWO

Maiasora Silvercloak stood on the banks of Luminara Creek and stretched her arms above her head. Her back cracked like snapping twigs, and she groaned. How long had the dryads kept her as a lamp this time? It seemed shorter than usual, though she couldn't tell from the sounds her back made.

Her gaze rested on the trail beside the creek and the rocks glistening in the pale light left from a recent storm. Her sisters should be waking up from their forced transformation soon and she'd have to listen to them bemoan their fates.

She and her eleven sisters had made one mistake.

Well, Inge made the mistake and the rest of us paid for it by being turned into lamps.

Inge had been determined to go visit the dryads every chance she got, and her sisters had trailed along for the party and dancing. But Inge had been seeing a lover, one of the dryads' holy folk known as a druid. The man seduced her into showing him dryad secrets to which he wasn't privy. How Inge knew them or where to find them, Maia never learned. But when he stole the artifacts and fled, Inge was blamed for her collusion, and the rest of her sisters were transformed into warning lanterns.

Literally. *But at least they gave us fancy stained-glass shades to keep the rain off.*

No rain today. Maia stared down at her dress and frowned. *Looking a little threadbare.* She doubted the dryads would give her new clothes, but it couldn't hurt to ask. At least the party dress she'd worn all these years remained clean. *Gotta love magic.*

She shot a look at the sky between the trees. Fat white flakes of snow fell through the branches, but didn't stick to the ground. She frowned. She couldn't recall a time when she'd seen it snow in the dryads' realm. She shivered as an icy wind curled along the stream in the fading daylight. *Odd.* The dryads had never awakened her in winter. Her gaze strayed to her other two sister lamps lining this creek. Why weren't either of them changing into their human forms?

Another frigid breeze snaked down her neck, carrying voices through the trees.

"Why are we to bring this one to the Grove? I thought we'd be done with them."

"The Keeper wants to speak with one. It has something to do with the assassin."

Maia gulped. *Assassin?*

"I don't know why the Keeper allows such dreck to live, even in lamp form. They made a grievous mistake allowing the artifact to be stolen."

"And it will be remedied. The Keeper has clues to its recovery and now wants to speak to one of them."

"Dreck, I tell you."

Two male dryads appeared and stopped within sight, their expressions hard. "The Keeper summons you, princess."

Maia swallowed her unease and gathered her skirts, wishing she had a shawl. Hard to look presentable in a tattered party dress. She suspected her appearance would be the least of her worries. She took a deep breath and raised her chin, marching after them. They'd have to take her as she came.

Neither of her escorts appeared to find the temperature uncomfortable, but men made of wood probably didn't feel much of anything. Her teeth chattered as they passed beneath the ornate arbor framing the entrance to the sacred Grove.

Tall Sequoias formed the apices of a twelve-sided space, creating a great hall of trees. Smaller species of scrub oak, fig, ponderosa, vine maple, apple, and alder filled in the gaps between the thicker trunks in artful designs. Maia suspected every species of tree had a place in the sacred grove.

The dryads led her to the end of the arboreal hall where the great spreading oak, the Elder Tree, presided over all. The roots of the giant had formed a more human-sized throne, complete with mossy seat for whoever sat there. Currently, a hard-eyed woman with a crown resembling a Bonsai tree occupied the seat and she offered no smile as Maia approached.

Not that I expected one.

Maia recognized the robes to the Keeper of the Grove, but the person had changed. This woman on the throne carried herself with less anger and more patience than the old man she remembered. Maia scanned the new Keeper, sensing something familiar about her, but the intimidation was the same since Maia and her sisters had come dancing that fateful evening. Trying not to step on the fringe from her ragged skirts, Maia curtseyed and waited to hear what the Keeper wanted.

"You're one of the women who came to dance the night the artifact was stolen all those years ago, correct?"

Maia raised her head. "Yes…Majesty."

The enigmatic woman looked her over with cold eyes. She wore the traditional wood grain tattoos common to the dryads and displayed the same superior attitude those with magic often offered to the "lesser" classes. *No, I'm not bitter at all.*

"We need you to find it, princess."

Maia bit her lip. "What, Your Majesty?"

"Don't play dumb with me. The artifact that was stolen by your sister's lover. We need you to find it for us."

How in the gods' names am I supposed to do that? Maia struggled to control her expression. "Why do you think I could be of service, Majesty?"

"Are you refusing to help, princess?"

"No, Majesty." Maia bowed her head. "I just don't understand how I can find it when I knew nothing about it even at the time it was stolen. Why do you think I have the skills you lack with all your druids and dryads?"

A small smile curled the Keeper's lips. "That's a good point. However, your family had connection to the artifact. That's why you were allowed into our world night after night to begin with. And how your sister had…relations with the Dark Druid." A grimace worked its way across the Keeper's face before it smoothed out once more. "The time of anger is done, but now we must recover the artifact the Dark Druid stole from us. Your family, and you in particular I've heard, have the ability to sense the magic unique to the artifact."

Maia frowned in thought. "I know my family was sensitive to magic. But I never saw this artifact you keep referring to." The ability had allowed them to come dancing with the dryads back when it had seemed a frivolous adventure. "Why do you think I'm the most sensitive to its magic?"

"Call it an intuition." An enigmatic smile curled the Keeper's lips and Maia suppressed a shiver. "Because of that sensitivity, we need you to go find this artifact and return it to us. I suspect it has a familiar energy signature."

"Wouldn't my elder sister Inge be better suited to this

task? She's seen the artifact and must have known more about it than all of us. Shouldn't she be the one to find it for you?"

The Keeper exchanged a look with one of her guards and the dryad looked away with chagrin. "They weren't told?"

"No, Keeper. There wasn't time."

"I wasn't told what?" Maia's gut sank as the silence stretched.

"Your elder sister was put to death for colluding with the Dark Druid."

Maia gaped. They'd killed her sister because the man they called the Dark Druid seduced her into showing him what he wanted? *So it was Inge's fault? That's hardly fair.* Maia hadn't particularly liked her elder sister, but she hadn't wished her dead. Anger simmered, but she recognized these people were far more powerful than she could fight. They still had control for the time being.

"You killed my sister and turned the rest of us into lamps to illuminate your forest creeks, but now you want me to help you? Why should I? What benefit could it be to me to help those who killed and imprisoned my family for a mistake made by your own people?"

"It was a dark time in our history and we seek to correct the destruction of those events." The Keeper gave her a compassionate look filled with sorrow and regret.

Damn right you should regret it. But Maia held her tongue. Maybe she could use this to her advantage. *They accused us of being manipulating and conniving. They ain't seen nothing yet.* She'd give them a taste of true manipulation.

"Do you still have this ability, princess, or should we continue our search for someone who does?"

Maia shrugged. "I don't know, to be honest. Do you have anything with the same energy signature of the artifact you're looking for?"

Another exchange of looks made her wonder what else they hid from her. *So much for openness and honesty.*

"We don't have anything left of it, but my energy and magic is similar, and while that is waning, it's something you can learn to see." The Keeper dropped her hands to her sides and tilted her head expectantly. "Do you still have the ability to see this energy?"

Maia stared at the woman, allowing her eyes to unfocus. Swirls of energy surrounded the whole clearing in muted earthy colors. They rose like wavering heat mirages in the desert, and she shifted her gaze to the current Keeper of the Grove. Brilliant green and gold light burst from the being in front of her. Outwardly, she appeared like a human woman, but within Maia's sight, she stood as tall as the tree of life, with roots and branches of undulating light spearing in all directions.

Yeah, I can still sense the energy.

Maia pulled her senses back until the Grove settled into normalcy. "I still have the ability, Majesty."

"I think I hear a 'but' in there." The Keeper tilted her head.

"Not a 'but' so much as an inquiry for negotiation." Maia met her gaze wearing her best polite impassivity. "Perhaps I might trade on my skills for something I want."

A half smile quirked the Keeper's lips. "What did you have in mind?"

"I suppose that all depends on what you need me to do. You say you need me to find this special artifact, but it was stolen some time ago."

"Three hundred years have passed since it's loss."

Maia jerked in surprise, but stored that information away for later consideration. "Three hundred years ago. Do you have any idea where the artifact might be, Majesty?"

"No, that's why we're asking you to start the search."

The dryness in the Keeper's voice could've cracked Maia's skin as the woman rose and stepped forward. She appeared to float down the steps of her dais. Maia shoved a spike of envy away. She'd practiced for years to get that kind of grace, but never mastered it.

And then I became a lamp, so no walking for me.

The Keeper strode around Maia, her gaze fixed on the tattered dress. Maia refused to be embarrassed. She would've had better clothes for this audience if they'd given them to her, but they never bothered. She raised her chin and stood tall. *Clothes don't make the woman or the leader.* Her father had once said that and she believed it. Living up to it took determination in the face of the Keeper, however.

"What I need from you is your awareness of this energy and your willingness to complete a quest to find it. We have a few leads on where to look, but we have no idea if it's in one piece or disguised. It may be in ordinary objects or otherwise unremarkable. I need someone who can pick out the correct signature."

Maia nodded slowly. "Do you believe it to be in this world?"

The Keeper paused and raised her chin, her eyes narrowing. "Why do you ask?"

Maia shrugged. "I know there are more worlds than just this one in which to hide something. Is that what happened to it?"

The Keeper shook her head. "We don't exactly know, but we don't think so."

"So you want me to wander this world and others looking for your artifact. That seems like a fairly tall order."

The Keeper snorted. "If it wasn't, we wouldn't be asking for help."

"True enough. Very well. Here's what I want in trade. I want my life back. I want to know that was the last time I'll be a lamp in the dryad's realm. Once I do this job for you, I'll be free, and so will my two next youngest sisters."

She raised her own chin. "And I want it in writing."

The Keeper matched her, stare for stare, for several heartbeats, but Maia refused to back down. She'd been their docile light fixture for long enough. They wanted her help? Fine, but they'd have to compensate her, and give her life back.

Eventually a smile curled the Keeper's lips and she nodded. "Done. Broadfir, make sure someone takes notes and gets this written up. I don't want anything to be missed."

Maia blinked. They actually agreed to her request. *Thanks be to the saints.* She wanted to ask about her other sisters, but now didn't seem to be the time to push things. The new Keeper struck her as someone who'd hear petitions, but pushing her too far too fast would end all negotiations. The dryads had been less than friendly and Maia made a practice of avoiding them as much as possible. But the Keeper didn't act anything like the others she remembered.

"The only problem I can see is I don't know this world as well as I should. Being a lamp rather curtailed my explorations." She chose not to smirk, but the Keeper coughed a laugh.

The woman clapped her on the shoulder with a smile. "Fortunately, we have someone who can help with the navigation. All we need from you is to sense the artifact wherever he takes you." She waved at her second. "Bring in the assassin."

I have to trust an assassin?

Two more dryad guards appeared, this time flanking a tall man in a white, hooded coat. He bristled with bow, quiver, knife hilts, sword, and a small hand axe slung all around his body, a body broad across the shoulders and silent in motion. The hair on the back of her neck rose with a combination of attraction and fear. This man was a predator, the most deadly kind, and Maia didn't like the thrill zinging through her. *He's not sexy. I can't even see his face.*

He stopped beside them and studied each of them without moving. Maia did her best to keep still, but his perusal unsettled her and she fought the urge to run. *Who is this man?* The dryad guards looked as uncomfortable with the stranger as she felt.

"I see you didn't kill anyone while waiting." The Keeper chuckled at the guards' tension. "This is good. Now we have a proposition for you, assassin. You want safe passage across our lands and asylum from the rabble following you. We need you to search for an artifact with the same energy signature as myself."

"Pardon, Keeper, but how am I to find this missing artifact? I cannot sense magic." The robed man spread his hands and the guards gripped their weapons tighter. Maia suspected they wouldn't get them up fast enough if he chose to attack them.

"That's where she comes in." The Keeper waved at Maia. "Quinn Tarlen, master assassin, meet Princess Maiasora Silvercloak, seeker of the artifact."

Quinn's chin rose and his icy green gaze slammed into Maia, surprise and animosity sparking in the depths.

"I'm sorry, Keeper. I shall take my chances with the mob. I cannot do as you ask."

Cold fury laced his voice as he turned his gaze on the dryad leader, and Maia swallowed hard against the snub as her anger kicked in. *What the hell have I ever done to you? I've been a lamp, for the Goddess' sake.*

"Why not?" Both she and the Keeper spoke at the same time, but Maia kept her gaze on Quinn.

He didn't meet her gaze, staring at the Keeper. "I cannot work with my brother's murderer."

Astonishment shut Maia up completely. Murderer? She frantically searched her memory, but she couldn't remember any violence after her transformation into a light fixture.

****

Quinn clenched his fists to keep from throwing a blade straight into the wicked bitch's throat. How could the dryad Keeper ask him to take the enemy with him on a mission? He'd sooner run naked through the deep snow than spend any time with the little whore who caused the death of his brother.

"That's rather rich coming from a professional assassin, isn't it?" The Keeper raised an eyebrow.

"I am not a murderer." The young woman in the shabby dress lifted her chin and crossed her arms over her ample chest. "I couldn't have killed anyone. I've been a lamp for centuries."

"Centuries?" He snorted. "You don't look old enough to have been here so long. And your father killed my brother, my *younger* brother, less than thirty years ago. I should know as I've been in this world that long."

The Keeper shrugged. "Time works different here than in your world, Tarlen. You may have arrived "soon" after they disappeared in your time, but time is not always equal across the rifts between worlds. It's true the princesses were cursed for their negligence centuries ago and thus they have remained."

"Negligence seems to be a common trait in her family," Quinn remarked and the princess glared at him, her coffee-brown eyes flashing. "However long it's been, my brother's still dead."

He remembered coffee—the sweet creamy drink warming him from the inside out. But he'd lost the warmth with his brother. All for one fateful night when the princesses hadn't come home from their stupid revelries and his brother had paid the price.

"Why do you think she killed your brother?"

"Because he was the last one she and her sisters drugged to escape her father's castle. And her father killed him when they didn't come home." He swung his fury on the princess. "Do you even remember Sean, princess? A man searching for his fortune only to fall prey to your machinations."

She shook her head. "You think I drugged your brother? I never touched the tea served to him."

"But you went along with it." He bit back his snarl and turned to the Keeper. "My brother would be alive if she and her sisters had returned." Quinn raised his chin and crossed his arms over his chest. "I'll take my leave of you as soon as I'm able."

"I didn't kill your brother. I have no idea who you are." The wench mirrored his stance, her feminine curves barely hidden by the ragged clothes distracting him. Yet she still managed to look regal.

"Nevertheless, your actions caused his death." His gaze flickered shamelessly over her body. "You're without honor and therefore, not worthy of my company."

"Without honor." The princess snorted and raised an eyebrow. "This coming from a man who sneaks up behind people and slits their throats? You have no room to talk."

"I didn't ask for your input or opinions, princess." Quinn returned his gaze to the dryad Keeper's face. "As I said, Keeper. I'll take my chances with the mob."

"I'm afraid that storm has passed." She didn't smile, but a hint of amusement showed in her expression. "I have a quest I need completed and you have the need of safe passage through the forest. Princess Maia can locate what we're looking for, and you can get her there. Plus you'll be able to avoid the mob. Sounds like a win-win situation to me."

Anger kindled in his chest, but he kept his expression impassive. "Are you threatening me, Keeper?"

"No, just making sure the consequences of your

choices are very clear." The Keeper tilted her head. "You have a problem with past actions done by this king. The princess can make it up to you if you let her."

"Work or wither. Is that my choice?"

The Keeper shrugged. "It doesn't have to be that way. We'd probably feed you, but you wouldn't be leaving our domain any time soon. Perhaps you'd prefer the luxurious accommodations of being a lamp along a stream." She narrowed her eyes. "Although, I think you'd make a much better weapons locker given the array of arms you have on you."

"You mean, work or die."

"It's not death, really. Ask Maia. She's been a lamp for centuries. Think of it as illuminated immortality." The Keeper grinned, giving her a surprisingly youthful appearance.

He switched his gaze to the princess. She wore a scowl and didn't appear afraid of him at all. *I can change that.* But for now the better part of valor seemed to be agreeable. If worst came to worst, he could kill her once they'd left the dryads' grounds and be free.

He returned his gaze to the Keeper. "Very well. I accept your terms."

"Excellent." The Keeper nodded. "We shall outfit you with clothing, provisions, and supplies, and whatever clues we currently have to the whereabouts of the artifact. Now, both of you take my hands, please."

"Your hands?" Quinn raised his eyebrows.

"Yes, this will bind you to each other in an effort to keep you both alive for the duration of the quest." A smirk curled the Keeper's lips. "And keep you honest with each other, at least about the other's well-being."

They each grasped her hands and she closed her eyes, humming a tuneless sound that echoed in his breastbone. Vibrations shot through him and the scent of cloves hit his nose just before everything settled and the Keeper let go.

"There, now it is done. You have the night to prepare and shall leave in the morning." The Keeper retreated to her throne on the dais. "Broadfir will show you to your quarters for the night and outfit you accordingly on the morrow. Thank you for your service and may the winds support your leaves." She waved them out, her expression settling into wooden impassivity.

Quinn shot a glance at Maia, but the princess straightened her spine and marched out of the Grove ahead of him, her head held high. He snorted. *I'm just biding my time, princess.* He wouldn't have to be bound to her forever. He'd make sure.

CHAPTER THREE

Maia settled her pack on her back and pulled her hood up onto her head. The dryads had given her exactly what they promised, including a long coat with fur lined cuffs and hood, and thick insulated boots. She had extra clothes in the pack along with a first aid kid, a fire kit, water skins, and light-weight but warm sleeping blankets. They also had travel food, something the magic had compressed to make for easy packing.

Definitely better than being a lamp.

But her companion left a lot to be desired. *Beauty to look at, but beastly to talk to.* Yeah, if anyone embodied a fairytale, Quinn nailed it. If he took the role of villain. Dangerous, scary villain. *But sexy.*

She bit back a groan. Why did women always think bad boys were wonderful? He spent his time either ignoring her or scowling, neither of which constituted pleasant company. *There is something so wrong with me.* He'd make a nice wall-hanging, something to look at or admire, but not a good partner. In anything.

She shot another look at him from under her lowered lashes. He wore his long, white hooded jacket over trousers and tall brown boots. The visible weapons made him bristle, but she knew there were plenty she couldn't see. *Not to mention the sneaky way he's proficient at killing.* She'd never hear him coming.

Maia shook her head and closed her eyes, trying to settle her trepidation. She took slow, deep breaths to find whatever center she had and on a whim, tested for the energy of the Keeper. As expected, bloom of energy pulsed to her left from where she'd seen the Keeper standing. But another, faded shimmer of energy came from behind her. It wasn't strong, but it was present.

Hang on, if I can sense the artifact, why can't they?

Before she could ask, the Keeper called for their attention. "Your quest is this: You must find the Key to the worlds' gates. It may be in one piece or several, but included in your map case is the known drawings of this item. Find it, return it to us, and your contracts will be fulfilled. Princess Maiasora, your younger two sisters have been included in your contract and they shall be free to go upon your return. You'll find it in writing as you requested."

Maia pulled out her map folio and opened it to check the contents. The contract sat behind the hand-drawn map and the illustrations of the Key. The images were vague and so were the descriptions. *Oh, that's much better.* She resisted the urge to roll her eyes. *Guess I'll just have to depend on my sense of the damn things.*

She glanced at Quinn, but he hadn't moved. He remained as stoic as a marble statue. *And just as friendly.* She sighed. This was going to be a long trip. She stuffed the folio with its contents back into her pack.

"Our guards will escort you to the borders of our domain in the direction we suspect you'll find the Key. We expect you to return by midsummer when the sun reaches its solstice." The Keeper gave them a benevolent smile, but Maia wasn't fooled.

"And if we haven't completed the task by that time?"

The Keeper's expression turned impassive. "Then your sisters shall be put to death."

And there are the dryads I know and "love."

Anger bloomed in Maia's chest and she raised her chin, but kept her mouth shut. The Keeper stared her down as if daring her to challenge, but Maia said nothing. She'd bide her time and figure out a way to save her younger sisters. Even if she had to steal the lamps and find a shaman or magician to break the spell herself.

"You have what you need and you have your instructions. May the Earth Goddess bless your way and give you fair weather." The Keeper looked so benevolent as she had the guards usher Maia and Quinn out of the Grove.

Too bad she's a manipulative, soulless bitch who will kill my family if I don't do what she wants.

Maia followed after the guards, keeping her head down and her thoughts to herself. She had no idea if Quinn came with them. She couldn't hear him at all. *How the hell does he move so quietly?* She tossed a look behind her to see if he was there and met his hostile gaze. *Good thing he's paying attention. I might have run off.* As if she could outrun him. He hadn't been a lamp for centuries and those shoulders sat packed with muscle.

Still sexy.

Focus on the journey.

They made it to the edge of the forest and the guards said nothing, not even "here you are" as they stopped at the treeline. Maia raised her eyebrows and waited to see if they'd do anything, but Quinn marched resolutely out into the snow without a backward glance.

Guess we're on our own from here.

She sighed and followed after him. A light snowfall floated from the leaden sky and she used Quinn's tracks to save some of her energy as he plowed through the drifts. She wondered where he was going since he didn't know the way, but she was content to follow him long enough to get away from the forest. She wouldn't be able to sense anything beyond the Keeper if they didn't get some distance.

They hadn't gone far, maybe two hundred yards, and her body already ached and cried out with fatigue. *Holy hell, being a lamp killed all my endurance.* She allowed herself to stop to catch her breath and turned to look at the forest. She had no idea if Quinn had stopped, but he'd figure it out soon enough. She needed a breather anyway.

"What are you doing? We need to get going." His snarled statement made her want to throw snow at him.

"Wait for it…" She turned her gaze back to the forest.

After about thirty seconds, the forest shivered like a mirage in the sunlight and lost all its color as if the life had drained out of it. The low hum that had been in the back of her mind ceased and the silence of the snowy world swelled into her awareness.

"Okay, now we should be able to figure out where to go."

Quinn scowled. "You couldn't figure it out before?"

"No, genius. I had to wait until I could no longer sense the Keeper since she has the same energy as the object we're searching for. No use in going backwards now, is it?" Maia shook her head. If he was going to be a jackass the whole trip, she could give as good as she got.

She took a deep breath and closed her eyes, opening her senses as she ignored her companion. The world shifted from dull white and gray to unusually vibrant colors. The ground slumbered in indigo blue while the snow appeared more turquoise. She turned slowly, looking into the distance. The forest wore drab olive green with brighter green leaking from between the trunks. *That's the Keeper's energy.*

Swinging to her left, she looked for similar light against the turquoise and indigo world. A faint glimmer beckoned to her against the horizon. *Guess we'll go that way.* She opened her eyes and met Quinn's scowl with a bland look. *Still there I see.* She hoped he wouldn't maintain it for long.

"That way." She pointed into the snowy wastes.

"You're sure?"

She sealed her lips over a snarky response. "Yes. Are you going to lead the way or do you want me to?"

He growled something about irritating bitches and marched off into the snow. *At least he got the direction right.* She followed after him, glad she didn't have to break trail.

****

Quinn tried to breathe through his deepening ire, but the woman following behind infuriated him more than anyone he'd ever met, including his Assassin's Guild brothers and sisters. He'd figured once they were beyond the reach of the dryads he'd be able to break the binding spell and kill the princess without repercussions. But all his attempts had been met with excruciating pain. Apparently the spell even reacted to intentions.

Fuck.

So she remained alive and behind him, moving painfully slow through the snow. Surprisingly, she didn't complain or ask him to rest every ten minutes. She slogged on without comment, her head bent to keep the snowflakes out of her face. He wanted to push her hard into misery just because he could, but even he had to stop to eat at midday.

They'd been traveling into the white nothingness for hours and he had no idea if they closed in on anything resembling shelter. His legs ached from constantly breaking the trail through the deep snow and his breath sawed in his chest from the exertion. *Damn, I hate walking in snow.* He took them down into the swale of a drift out of the wind and stopped.

"We'll break for a meal then be on our way."

He hunkered down, not caring if she followed suit or not. He didn't want to care about anything she did. It frustrated him that he couldn't figure out a way to rid himself of her company, but every attempt, even subtle ones, was met with blinding pain. Anything he tried to do to her came back on him double.

"Are we still going the right direction?" It galled him to ask, but he didn't need to be off course any more than she did.

"Yes, the right direction." Maia didn't look up, just worked on eating.

At least she didn't natter on and on, that was a relief. He preferred silence and the company of his own thoughts. Despite this, he found himself annoyed at her lack of response. He expected her to rail at him for not trusting her and expound on why he should. But she did neither and soon it was time to go again.

"Which direction, Princess?" He readjusted his pack as he prepared to set off.

She raised her face and closed her eyes, standing still for several moments like a snow maiden statue. Her beauty struck him in that moment and he had a flash of what she'd look like smelling flowers he'd gifted her or enjoying a rare sunny moment.

What the fuck is wrong with me?

Before he could berate himself more, the princess opened her eyes and pointed just over his right shoulder. "We need to go that way. The energy signal is getting stronger."

"Good. Hopefully, we'll find shelter in that direction, too."

Maia nodded, resettled her pack on her back, and waited for him to lead them on. His annoyance rose again, this time at her expectation, even when he knew she couldn't break the trail for them. He stuffed his anger down deep and headed out, shuffling through the snow to give her an easier path.

Which makes no sense at all. Except that her fatigue and painful body strain dragged at him. *I'm only making it easier so it doesn't mess with me.* Despite the legitimacy of the thoughts, it felt inaccurate.

He spent time puzzling over the dichotomy as he trudged along. Despite the meal they'd had, his exhaustion dogged his every step, but he pushed it aside to keep going. He lost track of time, the cold monotony of slogging through the heavy, wet snow creating a dangerous brain-fog of numbness. When the rocks appeared out of the gathering gloom, he whipped out a blade and a cascade of sparks decorated the snow from his strike.

Rocks. That meant they'd stopped walking the plains at some point. He looked up, trying to figure out where they were. A solid rock monolith rose out of the ground in front of them, but he spied a way around it to the left. Sparse trees dotted the hillside in black shadows obscured by the driving snow. The wind whistled through them, tugging at his hood and swirling the snow.

Storm is getting worse.

But the hillside and monolith gave hope to finding shelter and wood for a fire. Quinn turned and looked for Maia to tell her he'd find a place to hole up to wait out the storm. To his surprise, she wasn't in sight.

What the fuck? Was she so slow that she couldn't keep up with his easy pace? Where the hell was she?

"Princess?" The wind swallowed his voice in its increasing howl and no response other than its whistle came to his ears.

The snow fell harder now and if he didn't go look for Maia, their path would be swallowed up in drifts. *Sonuvaprick!* He retraced his steps already filling with new snow, his eyes scanning the monochrome world around him.

"Princess!" He shouted the word, hoping she'd hear and respond. *She can't be that far back, can she?*

He kept going, searching the landscape as the snow pelted his face. The longer he walked the more concerned he grew. Where had she gone? Had she fallen? Why hadn't he noticed? He knew the answer to the last question, but didn't like it. The fatigue he'd felt had dropped him into survival mode and he'd shut out everything else. But he realized the exhaustion had come from her and he'd ignored the moment she'd reached the end of her endurance.

"Princess!" He shouted it again as an oddly shaped lump appeared out of the snowy gloom. While the dryads had given her a "white" coat, it had enough gray in it to be seen against the snow.

He pushed his body into a run to reach her. "Maia?"

She lay face down in the snow, her body very still.

"Maia!" No response. "Sonuvaprick!"

He pulled her up, her body flopping bonelessly, and turned her over. Gray skin and blue lips met his gaze and his gut sank. Was she already hypothermic? He dropped is face close to hers and found her breath barely warming his skin.

Shit.

He hauled her up onto his shoulder in a fireman's carry and headed back the way he'd come. He had to find her shelter soon or she'd die, and probably take him with her. The fatigue had already started to drag at him again with her nearness.

"Hold on, Maia. Let me get you somewhere warmer."

He couldn't sprint through the snow with her added weight, but he made good time back to the monolith at the base of the hills. He thought he remembered the structure from an earlier time when he'd traveled in this part of the world. These hills had caves, giant vesicles left from when volcanic gases escaped the cooling rock. Some would be filled with other animals seeking shelter, but he suspected he'd find at least one unoccupied for their use.

The snow fell harder, the flakes growing smaller as the temperature dropped. He kept pushing on, climbing higher into the hills as he searched for an opening in the rocks. He had no idea what time of day it was, but the sun had to be sinking soon. If it went down before he found a suitable shelter, they'd be lost.

He ducked under the low hanging branches of a sturdy pine and damn near fell into the opening of a cave hidden beneath it. The yawning entrance was only tall enough for him to crawl inside with Maia on his back, but it opened up into a larger space a few feet in. He set her down against one wall out of the wind and removed her pack. He had his own blankets, but had no idea if the dryads had supplied her with the proper gear.

Quinn dug around in her pack for anything resembling cold weather gear and pulled out two thick blankets. How they'd fit in her pack and remained lightweight, he had no idea, but he wasn't going to quibble over them. He wrapped them around her shoulders and feet then ducked back outside to gather wood. A fire would help keep them both alive and allow for hot water.

Fortunately, the tree supplied plenty of deadwood under it and he dragged it into the cave to chop up into manageable pieces. He was running out of time and energy as Maia sank deeper into her hypothermic coma. His tinderbox provided sparks, but the wet needles and wood were slow to light. *Come on, come on.*

At last the tinder lit and he coaxed the flame to feed and grow, cupping his hands to keep the wind from destroying it. The meager heat warmed his fingers, but he needed more to help Maia.

He crouched in front of the entrance to deflect the wind and prayed to whoever listened that it would become self-sufficient so he could reverse the cold. He told himself it was just to save his own skin because they were bound, but some other part of him worried for her.

The fire finally caught and he fed it larger fuel before he scurried over to Maia's side. Her skin remained gray and cool to the touch.

"Come on, Princess. Let's get you warmed up. I'm going to move you closer to the fire before I work on the doorway."

She didn't respond and fear crept into his gut. He shoved it away as he dragged her closer to the fire. It had grown enough to emit heat several feet away and he hoped it would be enough to restart her inner furnace.

"Let it seep into you while I block the entrance." Quinn hoped she would open her eyes and give him a baleful look, but she sat as still as his patron saint, Death. "Stay with me, Maia. I'll be back to warm you up. Just stay with me."

He hated to leave her looking so damn gray, but the wind would take away all the heat the fire generated if he didn't put up some sort of shield. They needed a gap to allow the smoke out without losing the life-sustaining heat.

He headed out into the snow again, scanning the tree in the fading light. If he cut enough boughs, it would not only smell good, they'd keep out the wind without blocking too much of the smoke. He set to work cutting off some of the lower branches still holding green needles without losing the disguise of their shelter. *No doubt bandits and other creatures will be lured to such a place.* They wouldn't like what they'd find.

Quinn dragged the boughs and positioned them over most of the entrance. The wind cut off almost immediately and the heat of the fire filled the space. Satisfied they'd make it through the night, he dropped down beside Maia and unwrapped her from her blanket cocoon. He didn't like the coolness of her skin.

"All right, Princess, we need to get you warm." He

didn't know why he needed to hear the sound of someone's voice, but it brought him a strange comfort. "I'm going to take off your coat and wrap around you under mine. We'll add the blankets to help keep the fire's heat in, too."

Extracting her from her coat was harder than he expected. Who knew an inert body could be so difficult to move and undress? He swore several times and almost tore her jacket, but eventually he managed to set her gear aside and expose her body. She wore a long tunic belted to her waist and trousers much like his own, but the body had curves he couldn't ignore.

His cock swelled in his pants and he gaped at her a moment. His primitive mammal brain shut down all other intelligent thought for one crystal clear statement. *Beautiful woman.*

Sensuous curves, full breasts, round hips, soft skin. His mouth watered until he slid his fingers over her cheeks.

Soft, smooth, COLD skin.

Fuck! What the hell's wrong with me?

He snarled at his wayward body and shifted the princess into his arms, her back against his chest. He wrapped his coat around her then threw the blankets over both of them. As soon as he touched her, her exhaustion swamped him and the fear for her well-being returned.

Come on, Princess. Stay with me.

He sat with her against his chest for several minutes until he had to feed the fire again, but he quickly returned. The gray in her skin faded as her body warmed up, but she didn't wake. He inhaled the scent of her hair, something resembling lemon cakes, and willed his body heat into her. He hoped he'd done enough for her as his mind succumbed to exhaustion.

CHAPTER FOUR

Maia woke slowly, warm for the first time in decades. She rested against something soft, warm…and breathing? Maia opened her eyes and tried to take in her surroundings. Rough rock walls flickered in the fitful light of a fire no more than three feet from her. Pale light peeked through needle covered branches over an opening to her right. The only part of her feeling the chill was her butt and legs against the stone floor.

She glanced down at herself and found a pair of arms wrapped around hers, clad in leather and padded cotton. She followed the arms up to their source, twisting her head around until she damn near kissed the stubbled jaw of the man holding her. *Wait, Quinn's holding me? Why?* It didn't make sense. The man hated her. Why by all the saints was he holding her, keeping her warm?

As much as she enjoyed the heat, being this close to him made her nervous. She suspected he could kill her long before she could get away. She took a deep breath as she settled her mind, and inhaled his scent. *Sandalwood and warm leather.* Those were the scents she recognized and wondered how he managed to smell so good after hiking all that way through the snow. She knew she didn't smell that good.

She raised her gaze back to his face and found his glacial green eyes locked on hers. From no more than six inches away. The intense look made her throat dry out and her belly flutter.

"Hello." He said nothing and this close, she couldn't read his expression. "I didn't mean to watch you. I hope it doesn't bother you, as close as we are."

"Being watched doesn't bother me, princess." His low voice rumbled through her back and she ignored the pleasure it brought.

"It doesn't?"

"No."

She thought he would say more, but he sealed his lips together and just stared at her. She wanted to ask him why. Why it didn't bother him. Why he held her after she'd collapsed in the snow. Why he'd made the effort to rescue her. *Because he's bound to you magically, remember?*

That was a less than satisfying answer. But what had she expected? That he might actually like or tolerate her? She mentally snorted. *Not bloody likely.*

"Thank you for keeping me warm. I appreciate it." She returned her gaze to the smoldering fire. "Is there more wood? We should build the fire up."

He sighed and shifted to move, but she settled back against him to hold him still and he paused.

"I'll get it. I just asked if there was more. I didn't mean you had to do it." She gathered her strength, reluctant to stray from his warmth.

He grunted behind her, and it didn't sound friendly. "A princess doing work for herself and others? Who'd have thought?"

And there's the sarcastic jackass. She didn't bother to reply as she rolled herself onto her hands and knees out of his arms. The cool air hit her and she immediately missed the warmth of his body, but she didn't miss sitting close to him. *Whyever did I think he'd be nice to me?* Maybe because she'd woken up in his arms, cozy and comfortable. *Fool.*

She pushed aside her disappointment and focused on the task at hand. He'd made the cave fairly snug while she was out. He'd stacked the gear on the far side of the fire with the food bags hanging from jutting cracks in the rock wall. The firewood sat in a neat pile near the door, far enough away from the flames to keep from igniting, but close enough to dry out. Because of his efforts, their space remained warmer than outside.

Maia crawled over to the pile of wood and selected the driest sticks she could find before returning to the fire. She'd watched many of her father's servants blow on the coals to encourage the flames to return while feeding the dry wood into them. She added the wood to the fire and blew on the embers, gratified when the flames licked over its surface. *I did it.* Encouraging a fire was a small thing, but satisfaction swirled in her chest and she sat up with a smile.

"I'm surprised you knew how to do that, princess."

And there went her satisfaction. She stuffed her irritation down deep and shrugged.

"Not all of us are damsels without skills, Mr. Tarlen."

"*Master* Tarlen."

Maia rolled her eyes before she crawled over to her pack to look for food. If he wanted to be a master at something, she wouldn't argue. His ego wasn't her concern. She dug through her pack, carefully setting aside the clothes and minimal toiletries. But her food was missing. It had to be here somewhere. She'd only gotten into the pack once.

"Where are my provisions?"

He said nothing until she looked at him with raised eyebrows. He smirked and tilted is head toward the far wall. She followed his gaze and remembered the bags of their food hanging from rocky hooks in the wall.

"Nice." She climbed to her feet in an attempt to move to them, but dizziness assailed her and she swayed. "Oh goodness—"

Her head swam and the world shifted. *Where the hell did up go?* She lost her balance and fell, hoping the impact wouldn't be too hard.

"Whoa, princess. I've got you."

Somehow, she didn't land on something hard and unforgiving. *What am I talking about? Master Tarlen is totally hard and unforgiving.* But he'd managed to move so fast and so quietly, she didn't hit the floor. Her head still twirled like a ribbon dancer, even while her body remained steady in his grip.

"You need food and water and rest. You lie down and I'll get it for you."

"Why?" Why was he being helpful and kind? It didn't make any sense.

"Because if you weaken and die, I'll weaken and die." He helped her back to the blankets they'd been sitting on without expression on his face.

Of course. The dryads had magically bound them together. Tarlen's motivation was to save himself. *Fantastic.* Maybe she should die just to spite him. But then they both lost and so would her sisters. *Guess I'll just have to survive somehow.*

"At least I know where we stand." She lay back and closed her eyes.

"Food and water first, then rest." He still managed to make it sound like an order.

She wished she had the energy to scowl and spit at him, but her little foray to her pack had worn her out. She docilely took what he gave her and ate, barely tasting the food. The water was cold enough to make her teeth ache, but in the end she was too tired to care.

Exhaustion set in and she only roused when he took

the uneaten bread out of her hand. He smelled good despite his determined hostility and she thought she caught him smiling. *Can't be. The man doesn't have functioning smile muscles.* But the image of an amused quirk to his sensuous lips followed her down into her dreams.

****

Quinn tucked the thick woolen blanket around Maia's shoulders and sat back, bemused. She thought he smelled good? It had to be the bread or the fire. The dryads had provisioned them with savory travel bread and dried fruit, decadent as far as he was concerned.

He shook his head and made sure the fire had enough fuel before he ducked out of the cave for more. The cold slapped him harder than he expected and he gasped, already missing the warmth of their shelter.

He shot a look at the sky to gauge not only the time of day but the severity of the weather. The snow fell heavily, darkening the day to a dim twilight. He inhaled, testing the smells of the world around him. *Lots of moisture and cold.* A long-lived storm had set in, he recognized the smell. *Aw hell.* He slung his bow over his shoulder and took some time to chop up more wood for the fire.

Physical activity felt good after the hours stuck inside, but it wasn't just his body that needed exercise. His mind ran around in circles of confusion and frustration.

He wanted to hate Maia for the death of his brother, for the king she represented, for her reprehensible family. He pushed himself harder, chopping at the wood as if he could destroy the demons of her father's sins. But she'd tried to keep up with him. She hadn't complained about the weather, the terrain, the cold. And she'd pushed herself into exhaustion rather than whine.

He couldn't hate her.

Sonovaprick!

He threw the hatchet into the nearest tree and clenched his hands into fists. It wasn't fair. She should be snobby, selfish, whiney, and useless. She should be impossible to deal with. But she wasn't. Granted, he hadn't known her very long, but she'd proven to be a determined companion.

Quinn rubbed his face with his hands, the sweat from his exertions cooling in the frigid weather. Goddess help him, he'd started to respect her.

And worry about her.

Just wait till she starts talking. Then I'll know for sure.

Nothing more annoying than a chattering woman going on and on about inanities. But something in his gut suggested she wouldn't be that way.

Shut up.

He shook his head at his stupid thoughts and hauled the wood he'd chopped back to the cave. The heat hit him like a welcoming embrace and he sighed with relief. Damn, it had gotten cold out there. They'd need to bundle up together if they ran out of wood.

Now why did that idea make his cock twitch?

Traitor.

Yes, Maia had beauty and grace and determination, but none of those things meant she wasn't lying, conniving, or selfish. Except his gut said she wasn't.

He stacked the wood away from the door and checked on her. She rested like the dead, her body relaxed and her mouth slack. She slept as if safe and sound, not surrounded by enemies.

Except, he was her worst enemy.

Wasn't he?

Growling, he returned to the cold snowy day, shoving his compassionate thoughts aside. Where had they come from? He'd never been compassionate. Honorable, but not compassionate. Why would he care about her?

He snarled at the falling snow and set off, looking for game. Not that anything would be stupid enough to be out in the weather. But they'd need something beyond bread to survive this storm. He just hoped he could find something for a meal.

Quinn followed a trail between the trees, looking for signs of anything moving around in the storm. *Only idiots like me would be braving this weather.* But he kept looking. It helped distract him from his unnerving thoughts about Maia. The wind whistled through the pine boughs and the snow swirled in ghostly shapes, but otherwise the world sat quiet and still.

So much for distraction. His mind kept going back to Maia and her determination. He didn't want to respect or worry about her. His only concern for her should be her survival to keep himself healthy. Nothing else.

He almost growled and kicked the snow, but motion out of the corner of his eye made him freeze. He slowly sank down into a crouch and waited for continued movement. The dim light of the snowy day made him one with the other gauzy shadows.

After a few moments, a line of ragged men appeared between the trees. They looked haggard and worn, but filed along in silence, as if they sensed a predator on the mountainside with them. Quinn held his breath as they shot wary looks his way, but they didn't see him.

Two of the men carried something large and furry over their shoulders, and Quinn nodded. So hunting was possible. He waited until the ragged line disappeared around the edge of the hill then followed. Their tracks remained deep despite the continuing snow.

They moved slowly and Quinn had to grit his teeth to keep his patience, but eventually they arrived at another set of caves with smoke billowing out of the gaping maws. The men slogged into the dark depths as a shout went up from the sentries posted in blinds among the rocks above.

Quinn paused and scoped out the settlement. Whoever they were, these men lived comfortably in a harsh environment. *As long as they find food.* He scanned the spaces around the caves for where they'd keep their stores and found a pen made from branches and vines holding a small herd of goats. *So that's where they get meat and cheese.* The herd wasn't large enough for him to take a goat without notice, but in a pinch it would do.

Still, he reckoned he'd traveled a good couple of klicks away from his own cave and if he planned to hunt and get back without mishap, he'd best get going. Besides, he didn't want Maia to wake up alone.

There's definitely something wrong with me.

Taking note of the sentries' positions, he faded out of site from the cave village and picked his way back toward their own sanctuary. He'd hunt nearby, not only to keep from being noticed but also to be close in case Maia needed him.

Someone should just shoot me now. He snorted and headed home. If they didn't add to their provisions, the magical bond might just give him his wish.

CHAPTER FIVE

"Good glory, how much can it snow in one storm?" Maia peered into the gloom outside the cave and rubbed her hands together to return circulation. They'd been stuck in this cave for several days and she'd grown restless. *Which is pretty understandable given my time as a lamp.*

She'd rested and eaten and rested some more in the days they'd been stuck in this hole in the mountain. It had become rather cozy, if she didn't mind rarely saying anything despite her companion. They'd had to dig the entrance out a few times or risk getting sealed in when the snow hardened too much to break. The exercise had worn her out, but her recovery each time had grown shorter. *Thank goodness for that.*

"Are you never quiet, Princess?" Quinn's voice held no anger only exasperation and she gritted her teeth in response.

"Nope. Not unless it's warranted, and right now, it would be nice to hear more than my own thoughts, thank you very much."

"I'd happily never hear your thoughts." He drew a short, sharp blade across a little whetstone incessantly and she wanted to rip it out of his hands and throw it at his head. She only resisted the urge with the knowledge of his profession. *And I'm not dumb enough to try to disarm a master assassin.*

"Don't you ever get tired of silence?"

"I would if such a place existed. But I'm afraid I haven't experienced it in days." He gave her a hard stare. "You haven't allowed us much silence."

Maia looked out at the snow swirling past the cave's doorway again. "Yeah, well, you try being a lamp for centuries and see how that silence hits you."

At least he got to go out and kills something for us to eat. It had been a good thing. With the storm increasing in ferocity, they'd been stuck in the cave with little or nothing to do except sleep and eat. *And talk, if he'd be willing.*

Being paired with a creepy assassin to search for the Key, whatever that was, had seemed like a good way to get out of the dryad's forest at the time. *I regret nothing.* But his determined silences grated on Maia's nerves. She hadn't been the most gregarious of her sisters, but she still had the ability to talk.

She sighed and rubbed her hands over her face. They'd grown rough from digging the snow away from the entrance. She wished she'd thought to bring some sort of salve or cream to keep them from cracking. *Note to self: Bring salve for hands and lips.*

She still wondered why the dryads couldn't seek the artifact out themselves. If it had the same energy signature of the Keeper, they should be able to sense it no matter where they were. Why would they need her? Something didn't jive with the explanation, but there was no hope for it now. She'd agreed to help on a misbegotten quest in exchange for a return to her human life and that of her sisters.

"Do you think you could stop sharpening that blade? It's irritating."

"Almost as irritating as your incessant nattering." He

continued with the whetstone, his motions measured and even.

Maia sighed. It would be a long night, and an even longer blizzard.

She huddled against the cave wall and wrapped her coat tighter around her. She let her eyes unfocus as she watched their meager fire. Between the sounds of Quinn sharpening his blade on the whetstone and the dance of the flames, she settled into a fitful doze.

Memories swirled into clarity behind her eyelids. Little girls in a rainbow of dresses ran through flowered a garden. She recognized her sisters and remembered the joy, when all she'd had her heart set on was another cake after supper. Back before her sister fell for a druid and they'd been free to be human.

A sharp screech tore her into consciousness and Maia turned her gaze to Quinn, her heart galloping.

"Stop giggling."

"What?" Maia blinked.

"Stop giggling."

"I wasn't giggling."

Quinn sent her a dry look. "Who is Yarenoke?"

Maia gritted her teeth but tried to look innocent. "Who?"

"Yarenoke. You kept saying you had Yarenoke's tail."

"Oh." Her face heated. "Yarenoke was my imaginary dragon."

An odd sound filtered through the crackle of the flames and she stared. *Did he just chuckle?*

"Are you all right, Quinn?"

"Go to sleep, Princess. You'll need it for tomorrow." And the ice in his voice returned with her insistence on using his familiar name.

"Why? What do you think will happen tomorrow?"

Quinn nodded toward the door. "We'll have to dig out again."

"Bugger." Her shoulders slumped. "I wish it would stop snowing."

Hi nodded, his motions pausing for a moment. "I expect a break in the storm tomorrow."

She raised an eyebrow. "Why do you expect that?"

He tapped his nose. "The air smells different."

"Seriously?"

He dropped his gaze back to his hands and said nothing. Maia sighed. They really made the perfect match. She'd been locked away and couldn't talk for decades, and he made a habit of not speaking. *Holy Goddess, I'm going to go crazy.*

"What are we going to do tomorrow?"

Quinn resumed the cadence of his knife across the whetstone, but he raised his hooded head. "It depends on when the snow lets up."

"And when it does?"

"We will continue our journey."

She gritted her teeth at his staccato answer. Extracting information from him resembled visiting the dentist. "Thanks, I hadn't figured that out for myself."

"Ask a thoughtless question…"

She almost picked up a pebble from the cave floor and chucked it at his head. The idea had merit and she tightened her fist to keep from grabbing anything.

"Are you growling, Princess?"

"Do you have any idea where we're going?"

"Do you?" Quinn paused in his motions, the silence looming loud. "I'm following you, after all. You're the one who senses the dryad's artifact, correct?"

"Yes…except it's muted here. The weather is very distracting, and being locked in a cave doesn't help." Especially with the angry, but sexy man with her.

Maia groaned. There had to be a better way to travel than with this unrelenting animosity between them. "Can't you just give me a chance to prove I'm not who you think I am?"

"No."

"Not even a little one? Just one chance to show you I didn't try get your brother killed? None of us intended to stay with the dryads." She stopped when she thought of Inge. "Well, most of us."

"Typical."

"It's not typical." She shook her head. "That's the problem. Some of my sisters were flighty, but not all of them. And not me. The night the druid stole the artifact might have happened a long time ago, but I still remember something being off about it." She frowned as she searched her memories.

"I'm sure the revels kept you plenty distracted. Perhaps you shouldn't have imbibed so much." Quinn's tone held both contempt and disgust.

"Shove off, you sanctimonious prick. I didn't drink anything other than water that night." She raised her chin and stared him down, meeting his blazing green gaze. "And where were you when your brother searched for his fortune at the hands of my family? Talk about typical. A man figures the easy way through life is to purchase a wife, right? Since women are merely a commodity to be traded between men." She pointed at Quinn, her fury heating her chest. "If you think I'm so rotten, *Quinn*, why didn't you tell him to find a woman on his own? Why didn't you do anything to stop your brother's execution? I was stuck here. It's not like I could have changed things."

"You could have come home." He didn't shout, but the venom in his voice chilled her more than the blizzard outside.

"Don't you think I would have if I could have?"

"I don't know, princess. Your family's motivations baffle me."

"That makes two of us. I didn't drug your brother and I didn't intend to stay gone. But if I'd been there, I would've stopped the execution of my sibling."

"Like you did for your oldest sister?"

Maia reeled back as if she'd taken a physical blow. She had to hand it to him, his aim was true. Hurt and sorrow mixed until it boiled into cold disgust and she turned her face away.

"Just let me sleep and ignore any giggling. I don't mean to disturb you with any remembered happiness." She hunkered down in her coat and closed her eyes, willing sleep to overtake the hurt still burning.

****

Quinn didn't often feel like a complete jackass, but he had to admit mentioning her dead sister was a low blow. He shot a look from beneath his hood at Maia, but she'd rolled up in her blankets with her back to him. He grimaced and set the whetstone aside as he shoved the blade he'd sharpened into its sheath. If it truly had been centuries, bringing up her sister's death wouldn't change the past. *It won't bring Sean back, either.*

No, it wouldn't.

He'd been carrying the anger and grief around so long he'd forgotten what it was like to live without it. He wanted to hate Maia, but in the few days he'd been with her, she'd turned out to be nothing like his assumptions. Of course, they hadn't made it more than a day away from the dryads, but she couldn't be blamed for the weather.

I'm sorry, Maia. He had to say the apology, but he couldn't bring himself to speak aloud. He'd lose any power he had over her, and she already held most of the cards. Beautiful, determined, sexy, and the only one of them who knew where they were going. If he showed her that extra compassion, he'd have nothing but the blackness of his soul to offer her.

But he wanted her to think well of him.

Wha—?

Now he knew he'd been out in the weather too long. What kind of pathetic drivel was this? He rolled to his knees and stuffed another log on the fire, growling. Why the hell would he want a Silvercloak wench to think well of him? He shook his head and rose, grabbing his hatchet. They'd need more wood for the night, and they could leave whatever remained in the morning for anyone else traveling these hills.

Quinn pushed out into the snow, his grip tight on the hatchet. He attacked the deadwood under the tree with all his fury, frustration, and confusion. By the time he stopped, he had a large stack of wood, his breath sawed in his chest, and he was close to tears. The admission of his need for Maia's approval felt like betrayal to his brother, and his heart clenched with physical pain.

I'm sorry, Sean. Goddess of Death, I wish you were here. Quinn dropped to his knees in the snow and wept. He wept for his brother's loss, for the icing of his own heart, for the odd predicament of being bound to the woman who'd helped destroy his brother.

But she didn't support Sean's death. Hell, she hadn't even known about it. And even if she had, she'd been a lamp. The tears dripped off Quinn's nose and landed on his thighs as the cold seeped into his legs. He didn't want to forgive Maia, but she'd been nothing but determined and courteous, even when he was an ass.

He shook his head and wiped his face on his arm before he levered himself up. Damn, he felt old and tired and cold. Worse, he missed his brother's laughing face. Shoving the thoughts aside, he gathered up the wood and took it back to the cave. The snow had lightened up and the air smelled drier. Tomorrow the storm would be gone and they could move on.

He stacked the wood to the side and fed the fire a few more sticks before he settled down on his pack to sleep. He shot a look at Maia, but she remained with her back turned to him and he grimaced. He really should be kinder to her, but it was too late tonight.

I'll try tomorrow. He snorted softly. *Yeah, good luck with that.*

****

The first time I met her was in the woods, the dryad's woods. Sean's voice drifted through Quinn's dreaming mind. *She was more than I'd hoped and all I wanted. I couldn't stay away, Quinn. She was meant to be mine.*

Quinn wanted to scream at his brother for being stupid, for thinking with his dick, for following an errant princess to his death. Sean laughed, his eyes full of compassion. *Don't blame Maia, Quinn. She's only trying to help. And she always encouraged Sorsia to be with me as much as possible. It's not her fault I died. Forgive her...*

Quinn sat up, reaching for his brother as the dream faded. Dawn threatened at the edges of the horizon, the first clear sky they'd seen in several days. Gathering his wits, he spared a glance at his traveling companion, and thought over his brother's dream words. Had it been a true dream? Had Maia supported her sister's interest in his brother's suit? She'd certainly been stronger than he expected of one of the fabled Twelve Dancing Princesses.

He scrubbed his face and cracked his neck as Maia shot him a perfunctory smile.

"Sleep well?" She added another stick to the fire as Quinn shook his head. She sighed. "I think the weather is clearing like you promised."

He refrained from smirking. For some reason he didn't feel so superior after his smart remarks the night before. He settled for a nod.

"Maybe we can make some headway and you can learn the art of conversation. Remind me never to travel with an assassin again."

Quinn gritted his teeth. He should forgive *this* woman? He'd rather stab himself with his own dagger. But his brother's face flashed in his mind with an expectant look and Quinn shoved away his irritation.

"Forgive me, princess. I'm not used to traveling with others, and I find conversation often superfluous." He raised his gaze to hers. "And I'm sorry for being an ass last night. I had no cause to blame you for the death of your sister."

Maia raised her eyebrows. "Glory, did you just give me a full sentence *and* use a big word?" She placed a theatrical hand on her chest. "I'm stunned."

To his surprise, humor bubbled up rather than irritation. "What were you expecting? That I have no cordiality? I assure you, princess, while I may not be able to rival your loquaciousness, I'm fully capable of holding a complete discourse should the mood strike me."

A brilliant grin broke across her face and she laughed, the sound splashing off the walls of the cave. For the first time since the death of his brother, Quinn's heart lifted and he grinned back at her.

"You have unexpected depths." Maia wrapped her coat tighter around her shoulders and shook her head. "Will wonders never cease." Then she lost her lovely smile. "At least you spoke a little. Any conversation is worth hearing after spending centuries as a lamp."

"It's not too different from being an assassin, actually," Quinn mused as he rose to join her closer to the fire. "The only people we encounter are usually our targets, and there's no point speaking to them."

"That's a terrible analogy." She shivered. "And a lonely one. Didn't you ever get tired of death being the only thing around you?"

He shrugged, trying to ignore his brother's shade. "It was something I excelled in."

"Killing?" She shivered again.

"Yes."

"Do you enjoy it?"

Quinn paused, thinking it through. He didn't take pleasure in killing, per se, merely completing the task. The satisfaction of a job well done. "I get satisfaction in doing my job well and efficiently."

"Doesn't it bother you that you're ending someone's life? Don't you question why someone is asking you to kill people?"

"No. They pay me. That's all I need to know."

"All you need to know?" Maia pulled back from him and distaste filled her expression. "You're ending someone's life, for no other reason than currency. You don't have a cause or a reason. I might be able to understand killing to protect your family or your home. I might even understand killing in the name of a worthy cause. But killing just because someone said 'here's six thousand gold pieces. Go kill that guy over there' without asking why? Ugh."

"It's just a job."

"No, a job is something you do that helps others."

"I'm helping others. They pay me to make someone go away."

Maia's lips tightened. "Next time maybe you should ask yourself why that is."

"Why they pay me or why they want the person to go away?"

"Both." She rose and collected her things. "Let's snuff the fire and get going. We need to find the pieces of the artifact or key or whatever it is, and get back."

Her mercurial response puzzled him. One moment she was funny and engaging, then next cold and remote. *She'd make a good assassin.* He packed up his gear in silence, still uncertain why his profession should upset her so much. He hadn't killed a member of her family. *Yet.* He watched as she stomped out into the frozen sunshine, and made sure the fire was completely out before joining her.

"All right, princess. Which way are we headed today?"

She took a deep breath and closed her eyes. He took the moment admire her face in the winter sunshine, her hair shining like chocolate silk where it escaped from under her hood. She had a glorious serenity when she did her sensing thing and he enjoyed the pause in hostilities. The slope of her nose and the curve of her lips made him wonder what it would be like to kiss her.

Probably like death warmed over.

She'd knife him in the gut the first chance she got. He dropped his head as her eyelids fluttered and waited for her to give the direction. *Please don't let it be up.*

"We have to go up into the hills more. The first piece of the Key is up there."

Of course it is.

He nodded and swung his pack off his back. If they had to go up, he'd need some fuel to start off the day.

"Isn't it time to get moving? I figured once you knew which way, we'd set off." Maia crossed her arms over her chest.

"You might consider eating something before we trek uphill, princess. It'll be slower going because of the incline and the snow." He didn't bother to rise to her bait. She probably had never walked farther than a city block when she'd been home. He swallowed his disgust and threw his pack over his shoulders. "Now it's time to go. Ready?"

She huffed and gestured in the direction of the snowy hillside. *Wonderful.* They'd make it as far as they could, but he didn't have much hope for her stamina. Or his patience.

CHAPTER SIX

Maia trudged behind Quinn, seething. Why she was more upset today than any other day she'd been with him, she hadn't a clue. But between the constant uphill path and the glare off the brilliant snow, she found herself tired, irritated, and fighting a headache.

The wound their way upwards, passing trees and rock formations still gilded in a mantle of white. The breezes had been light and the day bright, but heat from the sun remained distant. Her shoulders and legs ached from the weight of her pack, and her head throbbed from the harsh light. She kept her mouth shut, though. No point in irritating the professional killer who kept her company.

Why killing? Why of all the things he could do with his life did he choose to end others'? The anger warmed her as they continued their trek upwards. She'd reached the apex of her fury when they stopped for a meal break and refused to speak to him beyond one word answers.

"Are you well, princess?"

"I'm fine."

Her terse response made him raise his eyebrows, but he didn't press. *Good thing.* She was ready to rip his head off. The weather took pity on her blinding headache by bringing in clouds. But the clouds dropped snow on them as they resumed their slog up the hill. *Mountain is more like it.* She pulled her hood up over her head and kept going.

The weather worsened as the day wore on and Maia swore she'd never seen snow as deep or as constant as they'd experienced. *Great time to travel looking for some special artifact.* She closed her eyes and reached out with her senses, hoping the direction they needed to go had changed. Unfortunately, her inner compass needle kept pointing up. *This is ridiculous. It's probably buried out there under the drifts.*

Maia had no idea where they'd gone after they'd left the cave. Her attention had been centered on the constant uncertain footing in the deep snow and the bone-breaking chill. She only knew they'd arrived somewhere when she ran into Quinn's snow-shrouded back.

"I'm sorry." Maia raised her gaze from the unrelenting white and gaped.

Gray veined walls of marble mirrored the cliffside, so well camouflaged she could barely make out the outline of the door. Snow flurries disguised the odd scrollwork on the portal and an eerie feeling skittered down her back. Quinn surveyed the doorway then shot a look at her.

"Do we go in?"

"Why would we stay out?" Her mind couldn't quite grasp why he'd asked.

He sighed. "Is the energy of the artifact directing us inside?"

Oh. She glanced at the eerie door again. "Yes. In there. That's where we have to go."

"You're sure?"

"Yes, why?" She frowned.

"Because you don't look like you want me to open the door." Quinn grasped the hidden latch and yanked. Despite the air of abandonment, the door swung open on silent hinges. "After you."

He didn't have to tell her twice. She trudged past him and he pulled the door shut, closing them in a deafening silence. Not even the scream of the wind cut the thick quiet. The air smelled stale and dry as if the door hadn't been opened in unmeasured time.

"Where are we?"

Her voice echoed and Quinn struck a match, the hiss bouncing off the vaulted ceiling.

"It appears to be a sepulcher."

Maia swallowed against bile as she took in the hideous construction before her. Skulls and limb bones of humans created a macabre chandelier and garlands around the ceiling. Four pillars topped by cherubs drew supplicants toward an altar in an alcove. A single angel stood upon a carved pedestal bearing a trumpet and a sword.

"Goddess above, this place is creepy."

"There's no justification for that assessment."

Maia swung toward Quinn with surprise. "What do you mean 'no justification'?" She waved at the morbid décor. "Those are human skulls. They were people once."

Quinn shrugged, his expression serene. "They're dead. The soul has long fled and they're nothing but bones. No vengeful spirits, no walking dead. Just old bones gathering dust. Quite peaceful, actually."

He's lost his mind.

He caught her look and raised his eyebrows. "Certainly better than being out in the howling wind."

"I'm not convinced of that." She glanced up at the bone chandelier and shivered. "Who do you think built this place and...that?"

"You don't know much about this world, do you, Princess?"

Maia dropped her chin. "I've been a lamp, remember?"

"And enlightenment didn't come with it?"

She stared at him and he cracked one of his rare

smiles. "You know, you should be careful. If you start making more jokes, you could be in danger of becoming friendly."

"We wouldn't want that." Quinn lit a torch resting in a sconce on the wall.

She huffed a laugh. "Definitely not." Then her levity died. "Ugh. Are those rib bones on the arch?"

"Yes."

"Lovely." She wrapped her arms tighter around her own ribs. "This place gives me the creeps."

Quinn sighed. "This was the only place out of the wind and snow for shelter on the path you led us. So tell me, Princess, where are we going? Do you sense the dryads' artifact here?"

Maia closed her eyes and opened her senses, struggling to take a deep breath without inhaling the scent of musty bones. The old sepulcher shimmered before her mind's eye in an iridescent rainbow of colors. *That's odd.* She'd never seen anything like it. It had the energy of the dryads, but different. Instead of blinding white, it had all the colors and some she couldn't name.

Turning slowly in a circle, Maia searched the glittering room and stumbled to a stop. She wanted to shield her inner eye from the searing glare of white light flooding through an arched doorway to her left and raised her hand to her closed eyes.

"Through there." She waved vaguely in the direction of the archway, but hitched a breath as Quinn walked through her vision.

Instead of dirty white robes with bristling weapons slung around him in dull muted colors, Quinn flashed red and gold of power and courage. Sparkles of white and green flashed throughout his form, showing honor and...love? Surprise made her stumble again and she "fell" out of her senses to stare after his fading silhouette.

My assassin is in love? She'd never thought the man

could feel anything, though she'd seen flashes of humor. She hadn't expected him to have a life outside of the week she'd known him, but she admitted the arrogance of the perspective. *Maybe he has a lover waiting for him to finish this quest.*

She didn't understand why the idea of Quinn's lover depressed her, but disappointment bounced around inside her as she followed him through the archway. A short hallway led them to a central room carved from more of the marble she'd seen outside, well-lit from above. The room reminded her of the Keeper's grove with its twelve sides, each with an arching doorway leading to dark halls. She glanced up at a crystalline roof much like the glass of her mother's atrium at home. Snow darkened some of the panels set in the metal I-beams, but others allowed the pale light of day into the hall.

Maia stepped into the very center of the room and paused, let her gaze slide around the vacant doorways. *Odd.* They left no footprints, as if the floor had been swept. The air no longer smelled musty or stale, and the room felt warm, warmer than merely being out of the wind. She frowned. *Something's off.*

She closed her eyes and settled herself back into her senses then "looked" at the room around her. Bright jewel-toned lights blazed from each doorway. They pulsed as if some living, breathing being rested within them. She stretched her hands toward each, curious what would happen if she touched them. When her fingers brushed the colored portals, each gave a different sound, like wind chimes, and a subtle hum reverberated through the floor.

Maia opened her eyes just as light filled the cracks between the stones in the floor and shot off directly to each of the twelve doorways. When it hit the portal, it illuminated it with the color she'd seen in her mind's eye and she stood bathed in rainbow light. The howl of the wind outside filled the hall and she swore she heard voices mixed in with its keen.

"What the hell is that?" Quinn's voice cut across the wind and Maia shook her head.

He stepped up beside her and drew his hatchet, his expression cold. She shivered and waited with him to see what would happen. The wind increased and sucked up the light from the doorways until they stood in the center of a rainbow cyclone heading for the glass ceiling. The wind rose to a crescendo before the light exploded everywhere and glittering bits of colored light drifted around the room, tinkling like tiny bells when they encountered the stone.

Maia blinked. "Did someone release pixie dust in here?"

Tinkling laughter filled the space and vague gauzy shapes appeared in the air around them. Quinn's grip on his weapon and the torch tightened and Maia swallowed hard. *Good glory, ghosts!*

"Be welcome, Maia Silvercloak, daughter of King Owen and Queen Ashlynn. We are honored by your arrival to Windbreak Keep." One of the gauzy shapes solidified into a legless woman drifting above the floor. "I am Moriah Wisp, Chamberlain of the Windbreak Keep." And she bowed.

Maia gaped. What the hell was she supposed to say to that? "What?"

Moriah looked up at her, eyebrows raised. "We've been expecting you, though not quite this late. Weren't you informed about your role here at Windbreak Keep as the Keeper of the Key?"

"Keeper of the Key?" Maia frowned. "Do you mean the artifact the dryads sent me to find?"

"Of course. Your mother sent the druid here to protect it until you came to retrieve it and take your place as the Keeper." Moriah tilted her head. "No one told you about this?"

Maia shook her head. "No. And you mentioned the

druid. Would that be the Dark Druid the dryads mentioned?"

Moriah's expression flattened. "Is that what they named him?"

Maia swallowed hard and nodded. "Yes. They told me he had seduced my elder sister and stolen the Key, for which my sister was put to death. And they charged me with its recovery."

Anger suffused Moriah's face and her features grew gaunt as if the life had bled out of her. *I don't even know if she's alive. She looks like a ghost.* Maia took a step back into Quinn and he held his weapons ready. *Not that they'll do much good against a ghost.*

Moriah took in Quinn's presence and some of her anger melted away. "I see you've brought your protector with you and this is good. It is exactly as predicted."

Maia and Quinn exchanged a look. "Predicted?" She swallowed again and raised her chin. "I don't really understand what's going on or how the dryads are involved. Perhaps you could explain things to me from your perspective so I can determine where I should go from here."

Moriah laughed, a hollow sound echoing around the chamber, and Maia clenched her jaw against the unease, but stood her ground.

"Your mother and her protector chose well in you, Maia Silvercloak." Moriah nodded her head. "Come with me. I shall show you your chambers and we shall discuss the Key that you seek." She gave Maia a smile. "I'm sure you'd both like a hot fire and some refreshments. We didn't know when to expect you so it may take a short time to provide you a meal, but the fire is ready now."

Moriah gestured toward a small alcove Maia had assumed was another doorway full of colored light, but it turned out to be a clever door made of the marble from the walls. It swung open on silent hinges and showed them another hallway lit by torches much like the one Quinn still held. He placed it in an empty sconce as they passed and gestured for Maia to continue.

For all his silence and hostile interactions, she was glad she had him with her. *Not that he can do anything about ghosts, but at least I'm not alone.*

They strode into what could only be termed a palace. It reminded Maia a little of her father's castle where she grew up. The walls and decorative columns came from the same stone she'd seen outside. *This whole mountain is marble.* Rugs and wood accents made it homey rather than cold, and elegant wrought-iron sconces offered plenty of light. Paintings and tapestries hung from the walls and small wooden tables supported vases full of flowers made from metal or crystal.

"Good glory." Maia spun slowly in a circle. "This place is magnificent. How long has it been here?"

"We're just a decade shy of a millennium." Moriah tossed a smile over her shoulder as she guided them through a set of double doors inlaid with different colors of wood. "This is your suite. There's a fire in the hearth. Please give us a few moments and we'll bring food and drink to you."

"You wouldn't happen to have Chai tea, would you?" She hadn't tasted the spicy creamy drink in ages.

"We do, Keeper. I shall have some brought to you." Moriah bowed again and drifted for the doors.

"Will you come back, Moriah?" When the ghostly woman looked surprised, Maia added, "I want to know the story of why you think I'm the Keeper of the Key and what really happened with the druid who took it in the first place."

"Ah, of course." Moriah nodded. "I shall return with your refreshments."

She faded out of the room and Maia wondered how a ghost could bring anything substantial as a tray with food on it. *Why would she even have food if she's a ghost?*

"Once a princess, always a princess." Quinn's dry words brought her back to the present.

"What's that supposed to mean?"

He gestured to the opulent apartment around them. "This place can't be too different from your home with your father and sisters. Was this all your "senses" led you to? Just another palace where you get to live in luxury without care or responsibility."

"What the hell are you talking about?" Maia crossed her arms over her chest. "I didn't know this was here and I'm certainly not staying beyond retrieving what we came for. I have sisters who need my help, Quinn. I want to know why Moriah thinks I'm a Keeper of anything, but until I retrieve the Key, I'm not staying put. I honor my word."

He snorted. "I'm sure."

"Okay, stop. Beyond the loss of your brother, what is your problem with me, specifically?" She raised her chin and stared him down. "I have just as much to lose if we don't complete this quest as you. More, actually. I have a family to rescue. All you have is your life, for all the good you've done with it."

"What would you know about doing good, Princess?"

"At least I'm trying to save someone beyond myself. It's not just about me here." She clamped her mouth shut, afraid she'd say something damning to herself. "Look, let's just wait to see what Moriah says and we'll figure out where we need to go next. I'm too damn tired to argue right now."

"Will wonders never cease."

Maia sat down on an ornate divan and scrubbed her hands over her face. Some piece of the key was here in this mountain palace, and while she did like the comfort offered, it felt more like a stepping stone rather than a destination. She had to get the key and return it to the dryads to save her sisters. Quinn could go fly a kite for all she cared.

It didn't take long for Moriah to return, but the silence in the suite rivaled the winter cold outside. Moriah shot a look between Maia and Quinn, but said nothing about their evident hostility. She'd brought a tray with hot Chai tea, bread, grapes, and cheese, and Maia's mouth watered at the fresh food.

"Here you are. I hope it's all to your liking, Keeper." Moriah smiled.

"Thank you for the food. Please join us and tell us why you think I'm a Keeper of anything." Maia reached for the food to serve herself and Quinn, not that he'd appreciate it. But she was too hungry to care.

"Your mother never mentioned the story to you?" Moriah wore surprise like a cloak.

"My mother died long before the night the druid took this key everyone is concerned about, so I can't see how she could've told me the story." Maia set out cheese, slices of bread, and grapes for Quinn, before rising and handing him a plate. He raised his eyebrows, but took the offering without a word. "So why do you think I'm the Keeper of the Key?"

"It's precisely because of your parents that you're the Keeper."

Maia shot a look at Quinn, but he wore his patented stoic expression.

"At risk of sounding pushy, could you explain that a little? My father was human along with my mother. Right?"

"Oh, my dear Keeper, that's not even close to true." Moriah shook her head, her expression turning compassionate. "Your mother was a dryad, one of the nobles within the Dryad's Garden. But unlike her family members, she never found someone to bond with. Because she was connected to the Archdruid, she had the Key to the Rifts that allowed her to visit the Twelve known worlds, of which this is one. You and your family came from one of the others."

"There are twelve worlds?" Again, Maia looked at Quinn, but his attention had sharpened on Moriah.

"Yes. Your mother Ashlynn visited your world many times because she liked the trees even if they weren't sentient in your world. She happened across a young man fishing in a lake. The young man was your father and they fell in love. I could bore you with the details of their love affair, but that's not what's important about this story. They had twelve daughters, one to watch over each world, and the one who would watch over this world would be the Keeper of the Key to the Rifts."

Maia opened her mouth, but she had too many questions to voice at once, and she let out a sigh instead as her mind whirled. "My mother was a dryad? And I'm the daughter meant to watch over this world? What happened to my mother? What does the Key look like? And why was it stolen by the Dark Druid? And why was it broken apart? Ugh!" She rubbed her eyes with the heels of her hands. "I have a lot of questions."

"It's to be expected." Moriah nodded. "What do you know about the druid who took the Key from the Dryad's Garden?"

Maia shook her head. "Nothing. Just that the dryads said he was the "Dark Druid" and he seduced my eldest sister Inge into showing him where the Key was so he could steal it for his own nefarious purposes."

Moriah's expression turned cold and anger crackled in icy blue sparks throughout her body. Maia clutched her plate and sat back, not wanting to receive any of her ire.

"They would concoct such a tale. Power-hungry fools." The ghostly woman shook her head and took a few deep breaths before her energy settled and she gave a sharp nod. "He did no such thing. The druid was named Reuben and he was your mother's protector. She'd charged him on her deathbed to watch over her daughters, particularly your elder sister Inge, for she would inherit your father's Kingdom and watch over your home world.

"Because of your mother's heritage, you were allowed into the Dryad's Garden as honored guests and for many years you were welcome. But as in most courts of the worlds, there are power-hungry individuals who'd do anything to seize power beyond their due, and one such individual was the so-called Archdruid of the Dryad's Garden."

"We didn't meet this Archdruid, only the Keeper of the Grove." Quinn's voice startled Maia and she blinked as her mind went over the new details. "Where is this Archdruid now?"

"He was killed by Reuben after he discovered the Archdruid had poisoned Ashlynn's anchor tree so she'd die before she could pass the Key to her daughters." Moriah wore calm satisfaction.

"What happened to Reuben? Is he still here?" Maia craned her neck to look around, but she hadn't seen anyone other than Moriah in the cliff palace.

"In a manner of speaking." Moriah tilted her head. "After your sister helped him decipher the clues to find the Key, Reuben took it and escaped the Dryad's Garden. But he knew they'd come after him as soon as they discovered its loss. So he broke the Key into three pieces and left them with specific guardians before he brought the final piece here. Then he asked our people, the Aerys, to keep the last piece of the Key until the true Keeper came for it."

Maia frowned. "Do you have one of the pieces here?"

"We do."

"How did you disguise it from the dryads? From what I've been able to understand, it has the same energy signature of the Keeper of the Grove." Maia sipped her Chai. "If I could sense it, I'm pretty sure they could, too. How did you hide it?"

"The Aerys don't have that kind of magic, but Reuben spent his life here in study, learning all he could about the Twelve Worlds so he could pass on the knowledge to you and your sisters when it was time. Before the end of his life, he asked us to take his energy and distribute it throughout the entryway of this fortress to better hide the Key."

"Take his energy…"

Quinn shared a glanced with Maia. "You mean you killed him and used his bones in the sepulcher through which we entered."

"Not quite. We did use his bones in the sepulcher, but he'd reached the end of his life when the ceremony was done."

Maia shivered. "He asked you to do this? Really?"

"He did. And he did it to protect you and your mother's legacy. The Key is for you alone, Maiasora Silvercloak, and you'll need it to help your sisters find their places in the other worlds."

Maia set down her mug and stood, striding away to look at anything but the ghostly woman. Anger surged at the unfairness of her past. Why hadn't her mother ever told her all this? How the hell was she supposed to teach her sisters about the other worlds when she didn't know anything about this one? And what about Inge? She died centuries earlier. Now there was no one from her family to watch over their original home world.

And that's if I believe all of this.

"Why should I believe you? How do I know this is the truth? So many people have lied to me recently and my parents never mentioned this to me when they were alive." Maia turned around to face her companions. "All of this is dependent on your story being the real one. What if the dryads have it right? Who am I to believe? I know none of you."

Quinn tipped his head and she thought she detected

some approval in his expression. *Hard to tell when he's not scowling.* Not that his approval mattered to her. Why should she care if he thought her smart? The problem was she didn't know who to believe. She'd never met Reuben or knew about the Key until now, centuries after the fact.

Moriah didn't say anything, her expression smooth and still. *Like death.* Maia shivered again and shook her head. There had to be a way to get the truth.

"Let's look at it this way. If I get all the pieces of the Key and fit them together, what do you gain from it?"

"We gain nothing, Keeper."

Maia scoffed. "Come on. I don't believe that. You've been waiting on me according to what you've said. No one does something for nothing, not even him." She thrust a finger in Quinn's direction. "He's not really my protector. He's just here because he's bound to me by the dryad Keeper's magic so he can't kill me without killing himself." She shook her head. "What do you gain?"

"Upon my honor, Keeper, the Aerys gain nothing. Our people cannot cross the Rifts between worlds. We'd lose our sentience and become nothing but ordinary wind and cloud." Moriah didn't appear insulted at all at Maia's disbelief. "But let me ask you this. Do you trust the dryads to tell you the truth?"

Maia snorted. "I don't trust them at all. The killed my sister and imprisoned the rest of us."

"Then why do you seek out the pieces of the Key for them?"

"Because it gave me my life back and they will free two of my sisters."

Moriah gave her a sultry smile. "If you piece together the Key and learn your true powers, Keeper, you'll have the ability to free all your sisters whether the dryads like it or not."

Maia stared at the ghostly woman. Was she for real? Could she really free and save all her sisters from their nonlife as lamps? She dropped her gaze to her boot-toes and tried to sense the truth from the woman's words. Even if the woman hadn't told her everything, she also hadn't asked for anything. Not like the dryads. They said, "get the Key or your sisters die." The Aerys, whatever they were, hadn't asked for anything at all. *Yet.*

Maia tapped her chin with one finger. "If I piece together the Key, are you going to show me my so-called abilities?"

"No, that isn't our role in your life, Keeper." Moriah shook her head. "Like the Key, the different aspects of your training were left to the different peoples who hold the pieces. We only hold one piece and our role is to provide you the story of your history as well as a place to live once you've concluded your quest."

"I'm supposed to come back here once it's all said and done?"

"Yes. This fortress was built at a nexus point for the Twelve Worlds. Only the Keeper of the Key can access the nexus and open the doors." Moriah tilted her head back toward the room they'd visited earlier. "Those twelve doors lead to each world and we hold them until you have reached your full potential."

"But you can't teach me that."

"No. That is the task of the holders of the next piece of the Key." Moriah shook her head. "We only have one piece and we only know of one other. You must journey to the holders' location to learn where the third and final piece is."

Maia groaned. "You don't know where it is?"

"No. To keep the Key safe, each people was only told of one of the others so that it couldn't be pieced together so easily."

"Wait, how would you know who was meant to find it and who wasn't? Anyone could pretty much walk in here and say they were the new Keeper. Don't you have safeguards in place?"

"Of course." Moriah's lips curved into a chilling smile. "If you weren't the Keeper, you wouldn't have survived the sepulcher."

Maia swallowed hard and shot a look at Quinn. He didn't say a word, but his shoulders had tightened.

"But that's enough. I have one more thing for you before I leave you to take your rest."

Moriah drifted to an ornate cabinet with intricate scrollwork on the front doors. She pulled them open and lifted out a book of papers held together by a leather folio. A great spreading tree had been stamped on the cover and a smaller leather strap wrapped around a silver button to secure it closed.

"This is for you. It's the Key Keeper's Book. In it you will find explanations about your mother, Reuben, and what you will need to do to recover and keep the Key safe." Moriah handed the book to Maia. "This book must not leave Windbreak Keep, but it will always be here for you to refer back to. It's meant for you, Keeper, but it must remain here."

The ghostly woman bowed her head over the book. "I shall leave you now. If you require anything, you only need ask."

Maia stood dumbly as Moriah whisked herself out of the door and closed it behind her. Her head swirled with all the information she'd been given and she wasn't sure what to do next. *Rest, probably. Or read the damn book.*

She glanced down at the leather-bound folio and slowly unwrapped the silver button. The leather smelled old and unused, but remained supple. She opened the cover and stared at the front page. Writing decorated the mottled paper from a few inches below the top to the very bottom edge and she stared at it a long time, trying to understand what she saw.

"Well, are you going to read it?" Quinn's voice came

out dry.

She looked up at him, her gut sinking. "I can't."

CHAPTER SEVEN

Quinn waited for Maia to smile and tease, but her face had lost all color and her eyes held panic. He frowned and rose, coming to stand beside her. The front page held writing in an ornate script that was difficult to decipher, but not impossible. His frown deepened. Hadn't she been taught to read?

"It doesn't look that difficult. Don't you know how to read?"

The look she shot him could've withered a dryad's tree. "Of course I do, but this isn't a language I know. What is it written in? Chinese?"

"No, it's an older form of Common Speech from this world. Weren't you taught any of it?"

Maia opened her mouth, but nothing came out and she merely shrugged. "I can't read it."

"Here, give it to me and I'll read the first paragraph to you." He held out his hands for the book.

"I—okay."

She handed it to him and he returned to the arm chair to decipher the passage.

"Dearest Maiasora. I'm sorry you have to learn about your destiny in this way, but you're much too young at the moment and I'm running out of time." He looked up as Maia sat down on one of the arms. She swallowed hard. "I'm growing sicker by the day so I must leave only this written record for you to follow when you're old enough. Hopefully my dear friend and protector Druid Reuben will be there to help you and teach you the ways of the Key."

Maia's lips turned down and she looked across the suite. "Oh, Mama." Quinn thought she'd say more, but when she looked back she only gestured for him to continue reading.

"But first let me tell you what the Key is. It is in the shape of a necklace made from platinum, titanium, and opals. The opals hold the magic, the metals are the conductors. When the one who is attuned to the energies of the worlds wears the Key, they are able to control the Rifts between the Twelve Realms. The Keeper of the Key can open or close the Rifts at will, and it's a great responsibility. It was my job before I met your father, and of all my children, the job falls to you because you were the only one attuned to the same energy as I am."

Quinn paused and tilted the book toward her. "There's an image of the Key, Maia."

She scanned the image of a necklace made from gleaming ornate metal and eleven drops of opal hanging from the lattice of the loop. A larger opal polished to oval perfection rested in the center above the middle drop. He couldn't tell from the drawing, but the opals of the necklace appeared to be different, some darker, some lighter.

"It's a necklace?" She tilted her head. "I guess that makes sense. Pretty easy to conceal as anything important beyond jewelry." She ran her fingers over the page. "It's lovely."

Quinn agreed and imagined what it would look like strung around her neck, the center drop dipping between her full breasts. *Focus on what's right in front of you, stupid.*

"Do you want me to read more?" He'd rather be looking at her, but it wouldn't be wise to give away his interest.

"Yes, please. I need to know what to do to find this thing and what to say to get it returned."

Quinn nodded. "Once you have the Key in your possession, you will need to select a protector to help you. Think of this being as a bodyguard of sorts, though she, he, or it will need to be someone you trust implicitly regardless of conventions and will be bound to serve you in this way until death do you part, whoever's should come first. Druid Reuben has been mine. He cares for me now as I fade. Please know that I love you very much, Maiasora, and I have no wish to leave you or your sisters, but I know my time is limited and I can't leave you without the knowledge of your birthright."

Maia wrapped her arms around herself and dropped her chin to her chest, her expression shuttered. Quinn wished he could make this easier for her, but centuries had passed and there was no going back.

"I'm sorry for your loss, Maia."

She barked an unhappy laugh. "I'm surprised to hear that from you. You're a dealer in death. Why would my mother's death trigger your compassion?"

He shrugged, studying the scrolling writing on the page. "Because I know what it's like to lose someone close."

She grimaced. "You bring that feeling to a lot of people when you kill their loved ones, you know."

He nodded. "It's what I'm good at. It doesn't mean I don't feel for you, though."

Maia blinked at him. "I thought you hated me. You called me a murderer when we started this quest. What changed?"

He shrugged again, not comfortable with sharing that information yet. "That's all that's written on these pages from your mother. She must have died after this point."

Maia looked like she wanted to argue, but she closed her mouth, narrowed her eyes, and nodded. "But there's plenty more book. What's next?"

Quinn turned the page and found more of the writing, but the font style appeared different, more bold and sure. "Can you read this?"

Maia shook her head. "No…turn the page back, though."

He did and she squinted at the writing, her eyes moving along the words. "I can read this now, though it takes some concentration. That's weird."

"But you can't read this?" He flipped back to the bolder writing.

"No."

"Hmm." Maybe someone had spelled the book to only be read by those who had a connection to the Keeper of the Key. *Which means what for me?* He'd never had a connection to this family back when the book was written. He only had a connection now, thanks to the dryads, with Maia.

"Are you going to read it for me?"

He cleared his throat. "Yes, sorry. May I please have some water?"

She raised an eyebrow, but got up to pour him some water into a cup. He used the time of her distraction to bring his confusion under control. First he'd started to like Maia, and now he suspected he had a deeper connection to her than just what the dryads created.

He thanked her when she handed him the cup and drank deeply before setting it aside to continue reading.

"Due to circumstances I was unable to stop, Queen Ashlynn has passed into the realms beyond reach and I must continue the instructions to the Keeper of the Key in her stead. My name is Druid Reuben T., and I was the Protector of Queen Ashlynn, former Keeper of the Key to the Twelve Realms."

"Reuben T.? I wonder what the T stands for?" Maia frowned. "I suppose it's not important considering his bones are in the sepulcher outside."

Quinn nodded, but a ripple of awareness tripped across his spine and he filed the fact away for later study. "It became slowly clear over the time of the Queen's marriage to King Owen Silvercloak, and subsequent birth of her twelve daughters, that her home tree, the sanctuary of her soul and long life, was being poisoned. By the time we realized what was happening, the poison had weakened her too much to recover, and her advanced age caused her rapid decline before her daughters were old enough to take over their duties. I cannot say for certain who has perpetrated this murder, but I can say it was at the hands of the dryads who claimed to be her people."

Maia's hands tightened into fists at her sides and her face had grown white as the snow outside. "Holy Goddess and all her wonders! Those bastards killed my mother and imprisoned us for centuries to hide it." She rose and paced around the room. "Son of a motherless stump!"

Quinn agreed. While he dealt death as easily as currency changed hands, he'd believed that somewhere, somehow his victims had brought the actions of an assassin on themselves. But this sounded like treachery in ways even he couldn't stomach.

"I've always been wary of the dryads, princess."

She spun to look at him with fire in her eyes. "You do realize I'm half dryad and you're bound to me, right?"

He nodded reflexively, but the truth of her words sank in slowly until his stomach tightened with unease. "Shall I read more?"

"Please. Let's get our task done so I know what more I'll be required to do to finish this farce."

"Farce?"

"Yes. The dryads sent me to find this key that had been

71

hidden from them on purpose, because they're murderers."
She looked ready to throw knives at something. "They still
have all of my sisters in their clutches. I have to figure out a
way to get the Key and free my sisters without giving it to
the very murderers who did all this damage to my family."

Quinn nodded. "I'm sure by the time you read this,
Keeper, the dryads will have made up a villainous story to
describe what transpired, but be assured it is only to cover
their treachery and destruction of Ashlynn and her children.
Inge Silvercloak was the only one aware of what was
happening to her mother and she took it upon herself to
help me find the Key and escape with it. I've since learned
that she was put to death for her cooperation and all of her
sisters were imprisoned, though I don't know the means by
which they're being held. I can only hope that if you're
reading this now, you've managed to escape and will set
this unbalance to rights."

"Imprisoned. Nice euphemism." Maia's words snarled
through the air between them, her anger making the
lanterns in the room flicker.

"Shall I continue?" Quinn watched her pace and hoped
there wasn't more to set her off. It frustrated him to see her
angry and he wished he could do something about it.

The thought was so alien to his lifestyle, his mind went
on a mental hiatus.

"Quinn? Are you going to read more?"

He blinked back to reality to find Maia standing in
front of him with her arms crossed over her ample chest.

"Uh, yeah. Yes. Where was I?" He frantically searched
the page in front of him to find where he left off. "I
suspected the dryads would send someone after me, so I
dismantled the Key into three pieces and took them to
different places here in our world. At each place I left a
piece with a phrase you must use to allow the guardians to
discern your authenticity. I can only assume the magic I
have placed on this folio will keep the usual riffraff from

reading it and only the Keeper and her protector will be able to decipher it.

"With that in mind, the last piece is here with me in the Windbreak Keep in the hands of the Aerys people, a group of air elementals who have sworn to protect the Key and me until such a time as it can be turned over to you." Quinn paused and met Maia's gaze. "I guess Moriah's people are air elementals."

"That would explain her ghostliness." Maia nodded, some of her anger dissipating. "What does it say about the phrases I need to know and the places I need to go?"

Quinn frowned as he found his place again. "Once you've received the three pieces, reassemble them. The Aerys have assured me they will serve you for as long as you remain in the Keep. Hopefully you've seen the room of the Thirteen Doors. One of them leads deeper into the Keep and your living quarters, another leads out of the Keep to the Sepulcher of Doubt and world outside. But the other eleven lead to the remaining Realms beyond ours, and matching Keeps like this one. I haven't investigated all these Realms as I'm not equipped to attend them, but that room is the hub of the Realms in this one, the one place you can access all of them. When your sisters are installed as the guardians of their respective Realms, that will be the place where you can connect with them."

"Yeah, that won't do any good if I don't have the phrases to say."

"I'm getting there, I'm getting there. This guy was long-winded." Quinn turned the page and shot a look at Maia. She didn't outright laugh, but a smile curled her lips. He wanted to make her smile more. "You must repeat this to the guardians when they ask you who you are:

"Sun and the Moon to light the realms.

"Wind and the Rain to nourish them.

"Fire to cleanse and prepare the way.

"And Earth to give place to flourish in.

"The Keeper will hold the Key

"To keep the Twelve Realms free."

Maia returned to his side and looked over his shoulder, reading the words printed there. She pointed to them and whispered their cadence as she dragged her fingers over the ink. He couldn't be sure, but they seemed to glow bronze as her finger slid over their forms.

She nodded sharply. "I can remember that. And I have to say it to each guardian?"

"Yes, that's what I read."

"All right." She frowned a little. "Does he say where he took the other pieces?"

"I'm sure you're wondering where I've left the other pieces of the Key, but that is not something I will write here. You must speak with the Chamberlain of the Aerys and she will be able to send you to your next piece. I have only told each guardian where to find one of the other pieces to keep the Key safe.

"Since I've stayed at the Windbreak Keep, I've learned that the guardian at one of the places has since died without a successor and the site was abandoned."

Maia's eyes widened and she sat back down on the armrest. "What happened to that piece of the Key, then?"

Quinn tried to ignore her scent of some kind of fragrant flower and pine, a combination he'd never considered delicious, but it teased his senses. "According to Reuben's account, you have to say the incantation over the "spelled stones" and they'll reveal the hiding place."

Maia blinked in surprise. "That's it? No directing of power or lighting candles on fire or some other kind of ritual? Just repeat the phrases he listed and that's it?"

Quinn shrugged. "It appears so."

"There has to be a catch."

"Perhaps the guardian at our next destination will have answers for you. This book is old and may be incomplete now that time has passed."

She chewed her lip. "Quinn, do you think any of this is really true? We're taking a lot of this on faith that it isn't a set up."

"You don't believe Moriah or Reuben?"

She frowned. "I don't know what to believe. My mother never mentioned any of this to me and I never met Reuben…I don't think." She shook her head. "All I knew was that we had this quarterly twelve day event where we'd go dancing with the dryads. Papa would get mad at us because we went through a wagon-load of shoes each quarter and keeping us 'well-heeled' was tough with twelve almost-grown women."

Quinn groaned. "Goddess, I can imagine. The horror."

She grinned at his teasing tone and warmth hit his chest.

"Yes, I know. The cobblers were our friends." She snorted as she threw herself down into a nearby chair. "But Mama never mentioned the Key or a special necklace or the Twelve Realms at all to me. Although it sounds like Inge knew a little about it. But she was in her thirties at the time and more privy to secrets as the oldest."

Maia sighed and rubbed her hands over her face. "So I'm supposed to repeat the phrase to Moriah and she hands me a bit of the necklace then we head off to the next place, right?"

"That sounds about right."

"Can we wait until tomorrow to do that or are you in a great hurry to get going?"

Quinn raised his eyebrows. "I thought you were in a great hurry."

"I was, but I'm exhausted and I'd like to sleep in a real bed and be warm. And possibly take a bath. I don't feel like going anywhere right now."

She did sound exhausted and he'd prefer to stay in one place for the night as well. But the idea of her in a bath, skin pink from the hot water and slick from soap had his cock sitting up and taking notice.

"Tomorrow is soon enough I suppose." He cleared his throat as he set the book aside on the coffee table and rose. "I'm sure Moriah won't mind if you wait until then to quote the phrases at her. I suspect that's what she's waiting for."

"Right. Because she hasn't given me anything beyond the book." Maia nodded and undid some of the buttons on her coat. "I'm really looking forward to a bath and a bed. They sound heavenly."

He couldn't agree more, but he merely nodded. Telling her he'd like to share the bath and bed with her wouldn't do at all. How would he be able to maintain his disdain for her and her family after that? For the first time in decades, it didn't seem worth it to hold onto the anger. It wouldn't bring his brother back and Maia hadn't sentenced Sean to death. She certainly hadn't tried to stay away.

Why in the Goddess' name am I defending her?

"Quinn?"

He blinked. "Yes?"

"Do you really think I'm the Keeper?" She'd taken her hair down and it fell in warm, mahogany waves around her shoulders. He wondered if it was as soft as it looked.

"I think we won't know that until you have the Key in your hands and in one piece." He tried to shrug away his sudden admiration for her looks. "No use worrying about it until we understand what we're dealing with."

Relief and gratitude flashed briefly in her smile. "Thanks, Quinn."

She turned away as if she didn't expect him to answer and headed for one of the bedrooms in the suite. He locked his knees to keep from following her and watching her undress.

Damn, it's been too long since I've had a woman. His usually ordered thoughts splintered as the vision of Maia in nothing but her long hair overwhelmed him and his cock flexed in appreciation. He mentally slapped himself and set about taking off his coat and weapons. Sleeping in caves necessitated the hard company of his weapons, but in this place he could get away with only a single knife. Hell, he didn't even need a knife. He could kill someone with anything, including a teacup.

"Quinn?"

He froze and rotated, both dreading and anticipating what he'd see when he turned. Maia's elegant form clothed only in a thin linen shirt and her trousers sent his blood decidedly south. Her dusky nipples pressed against the mildly translucent fabric and his mouth watered with the thought of sucking on them.

"Uh, yeah?"

"Can you ask Moriah to have a bath drawn for me?"

He blinked. "Why me?"

She gave him a goofy smile. "Because you're still dressed and I'm not."

Oh, he knew she wasn't. He could see it and it gave him all sorts of thoughts he usually ignored. Worse, if he went to look for Moriah, he'd telegraph those thoughts pretty clearly.

"Yes, of course." Wait, what had he said? He blinked as Maia smiled.

"Thank you." She turned and retreated back into her bedroom, freeing his mind from her spell.

What the hell is wrong with me? He seemed to be asking the question a lot lately, but he dutifully headed for the door to summon the Chamberlain. He grasped the door pull and paused. How exactly was he going to do that? Shout down the hallway?

In the end, he didn't have to do anything. Moriah stood outside the door just as he opened it and he almost leapt backwards in a defensive stance.

"Oh, forgive me, Protector Tarlen. I didn't mean to startle you." The Chamberlain bowed her head in apology.

"I came to see if you needed anything."

"Oh, uh, yes. Princess Maia would like a bath."

"Of course, I shall show her how it's done here."
Moriah tilted her head. "May I come in?"

"Uh, yes, please." He struggled to get his mind back
into coherency.

"Is there anything I can get for you?" The Aerys
woman floated across the floor toward Maia's room, but
paused at the door as she awaited his answer.

A stiff drink and a thump on the head?

"No, I'm settled, thank you."

"I don't think you are, but perhaps over time…"

Moriah disappeared into Maia's room with that
enigmatic comment and Quinn stood dumbly in the suite's
sitting room wondering what the hell she'd meant.

CHAPTER EIGHT

Maia settled into her bath with a moan of appreciation. Oh, glory, it felt good to be warm again. The keep boasted internal plumbing where the hot water came from heated tanks set into the wall with a space for a fire to be built under it. She turned simple levers and the water poured into the tub sunk into the floor. Another tank with cold water stood on the other side and the temperature of the bath could be adjusted.

Brilliant.

Moriah had shown her how to work the controls and set out fluffy blue towels that match the tiles of the bathing room. Maia hadn't felt this luxurious in…well, damn near forever. And she hadn't been warm since the night Reuben stole the Key to the Twelve Realms.

Glory, that sounds pretentious. She supposed it would be if the necklace didn't give the wearer the ability to open the Rifts. *Which I don't know if it really does or if it will work with me.* She sighed. So many questions and she hadn't even seen the Key yet.

At least Quinn had been willing to read to her. Despite his rather forbidding countenance, his voice had the smoothness of fine chocolate, deep and rich and hypnotic.

She could listen to it for hours on end. She'd enjoyed him reading to her, not minding at all that she couldn't read the text herself. *Maybe I should have him read all my missives aloud.*

She smirked to herself as she closed her eyes, imagining Quinn wearing a tight shirt that showed off his muscles and matching form-fitted pants, reclining in a window and reading. His green eyes glinted as he briefly sent her a smile before returning to his book.

Wait, that can't be right. Quinn never smiles.

She changed the look he gave her to one of quiet, sultry confidence. *What am I doing?* Quinn never looked at her with anything other than long-suffering disdain or disgust. So why the hell did she want him to look at her with attraction?

I've been a lamp too long.

But not so long that she couldn't remember how to use her imagination. If she couldn't have Quinn look at her with anything but disgust, she could still make up a fantasy Quinn with his flashing green eyes, his sharp angular face, and his sexy fit body. She closed her eyes and imagined him looking at her with interest and arousal. She remembered him holding her in his arms in the cave. True, it was only to keep her warm, but she could pretend it had meant more than that.

She imagined him laying her back on a bed somewhere with the warm summer breeze wafting the curtains on the windows as he leaned over her. His green eyes sparkled like the deep emeralds in her mother's crown and a sly, confident smile quirked one side of his mouth.

"Kiss me, Quinn."

She had no idea where the boldness came from, but this was her fantasy, dammit, and she could be as bold or as wild as she dared. His smile broadened and he leaned forward to brush his lips over hers.

He tasted of sweet wine and man, something she'd

wished for when she'd been young. While she'd remained a virgin to intercourse, she'd learned ways to pleasure herself and was no stranger to kissing or heavy petting.

The warm water relaxed her body and she slid her hand down between her legs. She gently stroked her nether lips until her finger found the sensitive bundle of nerves hidden amongst them. She let her mind fill in the blanks, painting fantasy Quinn staring down at her with a sultry smile as his hand massaged her sensitive flesh.

"Do you like it hard or soft, Maia?" His voice filled her thoughts and her pussy clenched with arousal. "Because I'll touch you just how you want and make you beg for more."

I'm already begging.

But she rocked her hips against his hand and moaned. "Touch me slow and soft, Quinn."

"My pleasure, my lady." He spread her legs wider and settled on his belly between them. His breath tickled the hairs on her nether lips and she shivered with pleasure. "So sensitive and responsive. I'll remember that."

Fantasy Quinn dipped his head and something hot and wet slid along her folds. *Good glory, is he licking me?* Fiery pleasure skirled its way through her body as he licked her most sensitive flesh.

"Oh, glory, Quinn."

He hummed against her pussy and flicked his tongue on her nubbin as his fingers stroked her inner thighs. Each touch ramped her arousal up higher and she rocked her hips in time to his motions. Despite the building urgency, he kept to a slow and soft rhythm, teasing her with erotic pleasure.

She whimpered and moaned, the heat from his mouth building into an exquisite burn. She tightened her hands into fists as he drove his tongue into her sheath and she lost her ability to breathe.

"Come for me, Maia. I want to drink your pleasure."

Fantasy Quinn sucked hard on her bundle of nerves and her orgasm shot through her like a bolt of lightning. He body bowed up out of the water of her bath as the pleasure swamped her whole being.

"Oh, glory, Quinn!" Her voice rang off the walls of the bathing room and only the echoes of it challenged her heavy breathing as she settled back against the rim of the tub. "Dear Goddesss."

She'd never had an orgasm that powerful. She opened her eyes and shot a look around the room, suddenly aware of her ghostly hosts. Shit, no one had come in to watch, had they? Shaking her head at her delayed awareness, she soaped up her body and cleaned the remnants of her interlude away before climbing out of the bath.

Despite her chagrin at how loud she'd cried out, she smiled to herself. The real Quinn Tarlen might be a stubborn, frustrating jerk, but Fantasy Quinn had been very useful. *You'll be starring in my future dreams from now on.* She laughed and dried her body as she prepared for bed.

****

Quinn's head came up at the first sound from the bathing room and he rose from the plush chair where he'd been drinking some warm tea. It sounded like Maia had moaned and he worried she'd been hurt on the hike up to the keep. He almost beat on the door when he heard the words, "Kiss me, Quinn."

What the hell?

He froze with his fist raised as the words sank into his awareness. *Did she just say kiss me?* He held his breath and listened hard. What was happening on the other side of the door?

Moans echoed and his cock perked up. *Damn, it sounds like she's having sex.* But princesses were necessarily virgins, right? He frowned as he searched his memories. Hadn't Sean said he'd met a family of twelve virgin girls? *Maia's definitely not a girl.*

More moans jerked him out of his memories and he pressed his back against the wall beside the door to the bathing room. Every sound she made encouraged his fantasies and his cock, and soon he'd undone the front of his trousers. *Goddess, she's making me hard.* His shaft strained against his fly and his balls tightened to the point of pain. He grasped his cock and stroked it, closing his eyes as she moaned again.

"Touch me slow and soft, Quinn."

Sweet Goddess, she's gonna kill me. He gripped his cock tighter and stroked slow and deliberately. He could imagine her in the bath, rubbing her sweet, sensitive flesh between her legs. Goddess, he wanted to be there, doing that. Touching her slow and soft.

Would she have mahogany curls down there like the hair on her head? Or nearly black like the soft darkness of a summer night? Or would she have some red like autumn leaves? Goddess, he would be happy with any color if he got the chance to look and touch.

"Oh, glory, Quinn."

Glory was right. He tightened his grip on his shaft and stroked harder and faster, his breathing coming in great gasped as he imagined her riding him. He could see her full breasts bounce with her perfect dusky nipples. He had no idea if they were truly brown, but it was all he could come up with as he built up his arousal.

Her whimpers grew faster and louder behind the door, mirroring his own race to the finish. He wished he could be in there, bringing her such pleasure. According to her own admissions, he was, or at least a fantasy version of him. *Bastard, I want that job.*

"Oh, glory, Quinn!"

Maia's exclamation set his release off and his pleasure overwhelmed him, shooting out of his cock to splash on his chest. Pleasure exploded through him and an overwhelming urge to enjoy this with Maia sparked in his heart. His hand was cold comfort, but it would have to do until he could somehow convince her he wanted to share it with her.

Splashing sounds came from inside the bathing room as he rested against the wall with his chest heaving. Damn, the woman winded him and he wasn't even near her. He'd have to change his clothes and perhaps convince someone to wash the ones he currently wore, but he couldn't bring himself to move quite yet.

It was only when he heard her get out of the bath that he scrambled to his feet and headed for his room before she realized he'd been outside listening. He ducked into his room just as he heard the door opening and thanked his lucky stars she hadn't caught him.

But would that have been so bad?

Quinn had no idea where the question came from. Would it be bad? He sat down on his bed and stared at his knees, the scent of sex perfuming the air. What if he admitted he liked Maia? What if he told her he'd heard her fantasy in the bath? He shook his head and rose to his feet. No, he couldn't intrude on her private moments like that.

But maybe he could work on being kinder, less harsh to her. He could try to see her as a strong and beautiful companion instead of the daughter of his brother's murderer. He pulled his shirt off and unbuttoned his trousers as he prepared for bed.

"Quinn, I wanted t—"

Maia's voice cut off in a gasp as he turned around to face her, his chest exposed. She stood gaping at him as if she'd never seen someone like him. He glanced down at himself, searching for what she found so surprising. He had scars from near-misses and training, but otherwise he appeared to be fairly ordinary. Naturally hairless except for the trail from his navel to his groin, his abs showed shadows in the light of the room, but they seemed ordinary to him.

"Are you all right, Maia?"

"I…yes, right. Of course." She blinked and nodded sharply.

"You said you wanted something?" He gazed at her, enjoying the softness of her dark hair cascading around her head and shoulders.

"I wanted…" She trailed off as her gaze dropped from his to scan his body.

He rarely thought of himself as something worth looking at, but he enjoyed her perusal. She didn't seem to be aware of doing it, but her nipples hardened against her shirt and she took a deep breath, pressing them tightly in the fabric. His hands tightened on the edges of his pants to keep the urge to touch under wraps.

"You wanted what?" He tilted his head as she licked her lips and told his cock to be quiet before it gave his attraction away.

"I wanted…to…" She swallowed hard and looked away as if to gather her thoughts. "I wanted to let you know the bath is free if you'd like to use it. I didn't mean to take so long."

He could definitely use a bath after his erotic explosion, but at the moment he was more interested in her sudden discomfort.

"Did you enjoy your bath?"

"Oh, yes." The response sat pregnant with meaning along with the secret smile curling her lips. She blinked and cleared her throat, raising her gaze to his. "Yes, very much. I'm sure there is more hot water. Rather ingenious really. Just turn on the valve and the water comes out already hot. It's marvelous."

"Can you show me?" He gestured for her to lead the way and her gaze dropped to his open trousers.

"Right now?"

"Yes, please, Maia. I'd like to see this fantastic bathing

room." He stopped beside her and her gaze seemed latched to his chest.

She swallowed hard. "Okay."

She spun around and marched back toward the bathing room, her back ramrod straight. He admired the curvaceous lines of her waist and ass as he followed along. *Like a damn dog.* But somehow he couldn't hate it. He had too nice a view.

Once she made it to the tub, she pointed at the odd valve grips. "You just turn them and the water comes out already heated."

"Really?" He stepped up beside her, enjoying the scents of flowers and woman. "How do you change the temperature?"

"This side brings the hot." She pointed to the red handle. "And this side brings cold. If you turn them on at the same time, they can be adjusted for the perfect bath."

Her company brought out the hot in him and he suspected he'd need a cooler bath than she took. Of course, from what he heard, his fantasies could heat up the bath as much as hers did. But he reached for the red handle and loosened it.

Steaming water poured into the basin set in the floor and promptly guzzled down the drain.

"Oh, wait, you need this." She leaned over and set a cork in the drain opening. The water began to pool in the bottom. "There. Now add the cold or you'll look like a tomato."

He laughed at the image and the sound surprised them both. Maia stared, her eyebrows hidden in her hair.

"Did you just laugh? I didn't know you could do that."

He shot her a frown and she grinned at him.

"I liked it. Your laugh is rich."

"Rich?" He had no idea what that meant.

"Yes, like chocolate or mulled wine, or well-aged cheese. It's like all the good things in life."

He stared at her, his mind running around in little circles. His laugh reminded her of all the good things in life? *That's foolish.* But the idea made heat bloom in his chest and he ignored the urge to pound his chest in triumph. *There's something wrong with me.*

"I don't think I've ever heard it described like that before."

"No?" Maia gave him a soft smile, one of those that spoke volumes but was indecipherable. "Someone should have and I'm happy to be the first."

She tilted her head, her gaze taking his measure, and he stood very still, waiting for her assessment. Would she say something about the sounds he'd heard?

"Well, I should let you get your bath." Her smile turned polite. "Thanks for the laugh. Enjoy your soak."

She nodded to him and slipped out of the room, leaving him with the echoes of her footsteps and the sounds of running water. He followed her to the door and closed it, bemused at her candor. What had all that meant? Why the hell had she used him for a sexual turn on? And why did he like it?

Shaking his head, Quinn stripped the rest of his clothes off and tested the water before he slid his body into the bath. Delightful heat encased him from toes to shoulders and he sighed with pleasure. He'd rarely been able to completely relax in his life, and even now he kept an ear out for any sounds of intrusion. But the hot water soothed his aches and encouraged his mind to let go of his worries for a short time.

He wanted to think about Maia and her strange behaviors tonight, but he couldn't focus and he let the heat take away his cares for a little while. He finally roused when his fingers had pruned and his balls felt as if they reached for his knees. He heaved himself out of the water and tugged the cork out of the drain before sloshing for the shelves of towels along the wall.

Quinn thought over all they'd learned as he dried himself off. From what he understood from the book, Maia and her sisters were pawns in the middle of a power-grab between the Archdruid and Queen Ashlynn. Ashlynn died and the Archdruid was killed by Reuben before he fled. But the question remained: Did the dryads know the events behind why the Key had been taken or did they believe the story told to make Reuben the villain?

Quinn shook his head. *If the dryads had known the real story, they'd never have sent Maia for the Key.* At least not alone. They couldn't guarantee she wouldn't learn what the Key was and how she was connected to it without guards or advisors telling her what to think. Maybe they'd hoped she wouldn't think about it or she'd find it and return it quickly, her concern for her sisters overriding her connection to it.

Quinn wrapped the towel around his waist, gathered up his pants and boots, and headed out of the room. He paused to check on Maia, but her door was closed and no sounds came from inside. He dropped his clothes in his room and returned to the main room to shutter the lamps as his thoughts cataloged all the different parts of the story. Though they'd yet to see the piece of the Key the Aerys people held, he couldn't see any reason for them to lie to Maia. What would they gain?

He settled himself in his bed and his body immediately relaxed. Damn, he hadn't slept on anything this soft in decades. The softness of the bed and blankets reminded him of Maia's hair and skin, and he wondered what it would be like to touch more than her cheeks. She'd evidently been thinking of him more than merely his sparkling personality. He liked what he'd overheard from the bathing room, but he didn't know how he could encourage it or even if he should. What would Maia's face look like when he told her he'd heard her little episode? A chuckle filled the dark room and he fell into sleep with a smile on his face.

CHAPTER NINE

Maia spent the next two days resting and exploring the keep. Quinn kept her company as Moriah showed them around, his presence soothing rather than forbidding. She liked him being there and some of her ongoing tension melted away.

"When you've assembled all the pieces of the Key, we hope you will return to the Windbreak Keep and guard the hub of the Twelve Realms here in our world." Moriah drifted along the corridor toward a new part of the Keep Maia hadn't seen. "We try to maintain the gardens and livestock so there is food for your people."

Quinn raised his eyebrows. "The Aerys people don't eat?"

"We take our nourishment from the winds of our birth, but we've cared for more corporeal beings for millennia." Moriah led them into a well-lit room full of plants and orderly gardens. "We've adapted our home to allow for the gardens to be around all year long."

Maia looked up to find the roof of the cavern made of girders and snow-covered glass. How they kept it from breaking when things fell or walked across it, she had no idea, but she loved the feeling of heat and life under the mountain.

"It's beautiful."

"Thank you, Keeper." Moriah gestured to another hallway. "We also keep chickens and goats for meat, milk, cheese, and eggs. This allows us to use the manure to nourish the crops and still gives the animals some range outside when the weather's good."

"That's clever." Quinn surveyed the enclosed green house with approval. "You can keep farming and growing all year round. How do you keep out the bandits?"

"Bandits?" Maia sharpened her gaze on him. He'd seen bandits?

"The keep is disguised by the natural formations, but also with wards set up by Reuben while he lived here." Moriah nodded as she led them back toward their living quarters. "The bands of scroungers who live nearby are unaware of our presence. We periodically leave some things out where they can "find" them, but mostly we keep to ourselves."

When they returned to their suite, Maia shot a look at Quinn and he nodded. They'd agreed it would be time to go find the next piece of the Key. Maia didn't want to leave the comfortable keep in the mountains, but they had a limited time before midsummer arrived and no idea how far or how long it would take to go where they needed to. They couldn't dawdle.

"Moriah, according to my book, I must repeat a set of phrases to retrieve the pieces of the Key that is meant to be mine. Is this correct?"

"It is, Keeper."

"Okay, then." Maia took a deep breath. "Sun and the Moon to light the realms. Wind and the Rain to nourish them. Fire to cleanse and prepare the way. And Earth to give place to flourish in. The Keeper will hold the Key to keep the Twelve Realms free."

A subtle ripple of power shimmered through the air

around them and a low-pitched sound, much like a gong, echoed deep in the keep. Moriah's smile broadened and she inclined her head as Maia's gaze slid around the room. The colors of the furnishings and walls seemed to be brighter and richer, as if they'd been hiding in a fog.

The Chamberlain drifted away to the same cabinet where the book had been housed and withdrew an ornate wooden box with a twelve-sided shape surrounding a spreading tree carved on its lid. She carried it to Maia and extended her hands, bowing over the box.

"For you, Keeper."

Maia shot a look at Quinn and he moved to her side to take in the treasure she'd been handed. She slowly opened the box and looked down into its velvet maw. White satin encased a small item and she pulled it out before setting the box down. When she unwrapped it, she held the center portion of the necklace she'd seen in the drawing. A large opal with blue and purple light rolling through it sat above a smaller tear drop opal of a more golden hue.

"Good glory, it's beautiful." She turned it over in her hands and felt the heat from the stone against her skin. "They feel alive."

"They are, in a manner of speaking." Moriah nodded. "They are attuned to your energy and that of the Twelve Realms. The large one in the center is from this world and therefore connects to you directly. The smaller one is from your father's world and belongs to you as well, though one of your sisters was meant to be the guardian of that realm."

"Was meant?" Quinn raised an eyebrow. "Was her eldest sister Inge supposed to guard her father's world?"

"Yes."

Maia dropped her gaze back to the fragment of the Key in her hand and sorrow hit her chest. *I'm sorry, Inge.* Nothing could bring her sister back and she certainly hadn't deserved such an infamous death. *I wish I'd known.*

"Thank you for keeping this safe for Reuben." Maia

raised her gaze to Moriah. "I think I'd like to be alone for a while."

"I understand, Keeper. Should you need anything, just call." The chamberlain bowed and wafted out the door, closing it behind her.

"Are you all right, Maia?" Quinn touched her shoulder.

She raised her gaze to him, grief and fear and anger rolling through her in waves only to spill out her eyes. She took a breath to answer, but the only sound came out was a sob.

"They killed my sister." And she threw herself into his arms.

****

Quinn hadn't expected Maia to throw herself at him, but he caught her and held her as she wept against his chest. He also hadn't expected to feel anything about a spoiled princess crying over her equally spoiled sister, but he found his own heart's grief recognized hers and he held her tight.

He guided her over to the couch and sat down with her in his arms, offering what little comfort he could. As the purveyor of death, he'd rarely had the interest or use for mourning family members. As far as he was concerned, the dead didn't care what the living did after they were gone, and he'd never been attached to his targets. For decades, he'd carried around the fury and a thirst for revenge on the women who'd caused his brother's death, but it had slowly eroded while in Maia's presence. Now the thought of her sorrow and grief brought him new pain, and this pain hurt worse because he could do nothing.

All he could do was hold her. Despite his lack of experience in the field of comfort and compassion, he enjoyed having her body in his arms. He didn't have words of solace or tenderness, but at the moment, she didn't seem to need them. So he held her and waited for the grief to ebb.

After a while, she grew still and quiet. Contentment filled his chest as he held her. He didn't need her to move at all. If she chose to stay in his arms, he wouldn't complain. Maia's scent filled his nose and settled his mind better than anything he'd ever used to calm himself down. All he needed was the smell of her hair and he'd relax.

"I'm sorry." Her mumbled words came from the vicinity of his chest.

"For what, Maia?"

She raised her head to look at him, sniffing. "For sobbing all over you. I'm sure you don't care about my sister's death."

Anger rose at her accusation, but cooled quickly. She couldn't know his perspective had changed.

"To be honest, her death doesn't affect me much." Maia grimaced and nodded. "But your grief does, and I'm sorry for your loss. You've never grieved for your sister?"

She shook her head. "I never had time. The dryads turned us into lamps before we knew what was going on. I didn't know she'd been executed until the day I met you in the Grove."

"Were you close with your eldest sister?"

"Not really. She always seemed so arrogant and selfish and strict about things." Maia sniffed again. "But I'm wondering if it was because Inge knew a lot of the secrets the rest of us didn't and was trying to protect us from them. Like about the Key. The dryads said she'd led Reuben to the location of the Key and that's why she was killed. And Reuben's account confirmed it. She must have known about it from Mama."

Maia sat back and rubbed her hands over her tearstained cheeks. "I wonder if she was the only one who knew, or if some of my older sisters knew, too."

Quinn hitched a shoulder. "You won't know that until

you free them from the dryads."

"Yes, right. I guess I'll try to save all my sisters rather than only the next two youngest in the contract." She shot a look over at her pack leaning against the wall, ready to go. "Will we start out again tomorrow?"

Quinn didn't say anything for a while, his thoughts churning. He'd enjoyed this idyll in the Windbreak Keep, quite a surprise because he rarely enjoyed doing nothing. But they needed to restore the Key and free her sisters. And then he'd be free of her. A frown pulled out his brows at that thought. Did he really wish to be free of her?

"What's the frown for? You don't want to leave?"

Quinn blinked. "No, I was considering the long term. I think we should leave tomorrow for the next piece of the Key, but what happens when you put the pieces together? Will you bring the Key to the dryads or will you bring it back here?"

Maia dropped her chin to her chest and bit her bottom lip. Quinn tried not to react to the action viscerally, but his body reminded him of the fantasy he'd had of her. *Keep your eyes on the prize, Tarlen.*

"I have to take it to the dryads. I have to save my sisters." She looked up at him. "If I can, I won't give it to them. If there's any way to save them without giving up the Key, I will."

"Remember, no one knows what it looks like but you."

"That's an assumption. We don't know if some dryad does remember and will recognize it when we return."

Quinn shook his head. "If one of the dryads remembered it, wouldn't they have gone to look for it themselves?"

"Looking for it and recognizing it are two different things." Maia rubbed her chin as she stared down at the opal jewelry lying on the satin pouch. "I think once the Key is back together, I shouldn't show it to anyone just in case someone does know what it looks like. Hopefully by then,

I'll have figured out a way to get all my sisters free."

"I'll help you, Maia." He had no idea where the words came from, but he meant them.

She raised her eyebrows. "You will?"

"Yes." He didn't need to make a long-winded explanation.

"Why?"

Or maybe I do. "Because as an assassin I can't right many wrongs, not without death. But it seems like a dishonorable way to win, and I don't trust the dryads with the Key to the Twelve Realms. Apparently, your mother didn't, either."

"Why would you trust me with it? Couldn't I be just as power-hungry as the dryads? I am half dryad."

Quinn nodded. "You could, it's true. But you don't strike me as someone who'd seek world domination."

Maia snorted. "You haven't seen me with the Key in once piece yet. I could be just as ruthless."

He shrugged and nodded. "That's true, too. But my gut says you're not. I guess we won't know until you have all the pieces together."

"Yes, I guess not." She nodded slowly and wrapped the opals back up in the satin. "So we leave tomorrow morning, early, right?"

He nodded, ready to be out of the keep for the next move. "We'll have to find out where we're going and get provisions for the distance. Moriah is supposed to tell you the next guardian she knows of, right?"

"Yes." Maia nodded and rose, carrying the satin bundle to her pack. "But now that I have this, I can feel a tug in a different direction." She closed her eyes and turned slowly in a circle. "That way." She pointed at one of the walls and opened her eyes. "I can't tell which direction that is while in the keep, but we'll have to head that way to find the next piece."

"There are two pieces." Quinn stood as well. "Can you

sense another one from here?"

She blinked then closed her eyes again, starting in the direction she'd pointed first. "There's the one I mentioned. And…" She shifted her body in small increments around in a circle before she paused. "I think there's another piece in that direction." She pointed to her left toward his room. "It's weaker as if it's farther away. But we'll see where that is once we get the second piece."

Maia reached to put the satin lump in the top of her back and Quinn caught her arm.

"Might I offer a suggestion?" He pointed to the satin. "That's rich fabric. Any thief or snoop will see that as a target and as something valuable. Here." He reached over and grasped some of the polished stones in a decorative bowl. "Put these in your satin pouch, and keep the opals either on your person or in something less noticeable like old leather or canvas."

She tilted her head and eyed him a few moments. "Had a lot of experience with this, I take it?"

Quinn flashed her a smile. "More than I care to admit. But we're going into new lands and not all people will see you as someone to leave alone. They'll see you as a mark instead."

Maia sighed. "I don't think I have anything that looks remotely ordinary."

"Give me a moment."

He ducked past her into his room and rifled through his pack. He found an old square of terry cloth he used as a washcloth and pulled it out. It was gray with age and use, but clean and sturdy. Anything wrapped in it would look like soap or more cloth.

"This should work." He handed her the terrycloth and watched her wrap up the center portion of her necklace. "Also, put it in one of the out-of-the-way pockets in your pack. One that takes extra effort to get into."

She frowned. "I wouldn't even know where that would

be."

"Let's look for one." He reached for her pack, but she drew back.

"What about you? Are you going to try to take the necklace once it's completed?"

He raised his eyebrows. "Maia, I don't want anything to do with control over any of the Realms, much less all twelve. I'm an assassin, not a thief. Just because I know how thieves think doesn't mean I am one."

She blew out a sigh of acceptance. "Right, of course. I'm sorry. It's hard to know who to trust right now."

He nodded as he helped her tuck the cloth wrapped bundle away. "That's true. But you can trust the dryads to get their magic right. I can't kill you without hurting myself, and the more time I spend with you, the less I'm inclined to do so."

Maia barked a laugh. "Well, I guess that's something." She nodded. "You're not so bad yourself when you're willing to talk to me."

He grinned. "I'll endeavor to talk a little bit more while we travel."

"A little bit would be a definite step up." She rubbed her eyes with her fingers and yawned. "I'm going to bed to get some rest before tomorrow." She tilted her head and gave him a tired smile. "Thank you for holding me and helping me with the opal. Good night, Quinn."

"Good night, Maia."

Warmth filled him as she disappeared into her room and he couldn't stop the smile from curling his lips. He'd helped her for no other reason than he could. Strangely enough, he liked doing it. He shook his head as he retreated into his own room and readied himself for bed. Something had shifted and he wasn't sure he wanted it to shift back.

CHAPTER TEN

Maia took a deep breath. "Are you sure we want to do this?"

"Are you?" Quinn shot back as he reached for the big stone door leading out of the keep.

"No, that's why I'm asking."

He snorted and pushed the door open. Snow fell in determined flakes, but at least the wind wasn't howling. The cold was a sharp counterpoint to the warmth in the keep, but Quinn didn't wait around and Maia had no choice but to follow him. *Damn assassin.*

Despite her grumpy thought, she no longer despised Quinn. He'd grown on her. *Yeah, like a fungus.* But he'd changed since they arrived at the Keep. While he hadn't been what she'd call overly friendly, he no longer looked at her like a bug he'd like to scrap off his boots with the tip of a knife. And she'd seen the knife he carried with him.

Damn, he's in danger of becoming a lot like Fantasy Quinn.

Today he wore his white coat and hood and she liked the way it gave him a sexy, mysterious look. *What is it about men in hoods?* He scanned the trees and snowy bluffs around them before he turned his hooded gaze back to her.

"Which way do we go from here?"

Maia settled her mind away from the alluring image of her companion standing in the snow like some sort of warrior hero and reached out for the energy of the Key. The piece buried in her pack glowed like a white star in her mind's eye, but another ripple of energy came from directly in front of her, straight down the incline. It appeared golden and warm like flames.

She opened her eyes and grimaced as she pointed. "That way."

Quinn nodded. "Let's get to the bottom of the hill first and reassess. I'm not a fan of learning to fly at this late in the game."

"What, not willing to take a leap of faith, and hope the snow provides a soft landing?" She grinned.

"Not this time." He smirked before he turned away and led her back along the trail they'd taken a few days before.

Despite their new-found camaraderie, they lapsed into silence as they traversed down the mountain. Maia's body complained about the weight on her back, hips, and knees with each step, but at least she didn't have to break the trail. Quinn moved with ease despite his gear and weapons and she followed him, trying not to enjoy the view of his broad shoulders, back, and strong legs as he hiked in front of her. *Too much Fantasy Quinn in that view.*

It took them a couple of hours' worth of daylight to make it to a low point from the Keep and Maia appreciated the decrease in constant down. She closed her eyes to catch her breath and check her inner compass. The energy pulled her a little to the left and when she opened her eyes, she found more hill in her view. *Great, up again.*

"That's not a good expression. Which way do we need to go?" Quinn braced his legs shoulder-width apart and rested his hands on his hips.

"That way." She pointed toward the next climb.

He followed her finger. "South?"

Maia shrugged. "I can't tell where the sun is in the snow, but that's the direction."

He nodded. "South it is. The only saving grace will be when we reach the warmer climate. Less snow."

"Let's hope." She nodded. "Do you want me to break the trail for a while?"

He paused and looked back at her from under his hood. "You want to break the trail?"

"If it'll help. I know how tiring it is. It might be better to switch off so we can conserve our energy." Maia shrugged, not wanting to do the harder work, but unwilling to let him do it all.

He nodded slowly. "Let's do it this way. You may break the trail in the valleys and flats, and I'll do the hills."

"All right." She started to move but stopped herself. "Thanks, Quinn."

He paused again. "For what?"

"For your help, but also your willingness to let me help you." She shrugged one shoulder as much as her pack allowed. "It's good to be given the chance." She nodded and swung into motion, breaking through the snow along the valley floor until the path rose once again and Quinn took over.

****

Quinn had to admit Maia had behaved better than he expected for a spoiled princess on this trek south through the mountains. After two days out in the weather, he'd expected her to whine about going back to Windbreak Keep, but she upheld the deal of breaking the trail when the ground leveled out and never complained.

On the third night from the keep, they had to find a windbreak using boulders and the trees around them. No caves provided shelter and they were in for a windy, cold night. Maia had learned how to build a respectable fire for their camp after a little coaching and she coaxed a small flame to catch the wood despite the wind. Quinn glanced over from his sentry position at the edge of their camp, returning his dagger to its sheath. Maia fed another stick to the fire, her expression lined and sad.

"Do you miss your family, princess?"

Maia glanced up. "Did you just ask me a personal question? As in a real conversation?"

"We've had real conversations."

"Not since we left the Keep. Apparently traveling makes you shut down tighter than a vault." Her remarks had no fire in them despite her goading words.

Amusement bloomed through his chest, but he only cocked his head, waiting.

"I do and I don't miss them. I think I'm saddest for Inge. She probably held secrets more than the rest of us and couldn't tell anyone." Maia shrugged as she returned her gaze to the fire. "She must have been terribly lonely and afraid to let us down."

"What about you? Are you afraid of letting them down?" He rose and moved closer to her and the fire.

"Oh, I have it worse than my sister. I not only have to worry about letting them down, I have to worry about letting twelve whole worlds down." She shivered and scrubbed her face with her hands. "That's a lot of responsibility for a sixth daughter. I don't think my other sisters would've been up to the task. Some of them were quite shallow. At least, that's what I remember."

"Harsh assessment of your own family."

Maia nodded. "I know, but make no mistake. We were princesses and privileged. We didn't have real tragedy or struggles before we were imprisoned as lamps. It's hard to be compassionate for people without the experience of hardship."

Quinn tilted his head, surprised to hear her words. "What made you change your mind?"

She fed another stick on the fire and wrapped her coat tighter around her to keep out the chill as the wind rustled the branches of the closest tree overhead.

"We had a maid, a serving woman named Gretchen, who would make sure we always had clean clothes and fresh fruit to eat in the summertime. At the end of the day, my father and sisters always insisted on having new untouched fruit, so Gretchen would gather up the uneaten fruit and take it away. Then she'd replace it with new the next day." Maia rubbed her hands together. "One day I found her putting it into a bag, and I asked her what she did with the unused fruit each day. She said she took it to the food bank in town for the less fortunate. I didn't know what she meant so I offered to help and followed her into the village." She grimaced. "I'd never seen people who didn't have enough and it was scary to me. But I kept going with her into town. Gretchen didn't have very much, but she had more than these people and she willingly helped them when she could. She taught me a lot after doing that. She never called me Princess in front of the others and I tried to make sure there was always a little extra to put in her bag every week."

Quinn raised his chin. "You're surprisingly charitable."

She shrugged and shivered again. "I'm no saint, but it taught me a valuable lesson about having enough. And it helped me understand that helping people is more satisfying than just living in luxury." She hissed as the wind blew harder. "Glory be, it's cold tonight."

Quinn moved to settle behind her, wrapping his arms around her torso. Having her in his arms felt right despite their clothes. He just wanted the physical company. Keeping each other warm was a bonus.

"What are you doing?" She froze in his loose embrace.

"Lean back. We'll both be warmer if we share body heat." He didn't tell her he wanted another chance to smell her hair and feel her body against his. "Relax, Maia."

"Are you feeling all right?"

Quinn just chuckled and wrapped his blanket around them both. For all her femininity, she had sass and he grudgingly admitted he preferred women with backbone. He'd never met anyone like this princess. She possessed a regality found in the usual royals, but under the façade was a person who cared about others beyond herself, and who wouldn't back down when something needed to be done. He hadn't expected that from a Silvercloak.

"Tell me about your family, about your brother. His name was Sean, wasn't it?"

Quinn stiffened in surprise. "You remember his name?"

"Yes, he looked a bit like you, but he had more red in his hair and blue in his eyes. Sorsia was totally taken with him, I think." Maia settled back against Quinn's chest and stared at the fire. "She liked his laugh and the way his shoulders filled out his shirt." She chuckled and shot a look up at him. "I'm sure you don't want to hear a woman's assessment of your brother. It had a lot to do with shoulders, arms, chests, and butts."

"While I admit I didn't look for those things on him, he did seem to catch the eyes of a lot of ladies when we were younger." Quinn recalled the women oohing and ahhing over Sean's reddish hair and striking blue eyes. The dark-haired, green eyed older boy was often ignored in the face of his brother's exotic beauty.

"Really? Sorsia wasn't alone?"

He snorted. "Not by a long shot. Women were often batting their eyes or smiling at him. They often didn't notice me at all."

"Maybe because you're an assassin and used to being sneaky and overlooked." Maia snorted.

Quinn laughed, though at the time he hadn't found it so amusing. "This was before I'd trained as an assassin." They sat in silence a few moments. "For the record, Sean confided in me that he'd met the woman who stole his heart, or at least his attention for longer than usual. Your sister Sorsia kept him coming back to try again. I think he really liked her."

"She really liked him. She'll be just as horrified to hear about his death as you were. It'll break her heart." Maia's voice settled into the sadness he'd seen on her face earlier. "I tried to help them get as much time alone together as I could. It wasn't much, but I know she really wanted him to like her. She didn't want him to marry Inge as the original degree stated." Maia tipped her head to the side, settling into the hollow of his shoulder. "To be honest, I don't think Inge was very interested in your brother, either."

"He never mentioned anyone but Sorsia." *And Maia.* Quinn's dream came back to him as they settled into another silence broken only by the wind and fire crackling. But he didn't want to admit that to her. *It was just a dream anyway.*

"I'm really sorry he's gone, Quinn. But even if he'd lived, he'd be long gone and Sorsia will be the same age as she was when she disappeared." She leaned her head back against his chest and closed her eyes. "Everyone we knew from home is dead by now."

He heard the sorrow and resignation in her voice. "Everyone except your sisters and me."

"And the dryads."

"Yes, and them. Or the Keeper of the Grove." He took a deep breath. "At least you have your sisters. Family is important."

"I will have my sisters. Currently, they're still lamps." She sighed and shook her head. "Do you think I can really save them from the dryads' spell?"

"I don't know. There's more to this adventure than I bargained for, that's certain."

"Yes, me, too. Thanks for coming with me, even if it

was under duress."

Quinn tilted his head and met her gaze. "You're welcome, Maia."

They stared at each other for a few minutes, neither looking away. Quinn wondered if she'd allow him to kiss her or if she'd break the moment and roll away from him. *Better not risk it.* He didn't want to lose her comforting weight and warmth against his body.

"Good night, Quinn." She tilted her head away and closed her eyes again.

"Good night, Maia." He settled back and watched the fire burn down as he inhaled the scents of her hair and her coat. Despite being outdoors and exposed in ways he preferred to avoid, he liked having her in his arms and contentment filled his chest.

****

The next day they made good time heading south and descended into a wide valley with a river meandering through it. The snow had stopped, but the sun remained hidden behind a thick mat of clouds. Maia had taken the lead and broke the path through the snow while Quinn covered her back trail. So far it had been a quiet trek, but unease crept through him and he kept his gaze roving around them. They were exposed and it made his neck itch, but they both wore white and he hoped that would keep them camouflaged enough to escape anyone's notice.

By early evening they'd made it to the mountains on the other and Quinn took the lead. Maia sent him a grateful smile full of exhaustion and determination. It didn't take him long to find a cave to settle into for the night. He had her wait until he'd checked it for occupants before they dropped their packs and set up the makings of a fire. They'd gotten into a comfortable routine, sharing the responsibilities to make the journey easier, and they always slept together to share warmth. Quinn didn't mind a bit. Her delicious scents made him sleep better anyway.

But something seemed off tonight and he didn't remove his weapons right away. If Maia noticed, she didn't say anything and continued to build a fire to give them heat and light.

"What would you like to eat tonight, dried meat and fruit? Or travel bread, dried meat, and vegetable chips?"

"Hmm, with such delectable choices, I don't know how I could choose."

Maia laughed, the husky sound warming him more than the fire. He'd made it his unspoken vow to make her laugh as much as possible. He liked the sound too much to give it up.

"Dried meat and fruit it is." She shook her head and pulled out two portions for them to snack on. "Come sit next to me for the meal. I know it's not the high table in a palace, but think of it more like an intimate engagement instead. I have a seat of honor for you right here." She patted the stone floor beside her.

Now it was Quinn's turn to laugh. "Are we having intimate dinners now?"

She raised her head and her eyebrows as he froze, surprised at the words he'd uttered. He hadn't meant to admit anything close to how he felt aloud. They were traveling together, no more than partners in an adventure. He hadn't meant to reveal his inner thoughts. *I'm slipping.*

She snorted and a smirk curved her lips. "Oh yes, so intimate. Come savor the goat jerky with just a hint of rosemary." Her sarcasm broke the tension and he settled onto the stone with a chuckle.

"Tell me more about your family." He had no idea where the statement came from, but now that it sat between them, he found he really wanted to know. "What were your sisters like? And how did your father get the idea to hold a pageant for men to find the love of their lives with you?"

Maia shrugged. "I think my father just didn't know what to do with all of us. Twelve girls of various ages would drive anyone mad. And four of them were two sets of twins. The older ones, Adeline and Madeline, were a little more tractable and willing to listen to father. But the younger set, Nara and Nora, were wild things, always getting into things. Addie and Maddie were fraternal twins, which is to say they had distinct differences, but Nara and Nora were identical and hard to tell apart."

"Sweet Goddess, that would definitely play havoc with men coming in to court you all."

"Oh, there were some high adventures with that." Maia snorted. "Nara and Nora were merciless. They once had two men fighting because they swore they'd each been promised a dance from the same woman, when in fact my sisters just wanted to see if they could tell them apart." Maia tipped her head and chewed thoughtfully. "In retrospect, it may have been their way of finding some individuality when they were always seen as the same. I think they would've liked the boys to know them well enough not to be fooled."

Quinn nodded. "I can see that."

"And all of us were a little disgusted that we were used as bait or prizes for men seeking their fortune." Maia grimaced as she let her gaze rest on the fire. "The first few times were rather exciting. New boys or men to meet, although Karissa and Clara weren't ever interested in them. Clara because she was too interested in nature and how things worked, and Karissa because she didn't find men attractive. She liked women."

Quinn blinked, his eyebrows rising. "She was...?"

"A lesbian, yes. Oh, she never said anything, but most of us knew and we tried to deflect Father's attempts to connect her with men. She was the next oldest to Inge." Maia shrugged again. "But after the tenth time a new guy would come in and start looking at us like a herd of prize pigs he hoped to purchase, it became less fun. Some of them were arrogant pricks figuring their swaggering and connections would win them some pliant woman. We got sick of that fast."

He'd never considered how the women felt before. He'd only seen his brother's attempts to find himself a better life through connection to the Silvercloak royal family. *Was that the way Sean was? Arrogant and swaggering?* He hoped Sean hadn't come across that way, but if he'd been put on display time and time again as the prize for someone seeking their fortune by completing some random task, he'd be jaded as well.

"Sean wasn't that way, was he?"

Maia turned her head to look at Quinn, and he squirmed under her somber gaze. "No, but I think he'd met Sorsia in the village a few times so he already knew who he wanted. And Sorsia liked him and welcomed his attention."

"I'm glad to hear that." Quinn blew out a relieved breath. "He thought the world of her. At least that's what he told me."

She raised her eyebrows. "Why didn't you do the same? Didn't you want to win your fortune by snagging one of the Silvercloak princesses?"

Quinn sat quietly for a short time, watching the flames as he swallowed down the dried meat. "That was Sean's thing. I wasn't ready for a woman in my life, though our parents were thrilled with the idea that we'd get married and give them grandchildren. But I wasn't interested in that. And then, when you didn't come back and your father put my brother to death for it, I definitely didn't have any interest."

Maia looked away. "No, I would bet not."

They didn't say anything more for a long time and Quinn wondered what his brother would be doing had the princesses returned. Would he have won Sorsia over and married? Would he have been disappointed when he fell asleep like the others and went home alone? Quinn couldn't imagine Sean morose. He'd always been the more jovial of them and somehow always landed on his feet.

Quinn missed his brother and wished he'd been able to stop his execution. The unfairness of Sean's demise threatened to ruin the peace he'd come to with Maia, but logic prevailed and he refused to blame her for it. Maia would've stopped her father if she'd been there.

"But it might have been a different story if you'd have come home."

Maia turned her head with her brows raised. "What?"

"If you'd have come home, I might have been tempted to follow my brother's footsteps." He met her gaze, enjoying the play of the fire's light on her hair and face. The shadows gave her character and mystery, and he found himself drawn to her more than he'd been at the Windbreak Keep.

She studied him for a long time and he wondered what she saw. Without a word, she turned her body and reached up to push back his hood, exposing his face to the light. He never looked away, though it was hard to meet her eyes as she examined him. Would she see the scars he'd accrued on his body? Would she see the ones on his soul?

She tilted her head a little as she looked away from his gaze. "You're turning silver at your temples."

He smirked as a laugh escaped. "The price of aging. My father was gray by the time he turned twenty-five. I'm well older than that and I should be grateful it's only my temples."

A smile curled her lips. "It makes you look experienced and distinguished." She dropped her gaze to his hands. She picked one of them up, tracing the white lines of hardship and the thick calluses from handling weapons. "Your hands tell a different story. But they're beautiful, too, in their own way. They show your experience and capabilities." She stroked his palm and his cock took notice of her caress.

When she reached up to skim her fingers along his cheek and jaw, he sucked in a breath of surprise. His heart fluttered with excitement and anticipation as her gaze studied his face.

"You're silver here, too, and the stubble is handsome." She paused, blinking, as her words seemed to sink in. "I'm sorry. That was too bold." She pulled her hand back, but he caught it.

"There's no one here but us, Maia. No one to say what's too bold or too forward. We're alone and we make the rules." Apparently, he was just as bold. *Who knew I was so poetic?* "I don't mind you touching me." He stopped before he admitted how long it had been since someone touched him intimately. Or how much he craved it from her.

She bit her bottom lip. "Do you trust me to touch you without hurting you?"

He blinked then laughed. "Hurting me? I can defend myself from men bigger than you. I'm not worried about you hurting me."

She narrowed her eyes and shook her head. "Yes, you are. But I'm not talking about your physical body. I'm talking about you." She dropped her hand to his chest, pointing at his heart.

He drew back from her, a frown lowering his brows. "Why would I worry over that?"

The intensity in her expression faded into stoicism and she dropped her hand. "No reason. I guess I was too bold after all. My mistake." She retreated from him and he felt her withdrawal like a punch in the gut.

He didn't know what to say, but he understood he'd missed an opportunity. *Dammit all to hell.* He frantically tried to come up with something to say to change the direction of the evening, but the moment was lost and she put distance between them. Silence yawned like a gaping canyon and he didn't know how to bridge it.

That night they slept apart and it was the coldest night he could remember.

CHAPTER ELEVEN

Morning came with a reminder of winter. Snow fell from the sky with a vengeance and Quinn woke up stiff and sore. *Damn, getting old sucks.* He forced his stiff body to move and looked around for Maia. She was already up and packed her belongings into her pack with economy of motions. This was the second time she'd been up before him while traveling.

She didn't say anything and he pushed his tired body into motion, hoping to warm up enough to loosen the stiffness. He wanted to reconnect to the easy camaraderie they'd had before, but he still had no idea what to say. Maia wasn't offering any kind of opening for conversation and they left the cave by unspoken agreement.

Quinn's mood darkened as they stepped out of their relatively warm sanctuary into the driving snow. Maia closed her eyes and searched for the direction they needed to go while he mentally prepared for a long day in the snow. He sincerely hoped moving south would reduce the winter travel they had to face.

While he waited for her to get her bearings, he heard something moving through the sparse forest. His mind stilled along with his breath and he listened hard. The prickle at the back of his neck made him pull out his hatchet. Something was wrong.

Maia opened her eyes and pointed along the length of the hillside as their direction. *Glad we don't have to go up first thing.* He nodded, but held up his hand as she started to move. When she opened her mouth to say something, he put his fingers to his lips and scanned the trees around him for danger.

The hiss of an arrow through the air was the only warning they had and Quinn twisted out of the way at the last moment. The shaft buried itself in the tree to his right as he ducked down. Maia threw herself to the snow-covered ground, her eyes wide.

"Glory, we're under attack."

"Yes. And they have an archer." He tossed the bow off his shoulder and notched an arrow of his own.

"Did you see where he fired from?" She lifted her head and another shaft hit the snow near it with a soft *thhock!* Maia squeaked and rolled behind a tree.

But the second shot had given Quinn the general location of the archer. Unfortunately, the man wasn't alone. Other dark shapes crept through the snow shrouded tree trunks, easily visible against the white. They closed quickly, but he wanted to take out the archer first.

"Quinn, give me the bow."

"What?" He shot a quick look at Maia before returning his gaze to the oncoming attackers.

"Toss me the bow and quiver. I'm not good at hand-to-hand, but I can fire the bow."

Was she serious? How could a woman who'd been a lamp for centuries know how to fire a bow with any skill? But his ruminations had taken up too much time. If they didn't do something, they'd both end up as blood-stains in the snow.

He tossed her the bow and threw off the quiver of arrows just as the first attackers reached them. He pulled out his hatchet and long dagger, and went to meet them, hoping Maia would be safe long enough for him to kill the men close at hand.

The fight commenced in eerie silence, the men coming at him making no noise except for the grunts of impact when their blades collided. The first man fell quickly, no match for Quinn's skill. He slit the man's throat before he'd done more than raise his blade.

But the second man had some ability and feinted to the left before swinging a harvest scythe in from the right. Quinn blocked it with his hatchet and thrust his long dagger into the man's belly. He jerked out of the way and swung a club at Quinn's head, but Quinn ducked and sliced at the man's knees with his hatchet. His opponent wasn't fast enough and went down, and Quinn drove his long dagger into his neck before looking for the next assailant.

He had a few precious seconds to check on Maia and found her taking aim at the hidden archer in a classic archery stance. Her beauty and elegance rivaled Artemis as she sighted along the arrow before she let fly. To his surprise, her arrow hit its mark and a man hidden in the trees beyond them fell hard to the snowy ground. If he'd had time to appreciate her skill, Quinn's cock would've hardened in delight. Maia resembled a warrior goddess and his heart kicked up in approval.

But he had to focus on the next man hoping for a quick death. He fought three more men in varying degrees of skill levels, but in the end, they all fell, leaving nothing but crimson bloodstains on his coat. He sliced through the last man's throat just as someone shouted for his attention. Quinn let his latest victim fall and turned his attention to the last threat

His fury settled cold and hard in his gut as he faced the man with his arm around Maia's waist and a knife to her throat.

"Drop yer weapons or I slit her feckin' throat." He

pushed the blade against her soft skin and the cold in Quinn's gut dropped deeper.

"Let her go and I'll allow you to live."

The dirty bandit holding Maia laughed with derision. "The way I figure it, you can't kill me before I give'er a second smile so drop yer weapons and we'll negotiate, all civil like."

Quinn shot a look a Maia and her mouth lay in a flat line, but her eyes held fear. That pissed him off more than the initial attack on them. Maia could face down anyone. Seeing her afraid made his decision for him.

"Go on now, drop them fancy blades." The bandit jerked Maia, pressing the knife harder and she whimpered.

Anger coalesced into fine fury, but Quinn sighed and dropped his hatchet into the snow, followed by the long dagger. But while he gave the appearance of defeat, he pulled his hand back and let fly with a throwing blade hidden in his sleeve. *Please don't move, Maia.* The knife hissed through the air to bury itself in the bandit's eye, right beside Maia's head.

She gave a cry and ducked just as the man grunted and released her. She fell forward, dropping face-down in the snow and Quinn sprang past her to make sure the man didn't get up. He gave the bastard his own "second smile" before turning to her.

"Maia." Quinn knelt beside her, his heart in his throat. "Maia."

She gave a sob and he yanked her to her feet, turning her to face him so he could scan her person. He'd never experienced such gut-wrenching fear, not even when he first started training with the Assassin's Guild just after his brother's death. *She must be okay. She must be all right.*

They stood in the snow, nose to nose, their breath steaming in the frigid air, and Quinn took in the beautiful woman standing before him. She didn't appear to be bleeding, though a small mark marred the soft skin of her neck. Maia stared back at him, her jaw clenched and her brows pulled together over her nose.

"Quinn..." The sound was barely a whisper, as if she didn't have the breath for more.

He slid his hands over her arms as the snow fell onto their coats and checked once more to see if she remained unharmed.

"You're not hurt, are you?" He wanted to check her whole body, but he couldn't look away from her eyes.

Maia shook her head, tears spilling over her lower lids as her reaction set in. She took a step forward and pressed her body against his chest seeking comfort, her hands fisting in his coat.

"It's all right, Maia. You're safe. I've got you."

"You killed him." She shivered. "You killed all of them."

"In defense. As per your request." He wrapped his arms around her. "We're safe for the moment." Holding her against his chest, Quinn wondered why he'd resisted touching her.

"Thank you, Quinn." She laid her head against his chest. "Thank you so much."

"You're welcome. You didn't do too bad yourself." He nodded in the direction of the bodies sporting arrows.

"Only because I had to. I couldn't let you be killed." She trembled in his arms, pressing her face into his chest.

"Let's get out of the open. It's cold and I don't want anything else to notice us here." He cupped her cheek and gave her his best reassuring smile. "Let's go back to the cave. I think we can afford a day of rest."

"What about the bodies? Won't someone see them?"

"I'll collect their weapons and move them. The snow should cover them soon. Let me get you back to the cave first."

Maia nodded and grabbed her discarded pack before she stumbled back toward their granite sanctuary. Quinn followed behind, retrieving his hatchet, long dagger, quiver and bow. He kept an eye out for more bandits, but whoever they'd been, there didn't seem to be more of them.

Quinn helped Maia into the cave and set the weapons and his pack against the wall.

"I'm going to go move the bodies. Start a fire and melt some snow for tea. I'll be back shortly."

"Quinn." Maia waited for him the meet her gaze. "Please be careful."

"I will."

He ducked back out into the rising snowstorm and let his fury carry him to the carcasses in the snow. He quickly stripped the bodies of weapons and gear they could use before dragging them several hundred yards east of their cave. The bandits had come from the west and he didn't want to broadcast their location to the cohorts should anyone come looking for them.

By the time he'd cleared the bodies and plucked the arrows from those Maia had shot, the sun had risen to the midday peak. Snow fell harder and he knew he was out of time. If he stayed out much longer, he'd never find the cave in the blinding whiteout. Using his knife, he cut a bough to use for disguising his backtrail and made his painstaking way toward the cave.

He checked for signs of additional intruders on his return, but the weather made it difficult. Fortunately the heavy snowfall would cover their tracks and the signs of the skirmish. The bodies would attract scavengers, but hopefully they sat far enough away.

He cut more boughs with his hatchet to cover the cave's entrance and settled them in a haphazard way across the opening. With any luck, the snow would cover the makeshift door and no one would know they were there.

"It's snowing harder. We should be safe for the time being." Quinn found Maia seated beside the fire, her arms wrapped tightly around herself. He crouched beside his pack and pulled out his bedding. "Nothing should show where we are beyond the smoke and the snow will obscure that. The bodies are out of the way."

"Good." She didn't meet his gaze.

"Are you all right, Maia?"

She tilted her head and shrugged with one shoulder, but said nothing. He took the time to spread out the bedding then moved to her side and grasped one hand.

"Come with me, please."

She followed him as he pulled her to her feet and tugged her to the bedding he'd laid out. They settled onto it beside the fire and he pulled her into his arms, her back to his chest. He held her, the silence stretching as the fire crackled with determined hunger.

"I was so scared, Quinn."

"I know. Me, too." He remained curled around her, enjoying the scent of her hair. "You're sure you're all right? No injuries?"

"Nothing beyond the scratch at my neck. That's it." She shivered.

"Let me look at it to make sure there's nothing wrong." He tipped her head back to look at her throat where the brigand had marked her. It was only a scratch, but the flood of relief surging through him damn near stole his breath.

"Were you really scared?" Maia's voice held surprise as well as doubt.

"Breathlessly." Didn't she know he had emotions?

"You didn't show it at all, which is probably a good thing." She squeezed her eyes shut and grimaced. "I'm sure it unsettled the bandits and put them off their game. I was shaking like a leaf."

He didn't say anything, unwilling to disabuse her of the steadiness he displayed. In truth, the only reason he hadn't been shaking was because of the rigorous training he'd sustained in the Assassin's Guild. But the adrenaline rush would end soon and he'd collapse in an exhausted heap.

"You're safe now and there's a storm coming so we'll have some time to rest."

"Thank goodness."

She snuggled down into his embrace and his cock stirred, reminding him he was in need of feeling her skin against his own. How he'd negotiate that when just an hour earlier she'd been furious with him he had no idea. But he needed her. It was his only way of being sure she remained unhurt. He closed his eyes and willed his cock to settle, but her soft moans filling the warming air echoed clearly in his memory. He skimmed a hand down her side, cupping her hip, and pulled her closer. If he could only hold her, he'd take it.

Maia whimpered and tipped her head back, pressing her face against his as she sought comfort. He tried to ignore the invitation to kiss her until she pressed her lips to his chin.

"Maia…" He didn't think he had the stamina to resist her if she teased him this way.

"Kiss me, Quinn."

Thank the Goddess. He sealed his lips to hers.

****

Maia fell into his kiss and didn't care. She needed to feel him, to touch him, to taste him as a reminder that they'd both survived. Quinn had been both the most frightening thing and the most magnificent while in the midst of the fight. He'd moved with fluid grace and ruthless efficiency. If she hadn't been so focused on taking out the archer and anyone still lurking in the distance, she would've paused to appreciate his skills.

But when the man came up behind her and held a knife to her throat, she'd lost all of her equanimity as panic clawed its way up her throat. Fortunately, it had frozen her in place because Quinn's next action would have killed her if she'd moved. She heard the knife go into the bandit's head, but thanked the Goddess she hadn't seen it.

Now she let herself sink into the sensation of Quinn's tongue wrapping about hers, warming her from the inside out, and banishing all the fear. She wanted to burrow into him and wrap him around her to protect herself from outside dangers. When he pulled back to catch his breath, she sat up and turned around to face him, pushing his hood off his head.

She took a moment to study his face, the sharp planes of his cheeks covered in salt and pepper scruff. She knew his eyes were green, but in the light of the fire they resembled dark jade with flecks of silver. The left side of his lips curved upwards, giving him a sardonic half-smile, and she often wondered if he hid his thoughts behind his constant non-expression.

"Quinn?" She met his green gaze.

"Yes, Maia?"

"Will you touch me intimately? Will you remind me that we're both alive?" Her boldness was unusual, but she didn't want to clutter the moment up with words that would make him retreat like he had the night before.

He didn't say anything for several heartbeats, but his eyes intensified as he stared at her. He swallowed hard then nodded with a dip of his chin. "Do you understand what you're asking?"

She resisted the urge to roll her eyes. Why did men think that women who'd had no sex had no idea about it? "If you don't want to have sex with me, all you have to do is say it. You don't have to patronize me."

The left corner of his mouth quirked before his brows came down. "I didn't ask because I didn't want to have sex with you, I asked because once I start pleasuring you, I'm not likely to stop."

His words shocked and thrilled her, but she raised her

chin. "All right."

He growled and swooped in for another kiss. She moaned as his lips teased hers, but she held onto his coat to keep from swooning. His hands speared into her hair and held her as he ravished her mouth. Pleasure leapt through her body, pooling at the juncture between her thighs, and her pussy clenched with unfulfilled desire. *Goddess, I want him.*

Quinn pulled back from the kiss and quickly unlatched her coat, revealing her body. She still wore all her clothes, but the way his gaze riveted to her chest made her feel completely exposed. He reached for her breasts, sliding his hands over the cotton-encased flesh, and her nipples tightened.

"Oh, Goddess, Quinn." Was that breathy voice hers? She'd be embarrassed except the sensations of his hands on her chest pushed away any discomfort.

"You're magnificent, Maia." He met her gaze. "Every curve perfect. You're like a gift I get to unwrap." He slowly undid the buttons of her shirt until her breasts sat exposed to the light of the fire. "Sweet Lady Death, you are glorious."

He dipped his head and pressed his lips to one nipple, sucking it into his mouth. Maia gasped as the heat and pleasure mixed into a bolt of arousal bouncing through her. Oh, she wanted this, needed it like she needed water. She threw her head back and closed her eyes as he suckled her breast, one hand kneading the neglected mound.

She wanted to touch him but he still wore too much clothing while his tongue danced over her nipples. When he pulled back to switch to the other breast, she caught his face in her hands.

"I need you undressed."

He quirked a brow and smiled. "Do you, now?"

"Yes." She couldn't remember a time when she was so breathless, but the idea of having Quinn naked before her for real set her heart to racing. "I want to touch you and feel your skin against mine."

"Then we should get undressed."

He sat up and pulled his coat back, but she stayed his hands as she rose with him. His eyes blazed as he took in her breasts, the nipples puckering in the cool air. He licked his lips and excitement built in her chest and she reached for his coat.

"Will you let me undress you?"

"You want to undress me? I thought you wanted me to touch you." His gaze rose to hers, but some of the fire returned to the irises.

"I do, but since I haven't had much chance to indulge in touching a lover, I thought I'd take advantage of the opportunity." She unbuckled the belt around his waist and worked on the buttons lining the lapels of his coat. She snorted as she worked. "How long does it take you to get dressed in the morning? This is daunting."

Quinn laughed and helped her with his clothes. "I dress for the weather. It's cold so I'm bundled up."

They got his coat off and he went to work on disarming himself while she laid her coat on their combined bedding. When she turned back he had removed his boots and unbuckled his belt. There was something so sexy about him sitting there with his trousers and belt undone and her pussy grew slick in anticipation.

She raised her gaze to his as she leaned into him, pushing the buttons on his shirt through their holes. "I want to see your chest."

He shot her a half-smile. "Why?"

"To be sure." She kept working.

"Sure of what?"

"That it's as beautiful as I remember."

She must have struck him dumb because he said nothing else and allowed her to open his shirt. *Yep, just as beautiful as I thought.* His skin ran smoothly over the hard

122

slabs of muscle, marred only by a few scars. Each abdominal muscle left a shadowed hollow in the light of the fire, but the dark line of hair running from his navel down into his open trousers teased her. She wanted to follow it with her hand or maybe her tongue, just to see where it led.

"And you're more glorious than I imagined." Quinn reached for her breasts and ran his thumbs over her nipples. "I've wanted to taste and tease these since your bath in the Windbreak Keep."

She paused. "You saw my nipples then?" Oh glory, had he seen her little fantasy in the bath?

"No, but I have a good imagination." He grinned as he pushed her back onto her coat and bedding. "I plan using that imagination to pleasure you now."

She loved the feeling of his body over hers, but she couldn't resist one more tease. "And you're sure you'll be able to pleasure me?"

His lips curled again. "I won't know until I try, but I'm willing to give it my all." He dropped his head and sealed his mouth over a nipple while his hands went to her trousers.

Maia helped him as much as she was able, but the hot, slick pleasure of his mouth on her breasts distracted her. He only pulled back long enough to tug her boots off and slide her pants off her hips, but then he paused and gazed down at her. She didn't know what he saw, but the long, hard ridge of flesh pressing against the fly of his trousers suggested he liked it.

When he sat there too long, she shivered and rubbed her arms to chase the chill away. Or to keep from reaching for that lovely bulge in his pants.

"Are you cold, Maia?" He tilted his head, his gaze on her breasts.

"Yes, a little."

"Let me put another log on the fire." He moved to do so, his back and shoulders illuminated by the light.

"Don't forget your coat." She could imagine him loving her while wearing the coat and hood. The very idea sent cream to her nether lips.

"My coat?" He raised an eyebrow. "You want to wear my coat?"

The idea had merit, but not at the moment and she shook her head. "No, I want you to wear the coat and hood while you pleasure me. It would be so...sexy."

His rich laugh echoed in the small chamber as he crawled back to her and picked up his coat. "You like my coat?"

"Yes, and the hood. More to the point, I like you in your coat and nothing else."

Quinn paused and looked at her as if to gauge her sincerity, but Maia didn't look away. The image of him fucking her with his coat fluttering around them made her pussy tighten and a shiver ran through her.

"That really turns you on." It wasn't a question.

"Yes."

"Very well, princess. I'll give you what you desire."

He rose to his feet and pushed his pants off his hips, exposing the long, curving shaft of his cock. She licked her lips in delight as a small drop of pre-cum beaded at the tip. While she'd played with toys made for the purpose, she'd never experienced a real, flesh-and-blood cock. *It's not a little thing on him.* Of course, she had no idea what big or little was on an excited man, but his cock looked big enough.

"Sweet glory."

"I've heard it called many things, Maia, but never that. However, I'm willing to give it a go to see if you reach that point." He grinned as he settled down between her legs and looked up her body at her. "Shall we begin?"

"Begin...?" What was he talking about?

"Yes, right here." He dropped his head and placed a soft kiss on her mound.

Is he going to—

Hot breath hit her nether lips just before the wet slick heat of his tongue tickled her sensitive flesh. She gasped and moaned, wriggling her hips. But he grasped them with his callused hands and held her still as he feasted on her pussy.

Erotic pleasure speared through her and she couldn't seem to find her breath or her voice. He licked and slurped at her tender flesh and she grasped the coat and blankets below her to keep herself grounded. But each lick and flick of his tongue drove the pleasure higher. She'd never experienced this kind of pleasure with her toys, and it had been so long since she'd played with them, she couldn't remember it being this good.

Maia whimpered and tried to hold back the rising arousal, but his deft motions left her incapable of control. The tide of erotic pleasure swamped her mind and before long she could do little more than wail. He moaned his approval against her sensitive nether lips and she shot into the stars. Her voice echoed off the walls of the cave as she sailed with her release. Pleasure unlike any she'd found with mere toys held her in its thrall and she knew she'd never get enough.

At last she settled back into the blankets beneath her as Quinn rose up to his knees. His cock proudly jutted out in front of him and she had the unreasoning urge to suck it into her mouth and explore the smooth head. He didn't give her the time as he crawled over her and took her mouth for a hot kiss.

"You are magnificent in your pleasure, Maia." He peppered her cheeks and neck with kisses. "I could do that again and again just to hear you moan."

"I won't stop you, but you have to give me a chance to play with your body as well." Her words ended in a whimper as he fit his hips between her legs and rubbed his hard cock against her wet pussy. "Oh, Goddess, I want to play with you, but not right now. Right now I want you to fuck me." She rocked her hips and he hissed as his cock rubbed against her wet flesh.

"Such language from a princess."

"I'm not a princess, I'm a woman who wants her hot lover to bring her glorious pleasure."

Quinn laughed and reached between them to arrange the head of his cock at her lips. "I will do as you ask, Maia, but I need to go slow because of your virginity."

She snorted and grimaced. "No need for that. I took care of it years ago."

He paused, his eyebrows rising. "You did?"

"Yes. Just because we couldn't have sex with men didn't mean we waited for them to give us pleasure." Maia skimmed her fingers over his jaw as she met his viridian gaze. "I had toys and I used them when the needs became too great. I haven't been a technical virgin for…well, centuries now."

"Oh, thank the Goddess." He kissed her hard and slammed his cock home.

****

Quinn had never felt such overwhelming heat and pleasure before in his life, but he held still to savor the deliciousness of being buried balls-deep inside Maia's pussy. *Just remember she's a virgin to lovers, not to sex.* He'd started with cunnilingus to ease the way for his cock, but it turned out to be unnecessary. *I'd beg to differ.* Enjoying her hot pussy cream had done wonders for them both.

She'd admitted to having pleasured herself with toys— and his mind filled in the blanks enough to make his cock flex—but toys only gave the physical pleasure, not the emotional connection. And he found himself wanting to give her more than just a quick fuck.

"Oh, sweet Lady Death, you feel so damn good around my cock." He'd never spoken so lewdly to women who weren't in the sex trade, but he couldn't seem to stop himself. "I could stay here forever."

Maia gave a short laugh. "That may be, but I want you to move."

He grinned down at her and slowly pulled his cock out of her tight grip. "Like this?"

She moaned and threw her head back. "Yes, but much faster."

"How about this?" He slid back in with a little more force and stars flashed across his vision. *Damnation, she's fuckin' tight.*

"Oh, Goddess, yes, but faster, harder."

He obliged her and moved with a little more speed, but kept his gaze on hers, learning her responses to his motions. Unfortunately, her inner muscles clamped down on his shaft, splintering his concentration with pleasure. Her eyes closed and she threw her head back as she wrapped her legs around his thighs to give herself more traction.

He loved when she clutched his arms and rocked her clit against his cock. She seemed to prefer when he slammed in hard, but dragged his cock out slower. Each time he followed the pattern, she grew wetter and slicker. The scent of her erotic musk rose between them as he thrust into her in a steady rhythm and he damn near succumbed to the building pleasure.

Must hold on. Must make her come again.

"Sweet glory, Quinn. I'm going to…to…"

"Look at me, Maia. Show me your pleasure. Come hard and squeeze my cock. Yes, yes!"

He slammed his cock into her as she came apart around him. She wailed her pleasure to the roof, her hands tight on the arms of his coat. She stared at him, her chocolae eyes losing focus as she got lost in the pleasure. Her pussy clamped down on him and he shot into the cosmos with her. *I want her forever.*

As an assassin, he'd never claimed anything. Most possessions were tools, only needed for other purposes. He never kept anything long term. But in that moment, Quinn realized he wanted Maia. He needed her, and he wasn't going to give her up for anything.

"See?" Maia's breathless words brought him back to himself, his cock still throbbing inside her. "I told you the coat and hood were sexy."

He laughed, a full-throated guffaw that shook them both, and she tightened around him, making him moan. "Damn, woman, you need to warn a man. I can't take much more pleasure."

"Hmm, I think we need to work on your stamina." She gave him a smirk before her inner muscles squeezed again.

Quinn groaned. "Great, more training." But he ruined his lament with a grin. "I promise I'm up to the challenge…just not at the moment." He reluctantly slid his body out of hers, but he meant what he'd said. He'd be more than happy to engage in endurance training with her.

CHAPTER TWELVE

The storm only lasted two days, but Maia and Quinn made the most of their time. While she'd had some experience in pleasure, Quinn taught her new and exciting techniques that sent her careening into the erotic cosmos more often than not. Maia enjoyed every moment.

By the time the storm let up enough for them to travel, Maia's pussy needed a break, but she counted it as a 'good pain.' When they hadn't been fucking, she'd gotten to know Quinn a little better, learning that his silences weren't always dour. He still intimidated her when he threw her a fierce look, but she'd learned it often meant he was puzzling and analyzing something, and didn't really see her at all.

They worked their way south, at least according to Quinn, and the weather turned more and more mild. By her estimation, they'd only been gone from the dryads' Sacred Grove about a month, but it seemed a lifetime had passed. While Quinn didn't chat a lot, he appeared more willing to break his silence as they traveled. The landscape and vegetation changed as well, the trees going from tall boreal natives to shorter, shrub-like conifers. Grasses made up the groundcover beneath their widely-spaced trunks and great ruddy-colored boulders stuck out of the sandy soil. The air held the scents of dry grasses and piney sap, and soon their coats weighed too heavily on their shoulders.

One afternoon as the sun shone in bright warmth, Quinn stopped and pulled off his pack in the shadow of some scrubby pines. Maia breathed a sigh of relief as she stepped into their shade and shed her own pack.

"Good glory, it's hot." She'd left her coat off earlier that morning, but now she needed a rest and water. She scanned the dry landscape. "Do you think there's a stream around here where we can fill up our water containers?"

Quinn did his own scan of the dry grass and scrub. "That depends. Which direction do we need to go from here?" He wiped his forehead with his sleeve and pulled out his water skin, drinking deeply.

Maia closed her eyes and searched out her own inner compass. The way ahead lay directly in front of her. She opened her eyes and pointed toward a clump of drooping trees just showing over the edge of the land.

"That way. Toward those trees."

Quinn followed her finger with his gaze and nodded. "Good. Those look like willows. Willows need water so there's likely to be a stream."

"Should we move down there? I'd like to put my feet in the water."

"Let's rest here a bit. I want to learn more about you." He gave her a lazy smile. Even without the hooded coat, he still held the attraction of a man in his profession.

"Haven't you gotten to know me very well already?" She cocked her hip and rested her hand on it as she tilted her head. "I seem to recall several days and nights where we shared many intimacies."

He laughed. "Yes, but I'm more interested in your fighting skills. You picked up and used my bow without trouble. I'm curious what other skills you have."

"Oh, those." She sobered and nodded. "Father didn't

have any sons, but he believed that if his daughters married neighboring princes and became wives of allies, they should have some tactical training."

"What you know is more than tactical."

"Yes, well, the captain of the guards who oversaw our tactical training preferred action over academics and for a few of us, granted weapons training along with the maps and strategy." Maia shrugged. "Inge, Karissa, Sorsia, Nara, Nora, and I wanted to learn how to use weapons. The others stuck to the more academic knowledge of war."

Quinn nodded. "That's unusual. But I'd like to see what all you know. Can you throw knives?"

She shook her head. "I didn't learn that skill. I learned the bow and some hand-to-hand moves with a short dagger. But I wasn't very good by the time I'd been transformed into a lamp. Karissa could move and fight like an assassin. The guards always complained she didn't fight fair, but the captain reminded us often that there isn't such a thing as a fair fight except in an exhibition."

"That's very true. You must use what advantages you have against your opponents, because in a real fight, they're trying to kill you." Quinn moved beside her and pointed out an old dried out stump. "Let's practice a new skill of throwing knives at your enemy."

Maia frowned. "Why?"

"Because sometimes the best defense against an enemy is not to engage them at all. If you can take someone down without getting close, you've already won." He positioned her hips and she did her best to ignore the sexual awareness that came with his hands on her.

"Or sneaking up behind them and slitting their throats before they know you're there."

"Whatever works. Remember, there are no rules when it comes to life and death situations." He chuckled. "All right. We're going to use that stump there. I'll show you how to throw a knife to disable a target. I don't expect you to kill someone, but if you can slow them down it could mean the difference between survival and death. Now watch."

Quinn tossed a dagger, expertly catching it with negligent grace. The bright blade winked as it tumbled end over end, making no sound against the air.

"How do you do that without cutting up your hand?" Maia watched him pluck the hilt from the air as if picking a long-stemmed rose.

"It's a matter of timing. You have to watch the blade and grab the hilt when it comes within reach." He flipped his hand over to show her the blade pointing out.

"What if you miss?"

"I don't." He winked.

"How long did it take you to *not* miss?" She wished she had such dexterity. He made it look terribly easy, but she was more likely to cut herself. Badly.

"Months, but I was learning more skills at the same time and there was no margin for error." His expression closed down and she decided not to push. "Catching the knife means you want to grab the hilt. But throwing the knife requires you to hold the blade. Like this."

Quinn snatched the blade out of the air and hurled it at the dry stump. The knife hit the wood with a hard *thock!* She gaped at his proficiency.

"Good glory, that was amazing." She shot a wide-eyed look at him. "Can you teach me how to throw it that way?"

"Yes, but don't expect to be able to do it after this afternoon. It'll take practice."

Maia gave him a resigned smile. "It always does."

He snorted. "True enough. Come. Stand before me and I'll show you how to hold it." He held out his arms to her.

Maia didn't know what pleased her more. To stand within his embrace or his willingness to teach her to throw a knife. After a few moments of adjusting her arm and explaining why, Quinn held up the dagger between his fingers.

"Now hold it."

"By the blade?"

"Yes. And aim…like this. Sight your target, and throw with a snap of your wrist." He pulled her arm back. "Throw."

She snapped her hand forward and the knife flew in a weak, clumsy arc to hit the dirt. "Oh."

"Try again."

She did, multiple times, but her attention remained split between what she was doing and where he stood. The scent of his sweat and the heat of his body kept distracting her from her task. Still, she rose to the challenge and did her best to ignore his allure. *I can do this.* Besides, if she mastered what he taught her, she'd win his respect.

The thought startled her so much she damn near threw the knife into her own thigh.

"Whoa! Okay, I think you've had enough practice for one day." Quinn pocketed the knife as if it never existed. "Let's grab our packs and hike down to the willows. We can get some water and rest in the shade."

She didn't argue. *Maybe the water will cool down more than just my feet.* She hoisted her pack onto her shoulders and followed Quinn. Neither of them said anything until they reached the drooping branches of the sweeping trees. Fortunately, a small stream trickled through the xeric landscape and provided a small mossy spot in which to rest. Maia sighed in relief as she set her pack down again and settled her butt into the moss.

She quickly pulled off her boots and stuck her feet in the water, hissing as the cold burned the raw spots from their hiking. The initial pain wore off and drew the heat out of her. She sighed and wiggled her toes in the water, grateful to be off her feet.

Quinn sat beside her and thrust his own feet into the clear stream. They appeared huge in the optical illusion of the water, but she couldn't resist sliding hers against him. He raised his eyebrows when they touched and she offered him a grin.

"Thank you for taking the time to teach me the trick with the knives." Maia rubbed her arm as the muscles protested from unusual use.

He nodded sharply, but didn't meet her gaze. "You're welcome." He took a deep breath and added, "You already have some natural talent. It won't take you long to get the hang of it."

"Think so? I was pretty sure I had no ability whatsoever." She reached down and rubbed between her toes in the water. "Ooohh, it's nice here in the shade. Can we rest here today do you think?"

Quinn scanned the landscape around them. The stream cut through the red rocks like a blade with steep walls to mark its course. The walls opened enough to allow the trees to grow in the place they sat and the rest of the course widened downstream. Blue shadows made by the rocks and trees offered decent cover should they need a place to hide. *Or our enemies do.* She shook her head with a grimace. *Now I'm starting to think like Quinn.*

"I think we can stay here tonight, but we should get an early start tomorrow. The heat makes traveling difficult here." He nodded to her water skin. "You should fill that and drink a full one before we rest. And I think resting now and continuing our journey at night might be wiser."

"Traveling at night?" Maia dutifully filled her water skin as she shot him a frown. "But we won't be able to see very well. It would certainly be harder to see attackers."

"And it'll be harder for them to see us as well. But the most important thing is to stay alive in the heat. And it's much, much cooler at night."

"But wouldn't it make more sense to walk around when it's warmer during the day?"

"Not when we have the gear to keep warm at night.

We're overdressed for the heat here." Quinn filled his own water skin and took a long drink before refilling it. "Besides, I could use a nap right now."

Maia raised her eyebrows and smiled. "You want to take a nap or was that a euphemism for something else?"

Quinn laughed as he unwrapped his bed roll. "As much as I'd like to pleasure you, I think sleeping makes more sense for our purposes." He gestured to her pack. "Hand me your bedroll and we'll sleep the afternoon away."

She did as he asked, but frowned. "What about keeping an eye out for bandits?"

"Not likely around here." He laid down on the roll and waited for her to join him.

"Why not?" She settled beside him, telling her libido to calm down and trying to get comfortable on the sandy soil.

"Because we're in Goblin country now. No one would dare come in here." He closed his eyes and wrapped an arm around her.

Maia swallowed hard. "What will they do to us, then?"

"Hopefully, nothing. But we'll see."

Somehow that wasn't an encouraging thought to bring on restful sleep.

****

Maia struggled awake just as the sun painted long shadows behind the rocks. The temperature had dropped enough to be comfortable, but an icy breeze snaked under the branches of the willow, reminding her winter remained. Despite the cool air, she remained warm and content where she lay nestled in Quinn's arms.

I'm in Quinn's arms.

It took her a moment realize the importance of that small discovery. Somewhere along their travels she'd become used to him. More than that, she enjoyed his company and now she enjoyed his embrace. She wanted to be in his arms at night, or at least when they slept, and she'd gone from being annoyed with his long silences and snarky comments, to content with his companionship. *And hopefully he's no longer interested in killing me.*

She sat up and scrubbed her face with her hands as she took stock of their situation. In addition to moving to the next guardian holding a piece of the Key, they needed provisions soon. Traveling took a lot of energy, particularly for her after being a lamp for so long. She swore her muscles had atrophied even if she hadn't worn her human form the whole time. She couldn't remember being so hungry at the end of the day or being so tired. But she'd grown stronger and no longer felt like death-warmed-over by the time they reached their daily destination.

Maybe Quinn would prefer that.

She allowed smile to curve her lips as she reached over to shake him awake. But she paused as she caught sight of him in the fading light of the sun. He lay with his head turned toward her and his long lashes creating shadows on his cheeks. The salt-and-pepper scruff on his chin and cheeks gave him a rough look she appreciated. *Here I am attracted to a bad boy.* Except, Quinn wasn't a boy by any stretch of the imagination, though he was bad, or he had been.

She frowned. It still unsettled her that his chosen professional equated to reducing the population one person at a time. Killing for profit was wrong. She couldn't find a way to make it okay no matter which way she looked at it, but Quinn himself wasn't inherently bad. The dichotomy stymied her. How could a good person kill others? It didn't make logical sense to her.

"You frown any harder and your bones will break."

Maia met Quinn's gaze and snorted at the smirk he threw at her. "Sometimes I have disturbing thoughts and it's better to frown than hold them inside."

He grunted and sat up before he slid the back of his fingers over her cheek. "I can imagine. What disturbing thoughts are plaguing you tonight?"

She shrugged, unwilling to admit her concerns over his skills. *Or kills.* "I'm worried about the Goblins and what they'll do when they discover we've come into their lands."

He nodded. "Hopefully they'll give us a chance to explain. We aren't skulking so they shouldn't shoot first and ask questions later."

"We're traveling at night. How is that not skulking?" She drank some water before rolling up her bedroll and shrugging into her coat.

"It's not skulking because we're not trying to hide." Quinn pulled on his own coat, black side out, and she shivered with appreciation.

What is it about that coat and hood? Whatever it was, it turned her on something fierce.

They packed up their camp and re-oriented in the direction of the Key's energy before setting off. The wind picked up and Maia tightened her coat around her. Who knew the desert could be so cold? She led the way along the stream for a few miles before her inner compass pulled her to the west. The trail grew steep and they had to pick their way through grumbling hoodoos and boulders. The landscape appeared like a giant child had forgotten her marbles in the sand. Some of them sparkled in the light of the crescent moon hanging in the sky above.

At sun-up, they found a cave to use as shelter, ate a little, and napped together again. Maia liked that Quinn no longer hesitated to hold her. He merely settled his body and opened his arms to wrap her up in them. She relaxed faster with his scent and strength around her than she'd ever done at home in her father's castle. He made her feel safe.

It took them three more nights to cross the Goblins' domain before the guards approached them. The sun had risen, but they'd yet to find a place to settle down when the first Goblin appeared. He wore a hardened leather breastplate over loose trousers and knee-high boots. Short, gnarled horns rose a few inches above his head, protruding through a dull bronze helm. He held a crossbow and a wicked-looking blade hung at his side through a loop in his belt.

"Quinn." She stopped and motioned him up beside her. "We have a visitor."

Quinn's head came up and he stood beside her with his hands loose, watching the Goblin guard.

"Who are you and why have you come here?" The gravelly voice didn't sound nearly as sinister as she expected, but she didn't doubt the guard could easily use his weapons.

How did they explain what they were doing without giving away the presence of the Key?

"We're just traveling through." Quinn stepped in front of her, his eyes on the lone guard.

Maia scanned the rocks around them as she sidled closer to him. There had to be more and she'd bet they weren't friendly.

"No one travels through the Goblin domain." The guard scowled. "You will come with us to see the King and Queen."

Us? Maia looked around, but Quinn kept his gaze on the one guard they could see. His shoulders remained rigid under his coat. She worried he'd do something drastic to affect their escape and stepped in front of him.

"Very well. We'll go with you to meet the King and Queen of the Goblins." She inclined her head as regally as she could. "You may let them know Princess Maiasora Silvercloak and her bodyguard are at their disposal."

Quinn said nothing behind her as the guard considered, but she could sense his surprise. To be honest, she'd like to take a bath and sleep in a bed, but she also had the sneaking suspicion the Goblins held the next piece of the Key.

Following them quietly might make them more willing to listen to her request when the time came.

At last the guard inclined his head. "Very well. Follow and do not deviate from the path."

"Where have I heard that before?" Maia muttered, but gave a vague smile when the guard shot her a suspicious look.

"What are you doing?" Quinn whispered in her ear as they marched behind the guard.

"Going to see the Goblin King and Queen." She nodded to the other guards materializing out of the gloom. "I'll bet you a shiny new crossbow that they have the piece of the Key."

Quinn said nothing for a bit, his footsteps quieter than hers or the guards'. "I'd like a new crossbow."

When she turned to rebuke him, she met a smirk and snorted. "Funny, smart guy."

They followed the guards through twisting and turning slot canyons of granite and red sandstone. Stripes of pale stone gave the impression of jewel-tones as the sun rose and painted mosaic-like colors along the walls. After an hour, the slots opened into a whole different country on the other side.

Green hills covered in grass and deciduous forests opened up ahead of them as they stepped to the edge of the sandstone plateau. Rising out of the bare trees laid out in a pattern stood a castle with high turrets and a decently thick curtain wall around the keep. Stone bridges connected some of the buildings within the wall, making her realize the castle was more of a city and far bigger than she expected.

"Damn, that looks like a long way."

The guards shot her a quelling look, but Quinn snorted. "I'd guess probably around five kilometers or so. Not so long in the grand scheme of things."

She nodded, quelling the urge to whine about how

tired and hungry she was. *What's one more hour of walking?* She resettled her pack on her shoulders and set off ignoring the forbidding scowls of the guards. *Oh, gentlemen, you got nothing on Quinn's scowls.* The snarky thought cheered her enough to keep her going.

The sun had risen to midmorning height and sweat soaked her back as they arrived at the gate with real drawbridge. Chains with links wider than two of her together anchored the bridge to the wall above it and a large iron portcullis hung suspended within the arch. More guards with horned helms and a rose-colored livery stood alertly at the front of the bridge and on the wall.

The guards conferred before they were allowed to enter the city and troop through the buildings toward the keep. Goblins of all shape, size, gender, and lifestyle paused to watch them go by. Children gawked and whispered to their parents. Maia experienced the feeling of being the freak show attraction in a local village.

"I'm thinking humans are still a rarity here." She tilted her head toward Quinn and he nodded. "I'd say they look at us as if we've grown horns, but that would make us fit in better."

Quinn snorted. "My only question is whether we're going the right way for what we need."

Maia nodded. "Hold my arm and guide me, and I'll check."

Quinn sidled closer and took her arm in a steady grip. She bit back the sigh of pleasure as sexual energy zinged between them, but settled herself by breathing deep and closing her eyes. She opened up her senses and squeaked a little at the flood of energy she could see. Brilliant colors like a kaleidoscope blazed around them. The Goblins had more magical energy than the dryads and she had to find the Key's signature among the sparkling residents.

"Hurry, Maia, we approach the keep." Quinn's whispered words made her frown and concentrate harder.

"What's taking so long?"

Where are you, dammit?

"Too much magical energy here. Everyone is blazing with it."

"Do you think it's somewhere else?" They halted and she was able to dig deeper into her memory of what the Key's energy and color looked like.

"No, it's here…" She took another deep breath and "reached" past the overwhelming rainbow of light and energy. "There." A shaft of white light pierced the brilliant rainbow and she focused on it. "Straight ahead."

"Inside the Keep. Guess you were right, Maia. The King and Queen must have it."

She opened her eyes as the passed through a huge set of double doors into the main entrance of a palace. While there was no question of its grandiosity, the stone columns and floor appeared to be a natural formation as if they'd been carved en situ. The halls held people dressed in all sorts of colors and finery, some with gnarled horns, some with short and straight horns, but almost all with the traditional courtier expressions. Maia inwardly sighed and schooled her expression into the impassive mask she'd worn as a girl in her father's court. *Never let them see you sweat.* Quinn didn't have to worry about giving anything away. The man was a sphinx.

The guards halted them outside another set of doors and conferred with someone just inside. Maia straightened her shoulders and waited patiently. Her feet hurt, her hips ached from carrying the weight of her pack, and exhaustion tugged at her eyes, but she held her head up and waited.

After a few minutes, her body started to revolt against her determination to stay upright and she had to clench her hands into fists to keep her eyes open. Quinn slipped up beside her and grasped her arm, rubbing the boney point on the inside of her elbow. The extra touch and pressure gave her some much-needed awareness, and by the time they were ushered inside, she'd regained her composure.

This room contained an audience hall with a true red carpet leading to a dais upon which sat two ornate thrones. The rest of the space remained open with windows lining the walls and a gold and cream checkerboard marble floor. At the moment, the room sat empty except for the two people seated on the thrones, the court herald, and the guards standing around the room.

"Announcing Her Royal Highness Princess Maiasora Silvercloak and her bodyguard to see the King Jakran and Queen Tricia of the Black Cloud Clan, Royal House of the Goblins."

Maia didn't understand why the herald shouted given how few people stood in the room, but she tried to keep her expression serene as she approached the dais and inclined her head to the royal couple.

"Welcome Princess Maiasora." The King waved at her to rise from her bow with a nod. He wore a pair of black horns rising a good foot and a half above his head. Gold inlays marbled them with intricate designs over long pale hair and golden eyes with slit pupils like a cat. "What brings you into the domain of the Goblins?"

"Thank you, Your Majesty." She let her gaze rest on the others around them before returning it to the royal couple. "My companion and I have been traveling in the footsteps of Druid Reuben. His journal instructed us to come here to the Goblin lands in search of something he left for us."

"Druid Reuben?" Queen Tricia raised pale blond eyebrows over her ice-blue eyes as she glanced at her husband. "I'm not familiar with this person."

The King nodded. "He was a holy man of sorts who visited us many centuries ago. You said you are following his footsteps in search of something, Princess?"

"We are, Your Majesty."

"Why do you believe it was here you should come?"

Maia shot a look at the herald and guards around them before returning her gaze to the King. "Originally, we'd planned on just passing through your domain without infringing on your hospitality, unsure if you were the people the druid spoke. But your guards discovered us and insisted we stop here to make your acquaintances."

Queen Tricia laughed. "Yes, they can be very persuasive."

"And you're certain you needed to come here?"

"Yes, Your Majesty. I was given his journal and instructed to find the guardian."

The King's chin rose and his nostrils flared as his eyes narrowed while Queen Tricia tilted her head in curiosity. Maia wondered how much could be shared, but she didn't want to give any listening ears the ability to take the Key before she got her hands on it.

"Leave us, everyone." The King's order made the guards hesitate before they filed out of the room. The herald remained, but the King shook his head. "You, too, Matten."

"But Your Majesty—"

"All will be well. We'll be fine."

Maia refrained from smiling at the knowledge of Quinn's abilities, and the herald reluctantly followed the guards out. Given the magic she could sense around the Goblin royalty, she suspected they'd be able to defend themselves pretty well. Still, she hoped Quinn wouldn't test them.

"Very well, Princess. We are now alone. You say you're in search of the guardian?"

"Yes, Your Majesty. I'm looking for the guardian of an artifact left by Druid Reuben in an effort to protect it for my mother, Queen Ashlynn of the dryads." Maia nodded. "Would you know where I can find this guardian?"

The King and Queen exchanged a glance and the Queen shrugged as if she would let him make the decision.

"I am the guardian of the artifact you seek, Princess. However, I believe there is a phrase I need to hear to grant you access to this artifact. Can you repeat it for me?"

Maia shot a look at Quinn before taking a deep breath. "Sun and the Moon to light the realms. Wind and the Rain to nourish them. Fire to cleanse and prepare the way. And Earth to give place to flourish in. The Keeper will hold the Key to keep the Twelve Realms free."

Silence followed her recitation and she resisted the urge to wipe her palms on her coat. She didn't know if she could trust these people, and she didn't want to give away anything to someone who wasn't the true guardian. But the only way to know was to give the clues and hope she hadn't made a grievous mistake.

"Thank you, Princess Maiasora. That is the proper set of phrases." King Jakran nodded and smiled, some of the tension leaving his shoulders. "Druid Reuben didn't describe you when he visited, but he said he didn't believe you would know how to control this sort of magic. Is this true?"

Maia swallowed hard. "Yes, Your Majesty. My mother died before she was able to teach me anything about controlling magic."

"I see. Very well. As we are the keepers of the magic needed to control the Key and the rifts between realms, you and your companion are welcome to stay with us as long as needed to master the skills to be the Keeper. Only then will we send you on to the next stop in your quest." King Jakran rose and strode down the dais to her to grasp her hands. "I'm very sorry to hear of your mother's loss. We expected you many years ago, but that you're here now suggests there was some trouble. Perhaps you would join us for the evening meal tonight to discuss your travels and history? By then we'll have found a teacher to help you understand your abilities."

"I can help her." Queen Tricia rose as well and her

husband shot her a look with raised eyebrows. "I have the time and I have the ability, Jakran. In fact, I'm probably the best one to teach her, don't you think?"

"Are you sure, *solara*?"

"Of course. I'm probably the only one in all of the Goblin domain who knows what it's like to be completely clueless." Queen Tricia gave a sardonic smile. "All of these people have had magic forever and never knew what it was like to not harness the magical energy. I was the only one with stunted growth."

Jakran sighed. "You didn't have stunted growth, my dear, just suspended learning."

"Uh-huh, and your brother has a mild medical issue that affects his good humor." She snorted and smiled at Maia. "I'd be happy to teach you how to tap into your magic and control it."

"Thank you, Your Majesty." Maia bowed her head in respect.

"Oh, please, we're all royalty here. Please call me Tricia." The queen waved her hand in dismissal. "Frankly, you both look exhausted. I bet you'd like a safe place to sleep and maybe even a bath and a meal. That sound about right?"

"Yes, Tricia. That's an accurate assessment." Maia frowned at her informal choice of words. "I'm not used to your frank and relaxed way of speaking. I feel positively stilted in comparison."

Tricia smiled and nodded. "That's because I grew up in the human world for half my life. Hell, I thought I was human until Jakran brought me here. But that's a story for another time. Let's find you a place to refresh yourself and we can trade tales this evening at dinner. What do you say?"

"Yes, thank you. That would be lovely." And just in time. Maia's fatigue threatened to collapse her knees.

"Excellent. I'll take care of them, Jakran, and see you

after for lunch, yeah?" Tricia kissed her husband's cheek and Maia didn't miss the flare of attraction between them.

"I look forward to it, *solara.*"

"Right. Let's get you into a suite. There are a few in this place. I still get turned around, though I've been here a while now." Tricia motioned for them to follow her, her ice-blue eyes crinkling at the corners as she grinned. "I'll ask Tiernan which rooms are available and to bring you anything you need. Towels, soap, a snack. You folks look like you were traveling at night to beat the heat, right?"

"Yes, that's right." Maia left off any titles because calling the Queen of the Goblins "Tricia" seemed too informal. "Quinn recommended it since we're more prepared for colder weather."

"Smart move. My brother was like that, too. He was always prepared like a good boy scout." Tricia shook her head, sorrow tingeing her smile. "I miss him."

"I'm sorry. You haven't seen him?" Maia tried to keep track of where they went after they left the throne room, but the hallways of the palace looked remarkably the same.

"No, unfortunately, once I left the human world, I haven't had any contact with my family there."

"Has it been a long time?" Maia bit her tongue to keep from asking how the Queen hid her magnificent pair of white and gold horns twisting eight inches above her head.

Tricia frowned in concentration. "I think it's been about fifteen years there, though it's been only five here. I never could figure out how time worked between the worlds. It doesn't seem to be a consistent ratio. But until a stronger connection between the worlds is restored, it's just the way it is." She ushered everyone through a door that led to a hallway full of more doors.

"That might be changing now." Quinn rested a hand on Maia's shoulder. "Maia's the Keeper of the Key to the realms."

"Yeah, I still don't quite understand that, but I'm sure

Jakran will explain it to me in time to talk about it at dinner." Tricia's tone of voice indicated she'd make it a point to get the truth out of her husband. "But first you should get some rest before we talk." A wide smile brightened her whole face. "This is a bit of an apartment minus the kitchen. But there's an attached bath and a sitting room. Go ahead and get some rest, and we'll talk to you at the evening meal."

"Thank you for your hospitality. It's very kind." Maia allowed Quinn to go inside first because she suspected he wanted to check for intruders.

"You're welcome and it's nice to meet you, Princess Maiasora."

"Oh, please call me Maia. I'm only a princess because of who my father was, not some inherent nobility." She smiled at the Goblin Queen.

"We'll have you called for dinner. I have no idea what time it will be. Guess it depends on what they serve this evening." Tricia waved her hand and shrugged. "It's always good, but not always at the same time of night. Go figure."

Maia laughed and nodded. "Thank you. We'll be ready."

"See you then." Tricia turned and sauntered away, and Maia realized a barbed tail twitched in cat-like contentment from beneath the hem of the Queen's long tunic.

"The rooms are clear." Quinn appeared behind her. "Come in and get some rest, Maia."

"What about you?" She strode into the comfortable apartment and set her pack down on one of the armchairs. "Aren't you going to sleep, too?"

He pushed his hood back, his expression stoic. "I will keep watch."

"No, that isn't going to happen." She marched up to him and pointed at his chest. "You're just as tired as I am and you need rest. The best way to protect me is to curl up and sleep with me. I'm sure you have ears like a bat and will hear anyone coming before they get near us."

"You have too much faith in my abilities, Maia." He shook his head.

"No, I know your abilities and mine. Don't worry. I'll protect you." She smiled and pointed at the bedroom. "Let's go to bed."

A smirk curled his lips. "Are you suggesting we go to bed?"

"Yes, to sleep, and..." She took her time unbuttoning her coat. "And I sleep better when I know you're close."

Quinn's brows went up. "Why?"

"Because I feel safer." There, she'd said it. She felt safer with an assassin than she did without him. She squared her shoulders and strode into the bedroom without a backward look.

CHAPTER THIRTEEN

Quinn stared after Maia's retreating back and tried to figure out what had just happened. *Did she just say she felt safer sleeping with me?* Ironic considering what he did for a living and his intent on killing her when they started this quest. But his focus and goals had changed. He liked Maia for all her quirks and faults, and he liked protecting her. And he definitely liked fucking her.

Get your mind back in the game.

He mentally slapped himself and headed for the bedroom. He couldn't let her words derail him so easily—

His mind stopped dead as he watched Maia pull off her boots and trousers before she crawled into the large canopied bed in nothing but her long undershirt. He could see the curve of her breasts and the shadow of her pussy through the sheer fabric, and his cock sat up with a vengeance.

He cleared his throat. "Where's the Key?"

"Protected and safe. Come to bed, please." She patted the mattress beside her.

Despite the allure of her damn-near naked body in bed, he went back through the apartment making sure the windows and doors were latched. When he returned to the bedroom, he found Maia already drowsy in the bed. *Holy Lady Death, she's sexy.*

He pulled his boots off and disarmed enough to slide into bed beside her. She mumbled something and snuggled right up to him, wrapping one arm around his waist. The scent of her hair settled his mind, though his ears kept straining for sounds of intrusion. But eventually the warmth of her body and her rhythmic breathing sucked him down into sleep.

When he woke, the day had advanced farther than he'd anticipated and he found the bed empty beside him. He sat up and scanned the room, looking for Maia. Nothing seemed amiss except for her absence. He found her clothes in a lumpy pile on the floor in front of a door he hadn't noticed when they'd gone to sleep. *So much for your keen observation skills.*

Quinn slid out of the bed and padded over to the door, listening for sounds of movement. When he didn't hear anything, he pushed the door open and stopped dead.

Maia scrubbed her body with a sponge as she hummed tunelessly to herself with her back to him. She'd never be a beautiful singer, but her body and personality made up for it in his eyes. In the light of the setting sun, he picked up faint lines much like the tattoos he'd seen on the bodies of the dryads. But hers only showed when the light hit her at a certain angle and appeared more like an elegant scrollwork than wood grains.

He leaned his shoulder against the doorjamb and watched her bathe, allowing some of his concern to slide away. She was safe and seemingly happy, and some of that happiness settled into his chest. He could see himself, old, tired, and gray, watching Maia bathing and singing off-key.

I've lost my mind. He'd never expected to grow old in his profession. But here he was wishing for something more than the next job. *I'm tired of killing.*

The thought brought him up short. Tired of killing?

Made for a lousy assassin. But if he didn't kill or continue as an assassin, what would he do? He turned away from his bathing beauty and retreated to the bedroom to change into the clothes someone had left for him. The pants were a deep chocolate brown and gathered at the ankles to billow around his legs. A pale gray vest fit over his chest and buttoned over his belly. The last piece of the ensemble was a deep purple sash that tied at his waist. Getting everything to fit comfortably took his mind off his uncertain thoughts, but they returned when he looked himself over in an old fashioned looking-glass.

Quinn didn't look like an assassin. Instead he resembled a southern trader or desert dweller, particularly with his feet bare. He hadn't shaved in days and his salt and pepper stubble gave him a rugged look he rarely noticed. Lines around his mouth and on his forehead spoke of his years, but he didn't remember smiling that often. *What did you do to get those?*

"Sweet glory!"

Maia's exclamation had him jerking around. She stood at the door wrapped in a fluffy tan towel with her mouth agape.

"What?"

"You're gorgeous." She blinked then shrugged one shoulder. "I mean, you look nice."

"Thank you."

He readjusted the sash and the vest to make sure they sat correctly before he realized she hadn't moved. He raised an eyebrow.

"Are you going to get dressed? There are clothes here for you." He gestured to the more brightly colored fabric on the bed.

"Uh, yes. Right." She nodded and entered the room, studying the clothes on the bed. "These are pretty. It'll be nice to have clean things to wear."

He couldn't argue with that. He remained facing the

mirror, but he shifted a bit to the side to see her get dressed. She dropped the towel and his cock tented his trousers. Her body was made up of smooth, elegant lines showing full breasts, curving hips, and round ass. He remembered what they felt like and how much he wanted to touch her again.

Maia pulled on the peach-colored pants that wrapped around her waist and tied at the front, leaving tantalizing glimpses of her legs from the knees down. A long tunic of deep coral with a fitted bodice and v-neck collar slid over her full breasts, hugging them to perfection. She settled a burgundy vest-like top that fastened beneath her breasts, but pushed them up and together just enough to give her a cleavage line.

"Do you have pockets, Quinn?"

"Wha-huh?" He gaped at her when he turned around, trying to rein his mind in from her lovely form.

"Pockets." She pointed at his pants. "I want to carry the piece of the Key on me because I don't want to leave it here in our room. Too many people who might find it. But this outfit doesn't have pockets."

"Oh." He patted himself hoping to readjust his wayward cock before she noticed. "Uh, yes, I do have one here under the sash." *Maybe I should adjust it to sit over my groin.*

She came over to him and handed him the little scrap of terrycloth holding the opal piece of jewelry. He tucked it away inside his hidden pocket and settled the sash over it so it would remain concealed.

"Thanks." She kissed his cheek and his cock roared with approval. "Let me put on my slippers and we can go."

"Right, yeah, me too." He bobbed his head like an idiot and looked for his own shoes. They appeared to be some low, flat slip-on soles with silk over the toes and heels to anchor them to his feet. And they were surprisingly comfortable. *As long as you don't have to run, hike, climb, fight, or dance.*

"Ready?"

"Yes, after you, my lady." He gestured to the hallway.

"My lady now, is it?" She snorted and shook her head with a smile, but swept out the door.

Always mine. He didn't know where the thought came from, but he wasn't going to argue.

****

Maia spent the whole dinner with the King and Queen of the Goblins hyper-aware of the handsome man sitting beside her and trying desperately not to drool over him. How the hell had he gotten that beautiful since they arrived? By the end of it, she wanted to run her hands over the muscles of his arms she could see, and the ones in his legs that she couldn't.

"So, Maia, you've obviously visited the Aerys people of the Windbreak Keep and know the story of the Key. Why has it taken you all this time to come retrieve it?" Jakran sat back in his pillowed seat near the low table and twirled a glass of some sort of fruit wine.

Maia yanked her attention back to the present and swallowed the bit of cheese she'd eaten. "It was never my intention to take this long, but I honestly had no idea about the Key or my role with it. And the dryads imprisoned me and my sisters for the loss of it. They only recently set me free."

Tricia's jaw dropped. "Wait, wasn't your mother a dryad?" She shook her head. "Why the hell did they imprison you and your sisters?"

"They blamed my sister Inge for colluding with the man they call the Dark Druid in the theft of the Key. They put her to death and turned the rest of us in to lamps."

"Lamps?" Tricia couldn't get her mouth closed.

"Yes. I had a lovely stained glass shade to keep the rain off." Maia couldn't help her sarcasm.

"Holy shit. That's barbaric."

"You said they freed you. Was it just you or are the rest of your sisters in their natural forms as well?" Jakran's brows lowered.

"No, just me. They needed me to find the Key and bring it back to them."

A frozen silence descended and the candles around them flickered as if a breeze had shot through the room.

"And will you? Will you bring the Key back to them and give them the power over all the Rifts to the realms?"

Maia met his gaze and employed all the training of royal impassiveness she'd had at her father's knee. "No. I'm the Keeper of the Key, and the responsibility of it is mine."

The candles flickered again, this time with a sense of relief.

"This is good to hear."

"But..."

"But?" Jakran's voice sharpened and Tricia laid a hand on his forearm.

"But my sisters are still imprisoned and if I don't give the dryads the Key, they'll be put to death like Inge." Maia straightened her shoulders. "I can't do that to them. They never deserved any of this. I have to find a way to save them without giving the Key to the dryads."

Tricia nodded slowly. "That's true. They're the guardians of the other worlds from what Jakran told me. If they're stuck here, those other realms are in danger and unprotected."

"Right." Maia sighed and shot a look at Quinn before returning her gaze to the King. "I don't know what I'm going to do, but I know I have to save my sisters and find a way to keep the Key from the dryads. I just don't know how."

"I might have a solution to that." Tricia shot a half smile at Jakran before she met Maia's gaze. "Give me a little time to do some research and talk to a couple of people, but we might have a win-win solution." Her lips curled into a smirk. "Goblins are nothing if not inventive and sneaky."

"No one is more devious than you, *solara*." Jakran nodded to his wife.

"Hey, I had to hide your birthday gift somehow."

"By growing an entire tree around it?"

"How was I supposed to know that was a spitting willow? The gardener never labeled the seeds." Tricia crossed her arms over her chest.

Despite the seriousness of the coming confrontation, Maia laughed. "A spitting willow?"

"Yes, it's a local tree here in our kingdom that spits seeds, sap, dirt clods, and rocks if it feels threatened." Jakran leveled a dry look at Tricia.

"I said I was sorry. I didn't know it would do that when I tried to retrieve the parcel." She shook her head again. "I had to cut all my hair off because of the sap. But at least you got your birthday present."

"I don't think a spitting willow will help in this situation. The dryads have a unique understanding of trees." Maia smiled to show she joked.

"No, we won't use a spitting willow. But we will use magic. Or more to the point, you will." Tricia matched Maia's smile, but showed a little teeth. "I like the opportunity to fix an old wrong."

"Speaking of that." Jakran rose from his seat and retrieved a small carved twelve-sided box much like the one Moriah had given her. "This is the box Reuben left with us. I've held it in our treasure vault until you arrived. But it's now yours." He extended the box to Maia.

"Thank you."

She opened the lid and found golden satin wrapped around a malleable object inside. She pulled out the satin and exposed the left side of the necklace. The lattice held five drops of opal of various colors, each with iridescent fire across their surfaces. A length of silver chain with a small ring at the end extended from the ornate lattice-work. She found two small hooks on the widest portion of the lattice and realized it would hook into the side of the big central opal she'd received from the Aerys people.

"Wow." Tricia leaned over to look at the jewelry. "That's gorgeous. But it looks broken. What is it for?"

"It's part of a necklace. When all the pieces are together it hangs around the neck." Maia shrugged. "Or so I'm told. We don't have all the pieces yet."

She carefully wrapped the treasure back in the satin and stored it in the twelve-sided box. She could feel energy in the stones and lattice, but she had no idea what it meant for her or for controlling the twelve realms.

The conversation shifted back to more mundane and easy topics until Maia hid a third yawn behind her hand.

"I believe we've kept you long enough. Perhaps on the morrow we'll be able to make some progress on the question of how to rescue your sisters." Jakran rose and offered a hand to his wife. "We've enjoyed your company and would like to offer our hospitality for as long as you need."

"Thank you, Your Majesty. Before we go, we'll need what you know about the next guardian of the Key." Quinn bowed his head a little, but never took his gaze from the King.

"Yes, of course." He hesitated as if he wanted to say something else, but smiled. "As soon as we've found our solution to your dilemma I'll give you the next clue."

"Thank you." Maia nodded and headed for the door with the Queen. "I really appreciate your help. I have no idea what we can do, but I can't leave my sisters with the dryads and I can't give them the Key."

"We'll figure out what to do." Tricia waved her worries away with a smirk. "I got some ideas, but I need to check with some people before I make any real plans."

Maia smiled as she watched Quinn and Jakran speak earnestly on something across the room. Quinn's eyebrows went up and his shoulders stiffened at something Jakran said, but before she could move to his side, he thanked the King and headed her way.

"Ready to go?" He gave her a meaningful look and took her elbow.

"Yes." She turned to the Queen and King, and smiled. "Thank you for dinner and the place to stay. We'll see you tomorrow. Good night."

"Pleasant dreams."

Quinn escorted her out into the hallway and back toward their suite, his silence more withdrawn than usual. She wanted to ask him what the King had said to set him off, but she got the impression the information was important, too important for unscrupulous ears. They passed a few servants on their way and held their silence until the returned to the rooms.

Once they stepped inside, Quinn closed the door and removed his sash before he retrieved the central portion of her necklace from his pocket. "Your treasure."

She took it, but didn't move, watching his body language. *Oh, who are you kidding? You're watching his body.* He still wore tension and unease, and she closed the distance he tried to put between them.

"Thank you. What did the King say to you, Quinn?"

CHAPTER FOURTEEN

"Nothing." Quinn's mind repeated the King's words, but they'd been too vague for him to find the point to them.

Maia dropped her chin and shot him a dry look from under her brows. "Seriously?"

"He said he'd like to talk to me about something affecting your ability to be an effective Keeper of the Key." Quinn shrugged. "He said it had to do with my family when I pressed him, but he wouldn't say anything else. We're supposed to get together while the Queen is training you to talk more."

"Oh, okay." She nodded as her brows lowered. "Do you think it's something bad?"

"I don't know." He unbuttoned his vest. "He was very close-lipped about it. I can't imagine what it could be. I had a very small family, just my brother and me. My father was a tailor, which is why my brother Sean knew about the opportunity to marry into the King's family. My mother worked with him as a seamstress. She constructed dresses for the aristocratic women and their various events. They made a decent living." He shrugged.

"What about other members of your family? Like extended members. Did your parents have siblings?" Maia settled onto one of the settees and pulled out the twelve-sided box the Goblins had given her.

Quinn frowned and sat beside her. "My mother had a large family, but they were in a village across the kingdom from us. She'd married my father and moved with him until they came to the capitol city where they could make a living with their exceptional skills." He shook his head. "I didn't know her family hardly at all and they seemed to have written Mother off as a lost cause."

He shrugged, dismissing them. *No use worrying about them now.* "But my father had a couple of brothers as I recall. One became a blacksmith nearby, trading clothing for cooking utensils and artistic work on railings, fire grates, and other tools. He was bigger than my father and heavier built, but kind for all his appearance of a thug."

"What about your father's other brother?"

Quinn shook his head again with a frown. "I don't know much about him. He disappeared when I was no more than five years old. I don't even remember his name. They didn't speak about him much, but I got the impression my father thought he'd run away on a fool's errand. I just don't know what that was."

He met Maia's gaze. "It doesn't matter now, I guess. And I'll find out what the King wants to tell me when he's ready." He nodded to the box in her hands. "Ready to put the pieces of the Key back together?"

She hesitated with the box and the scrap of terrycloth on her lap, her bottom lip caught between her teeth. "I don't know. I don't know if we should. What if someone finds it? I can't wear it yet, we only have two-thirds of it. Maybe it's safer in pieces."

Quinn nodded, gathering his thoughts before he said anything.

"The choice is yours, Maia. In this, you're the expert, even more so than the guardians who've held the pieces. And whatever you decide, I'll back you." He patted her hands wrapped around the box. "But there was a reason Reuben came here and left a piece of the Key with the Goblins. They're a people who use and understand magic, and the Key seems to be magical or at least a tool of it. Maybe connecting it will give you a better understanding of the magic you'll be using when it's complete."

He closed his lips and waited for her to meet his gaze, but her face remained down as she stared at their hands. He'd gotten better at speaking since meeting her, but still, his little speech contained more words than he usually used in a day. Despite that, he liked sharing his words with her and he didn't feel he wasted them on someone who spent their life jabbering without meaning. Maia used words to her advantage, but never frivolously.

At last, she nodded and took a deep breath before unwrapping the central portion of the necklace. She laid it on one knee and opened the box, peeling apart the golden satin to expose the left side of the necklace. She lifted it and set the box aside before she met his gaze.

"I don't know what's going to happen. I don't know if there will be something magical or nothing at all."

Quinn nodded. "Does it matter?"

"I suppose not. I mean is it ego to expect it to give fireworks and have bright light flash all over the room like pixie dust?"

He laughed. "Maybe a little."

She grinned. "Okay, then. I guess I do have a little bit of arrogant princess in me after all." She lifted the central piece and found the loops along the side where the collar pieces would fit together. Matching hooks sat on the left piece in the places they should. She met his gaze. "Ready?"

"Are you?"

"Not in the slightest." And she hooked the left piece into the central portion.

At first, nothing happened. They held still, their breath suspended as they waited for some sort of reaction. Quinn let his gaze rove around the room in case something showed itself, but for the first few moments, all remained quiet.

Then a subtle *pop* sounded just below normal hearing range, like they'd changed elevation, and another one of the invisible waves of energy rolled across the room from their location. The candles flickered in their sconces and the room became a little brighter. Details he hadn't noticed in the wall paper and décor became clearer, and the urge to get closer to the woman beside him grabbed him by the cock.

Maia sat with her eyes wide and her hands curled around the necklace. "Sweet glory, Quinn. I can see the magic."

"What?"

"The magic. It's like swirls of smoke or pulses of light running along the walls and floors. I can see it." She tapped her foot against the floor. "It makes up everything and gives us a framework to live in, like it's solid. But it flows without moving." She shook her head. "It doesn't make any sense and yet it is what it is."

"I don't really understand. Are you saying this castle is magic?"

"Yes, but not just that. All of us and everything is some form of it. Most of the time we can't see it, although I bet lots of people can feel it." She shook her head and took her hands off the necklace. "Whoa."

"What?"

"The world's so…" She frowned as she looked around the room. "Flat. Not quite colorless, but less vibrant or…sparkly?"

He snorted as a half-smile curled his lips. "Sparkly?"

"Yes." She shot him a grin as she picked up the necklace again. "Even you. You glitter like a dragon's hoard of gems. Who knew assassins could be flashy?"

For some reason her assessment of him combined with

the grin warmed him all the way to his heart. "Assassins use their surroundings to blend in. If the situation calls for flashy, we're flashy."

She chuckled. "I'm sure." She nodded and sobered. "What shall I do with this now? It's not long enough to wear, but I can't separate it again to make it smaller."

"You can't separate it?" He reached for the necklace, but hesitated touching it. Magical artifacts weren't something a smart man grabbed lightly.

"No. The hooks have fused into closed loops." She held it up.

He used her hands to turn the necklace so he could see. The pieces of the necklace were joined by linked loops of metal as if they'd never been apart. He nodded slowly. *Note to self: never mess with magical items that fuse themselves back together.*

"We'll do what we did when we traveled. We'll either put gravel in the satin within the boxes or just leave the satin there if someone comes looking." He gestured to the necklace. "Wrap this up in the soft terrycloth again, and keep it on you."

"How? The clothing here isn't exactly thick or concealing."

"I'm sure the Goblin women don't wander around unarmed. I bet they each have a knife or weapon on them that's concealed within those gauzy clothes." He waggled his eyebrows. "We had a Goblin woman in the Assassin's Guild. She wore some of the most revealing clothes I've ever seen, but no one ever touched her without her permission. The one who tried never made it through training."

"That wasn't you, was it, Quinn?"

"No-oh. I decided sex wasn't nearly as important as living to kill."

He regretted the words the moment her face fell and she looked down at the necklace. "I'm sure you completed your training with flying colors."

He nodded. "I did. I was very good at it. But I think I'm done with that now."

"What?"

He met her gaze, scared for the first time in his life. The fear came from somewhere deep, but he didn't know what he was afraid of. Rejection? Abandonment? Solitude? He wanted to scoff. He'd been alone since he stepped across the dimensional boundary into this world from his. The idea of fearing solitude was ludicrous.

"I don't want to kill for a living anymore."

Maia scrutinized him, her expression solemn. He expected her to laugh or scoff, but she studied him with calm attention.

"I think you mean that."

Quinn nodded. "I do."

"Why?"

He looked away, trying to put his feelings into words that made some sort of coherent sense.

"I think I was just killing time." She snorted and he laughed a little before sobering. "I was waiting for something better to come along. I don't regret the choices I've made, but killing people isn't something to do long-term. At least, not for me. I don't regret the skills I have, but I don't want to use them that way anymore. I'd much rather be useful."

She nodded. "How will you do that?"

"By using my skills to protect you."

She grimaced and rolled her eyes. "You want to be my bodyguard. Protect the Keeper of the Key, right?"

"Of course." He frowned. Why wasn't she pleased?

"Good. That's good." She sighed and ran her fingers over the large opal in the center of her necklace. "I'm happy for you."

"But?"

"Why would you think there's a but in there? You've

made a monumental decision."

"I'm not sure you're very pleased."

"Oh no, I am." She gave him a wide-eyed, innocent look.

"Maia, your sarcasm is showing through again." He frowned as he tried to figure out what about his revelation might have disappointed her. "Don't you want me to protect and defend you?"

She sighed. "Yes, of course."

"But?"

She snorted at the repeat of his question. "But I was hoping you'd want to stay, not because I'm the Keeper and need protection, but because...well..."

"Because?" He turned to face her, laying one hand on her knee as he tried to meet her gaze.

She shrugged and squirmed a little. "Because you like me as me. Not just because I'm the Keeper or the daughter of the King or because you're bound to me. But because you like me, Maia. The woman with the imaginary dragon named Yarenoke."

He laughed as his tension fled. "I do like you, Maia. More than I thought I would. You're more courageous than I gave you credit for, and I like to share my time and space with you. Especially because you have an imaginary dragon named Yarenoke."

She laughed and her shoulders loosened. "You don't regret coming with me on this quest?"

He shook his head. "Best adventure I've had in a long time, and I get to spend it with you." He pushed a strand of dark hair behind her ear. "You're beautiful, Maia. I've thought so since the moment I saw you the first time."

"I feel a bout of sarcasm coming on. Seriously?"

"Yes, I'm serious. I didn't like you, then, but I thought you were beautiful." He let a half smile curl his lips. "It's possible to like a person's looks without liking the person."

"Oh, I know that." She snorted and shook her head. "I

liked how you looked too, but I thought you were a bastard."

"Not a bastard. Both parents were alive and married when I was born." He grinned.

"You know what I meant." She thumped his shoulder with her closed fist before folding the terrycloth over the necklace. "I should find a place to put this for the night. What will we use to fill the gold satin?"

Quinn cast his gaze around the room until he found some silk flowers in a tall glass vase. Clear glass marbles held the flowers upright at the proper angles for the ultimate beauty. He rose and poured some of the marbles into his hand. "Use these."

They tucked the marbles into the gold satin and closed the lid of the box. Maia shook her head with a smile as she took the box and placed it in her pack on top of the other one holding the decorative stones from the Windbreak Keep.

"Do you think it'll fool anyone?"

"It doesn't have to. It just has to distract them from the real necklace." Quinn stood behind her as she packed everything away. "Thinking about it, maybe we should put the real one in my pack. No one would look for it there as I'm not the Keeper or royalty. I'm just a lowly bodyguard."

"No one would be fooled into thinking you're a lowly anything, Quinn." Maia shook her head, but she handed him the terrycloth bundle. "Will you keep it safe for me?"

"I will, as safe as I can keep you, too."

He wasn't used to such tender words, but even stranger was that he meant them with every fiber of his being. He wanted her, wanted to be with her, and wanted to keep her safe. The source of these emotions seemed alien. He'd never felt this way so strongly about anyone.

She's mine.

Possession wasn't his style. He didn't own things, only used them, and replaced them when they became obsolete.

But Maia wasn't a possession or an object to use. She encompassed more than an object. She held half of him, a delicate and fragile part, yet more precious than most of the weapons he carried on his person for everyday use. He didn't want to look at what the word 'mine' meant in this context, but he'd only be able to push away the definition so long. For now, he'd take the words at face-value and deal with them later.

She seemed just as unwilling to delve deeper into his statement. "Thank you." She handed him the combined piece of the necklace and kissed his cheek. "That means a lot to me."

She pulled away, but he caught her hand and held her close. "Let me make love with you, Maia."

"What? Now, here?"

"Yes, now, here, tonight. I want to spend this evening with you in my bed, pleasuring you."

Maia tilted her head. "Are you sure you're not too tired?"

Quinn smiled. "The nap helped. Besides, I have a feeling I won't be seeing much of you for the next several days."

"What makes you say that?"

He shrugged. "Training takes a lot of time and energy. More than likely you'll be coming back to the room and falling into bed already asleep."

"Come on. It's not like it'll be weapons training or running an obstacle course."

"You don't know what it's going to be like, except that it requires energy." He backed away to pack the necklace into an obscure pocket of his pack before he returned to her side. "You said it yourself, magic is in everything, the energy you saw." He ran his hands over her arms as he leaned in to kiss her neck below her ear. He was gratified when she shivered. "My guess is you'll be exhausted until you get the hang of your training. Before you become too engrossed in it, I thought I'd take the time to remind you of my pleasure in your company."

"Oh, and how will you do that?"

"By giving you as much pleasure as I can." He drew her with him toward the bedroom.

"Does that include my wishes?" Maia gave him a sultry smile as she followed.

Quinn chuckled. "It might. What did you have in mind?"

Her smile morphed into a smirk. "Remember how I feel about your coat?"

He laughed. "Yes, princess, I do. Do you want me to wear my coat here in the bedroom?"

She strode up to him and skimmed her fingers over his shoulders as if mapping out the muscles. He tried not to shiver, but her touch sent delicious sensations zipping through his body.

"That's very tempting, but tonight I think I'd just like to see you completely naked." She stopped and settled her hands on his hips. His cock took notice and filled out the remaining space behind his fly. "Seems like you think that's a good idea." She grinned as she untied the sash around his waist. "This is good because I really want to suck on your cock."

He moaned as she made quick work of his clothes and he stood before her completely naked. She paused and looked him up and down, taking in the scars and marks on his body. She didn't seem repulsed by them, but this was the first time she'd seen him completely naked and he hoped she liked what she saw.

Not that I can change what I have.

"You're beautiful, Quinn."

That's not a word I would've chosen.

She slid a finger down his chest and over one nipple, tweaking it enough to make his cock flex. That caught her attention and her hand dropped lower, down the line of hair below his belly button, and straight to his straining erection. She licked her lips and knelt before him, tangling her fingers in the hair around his balls.

Sweet Lady of Death, he'd never felt anything so sensual in his life, and he had to lock his knees to keep from toppling. His cock jerked threatening to unbalance him as she wrapped her fist around it.

"I like this part of you." She eyed the slit as a bead of pre-cum pooled at the tip. "I want to taste it."

"Perhaps you'd let me lie down before you do that?" He backed away enough to sit on the bed.

She rose from her knees and followed him, a smirk curling her lips. Damn, the smirk lit his fire. She stopped and returned to her knees, pushing his thighs apart as she dropped her gaze to his straining cock. He gripped the bedding beside him and held on to keep from grabbing her and easing her up his body.

Maia raised her gaze to his and her smirk returned. "I'm going to enjoy this." She gripped his cock and slid her mouth over it.

Holy fuck.

Wet, delicious, heat enclosed the head of his cock and he thanked every deity he could think of he was sitting down. The pleasure of her tongue on his shaft stole his ability to stand and he damn near melted into the bed. She hummed against his flesh and he damn near lost his mind.

She took her time fondling the head and shaft with her tongue, the rough surface sparking sensation as she dragged it over the sensitive head. She kept her eyes closed, but her expression filled with delight rather than nervousness.

Quinn watched her cheeks hollow out as she sucked hard on his cock. Goddess, she was so sexy and he gave into his need to tunnel his fingers into her silken hair.

Must be gentle. He had to repeat it because each time she tightened her mouth around his cock, he tightened his grip on her hair. She moaned as he tugged on her tresses and the sounds vibrated through his flesh. When she burrowed the tip of her tongue in his slit, his eyes rolled back in his head.

He hissed and threw his head back as pleasure ricocheted through his body. When she trailed her fingers over his taut balls, he saw stars. She moved her hand in time with her lips and set up a steady rhythm, his flesh shuttling in and out of her mouth.

He'd never had a slow blow job. All the women who'd ever sucked his cock were paid to get the job done and did well enough to get him off. But Maia took her time, moaning as she alternated with her hand, and his release built with relentless tenacity. His need to race to the finish and soar with his orgasm warred with his desire to enjoy her erotic ministrations longer. He didn't want her sensual assault on his cock to end, but he found it increasingly difficult to hold back.

"Maia, stop." She sucked him deep into her throat and he damn near lost control. "Oh Goddess, please stop." He pulled her off his cock with a wet pop and held her out of reach.

"Why? Did I do something wrong?" She pouted as she looked up at him with concern.

"No, no, far from it." He lifted her off her knees. "You were too good and I want to make sure I give you pleasure."

"That was pleasurable for me." Maia frowned. "Didn't you like it? I know I'm not a professional whore, but you seemed to be enjoying it."

"Oh, I was enjoying it too much." Quinn gave her his best smirk. "In fact, you gave me the best fellatio I've ever received."

Her frown deepened as he helped her undress, enjoying her curves being slowly revealed. "If it was the best, why did you stop me?"

"Because..." He lifted away the sheer fabric encasing

her breasts and sucked one nipple into his mouth. She gasped as he teased it to hardness before releasing it. "I would've come and been unable to pleasure you the way I wanted."

A slow, sultry smile curled her lips as her clothing fell to the floor. "And how do you want to pleasure me, Quinn?"

Sweet Lady Death, she's so beautiful. He took a few moments to enjoy the way the light caressed her curves. Her full breasts appeared rosy in the golden light, creating temping shadows on her smooth skin. Dark curls at the juncture of her thighs sparkled in the light from the wetness engendered from her sucking on him.

"Come, straddle my hips and sit on my cock, princess. I want you to ride me into ecstasy."

"Like this?" She crawled onto the bed and set her knees on either side of his hips.

"Yes." He guided her lower with one hand on her hip and the other holding his stiff shaft upright. "That's it." The tip of his cock kissed her nether lips. "Are you ready for me, Maia?" He brushed the head against her labia and they both moaned.

"Oh, sweet glory, yes, Quinn."

"Sink down on me, princess." He held his cock up long enough to enter her tight sheath and removed his hand just as she sat down on his lap, his cock encased in heaven. "Oh yeah."

He closed his eyes and allowed himself a few moments to enjoy the simple eroticism of having a woman on his shaft. He never grew tired of it. When they'd shared intimacy in the cave it had been quick and hot. But now, with her here in a safe place, he planned to take his time, and give her a slow deep orgasm.

"Oh, Goddess, Quinn." Her pussy gripped him like a vice and held him deep. "You feel so good inside me."

"And you feel damn good wrapped around me. But

now I'm going to move and we're going to take this slow." He lifted her slowly off his cock and her body fought to hold onto him.

The slide along her inner walls set off fireworks of pleasure along his shaft and he almost thrust back into her hard, but he forced himself to lower her back down with measured motion. Her eyes blazed with desire as he rocked his hips, thrusting into her hot sheath.

"Oh, Goddess, Quinn. You're so thick."

He barked a short laugh as he lifted her again. "I'm hoping you're not referring to my intellect."

"No…I'm referring…" She paused as she came back down on his cock. "To your cock." And she squeezed his shaft with her inner muscles.

Holy fuck, she's so damn tight.

"Oh yeah, princess. I'll give you this cock any time you want it."

He meant his words, but the pleasure of her riding him took away his coherency, and he could do nothing more than moan. Fortunately, she didn't seem inclined to talk more either and she rode him with measured slides, whimpering each time he seated himself to his balls. He tried to watch her eyes, but her breasts bounced when she landed on his lap and he couldn't ignore them.

Quinn dipped his head and sucked one nipple into his mouth, curling his tongue around the tip. Maia gasped and her pussy squeezed his cock hard. He groaned and threw his head back before he helped her rise off him and returned her to his shaft, harder and faster.

"Great Lady Death!" He couldn't keep the words in as his balls tightened under her sensual onslaught. "I'm going to come, princess. Come with me." He reached between their bodies and strummed her clit.

"Oh yes, yes, yes!" Maia threw her head back and clamped down on his cock, coming hard as he let go of his release.

Hot jets of cum shot into her as he joined her with his own howl of jubilation. He flew into pleasure so deep he didn't want to come back to the world where he sat alone in his skin. She was his other half, the connection he'd been missing since his brother died. He wanted to stay here, with her, forever.

"Oh, Quinn, that was…" Maia's voice remained breathless minutes later and she kissed his forehead. "Thank you."

"My pleasure, Maia. Anytime you need loving, I'm happy to help."

She laughed, and clamped down on his cock, which made him groan. "You're dangerous when you do that."

"Do what?" She raised an inquisitive eyebrow. "This?" Her inner muscles squeezed again.

"Yes, that." He shivered through her ministrations.

She smirked. "I'll have to remember that given how dangerous my current lover is."

He didn't like the word "current" at all. That implied she might find someone else later. And he'd be damned if he lost her to another male out to get his dick wet.

"No one more dangerous than me when it comes to you." He kissed her soundly, allowing all his emotion to bubbled up through their connection. *She's mine and I'm not giving her up.*

He allowed her to climb off his lap and followed her into the bathing room where they cleaned themselves up. They didn't say anything, but shared quiet smiles. It would have to be enough in the coming days.

Quinn knew her training would be rough, but he'd find a way to remind her what she meant to him. Not just as the Keeper of the Key, but also as the woman he'd come to love.

Love? That word rarely entered into his vocabulary, much less his thoughts. But it fit perfectly with his perception of Maia. He followed her back to the bed and held the blankets up for her, before skirting the foot and sliding in on the other side. He gathered her into his arms and smiled at the contented sigh she gave as her back settled against his chest.

He aimed to keep her sighs contented for the rest of his life.

CHAPTER FIFTEEN

Quinn wasn't wrong. Maia's training wore her out and then some. When she dragged herself into bed each night for the next four weeks, she could barely stay awake long enough to pull the sheets over her. Quinn smiled knowingly as he tucked her in and that was really all she saw of him.

From the moment Tricia started training, she went from elegant, regal queen, to hardass drill sergeant with an implacable mein. They started, improbably, with meditation and centering. Tricia explained the magic resembled a river and like rivers had a habit of flowing in the path of least resistance. Maia had to offer it an easier path than all over the place or she'd never be able to direct it where she wanted it to go.

But to be able to provide a smooth and directed path, she had to be far more resistant to distraction. Tricia taught her how to find her center in her mind and to picture it until it appeared clearly as if she'd stepped into her own garden. Once she had a clear picture, Tricia did everything in her power to distract Maia, even going so far as to nudge her with her hip. It took the better part of two weeks to reach a point where not even magical nudging could make Maia lose focus.

"Excellent." Tricia smiled for the first time since training began. "Now that you have your center, I'll let you play with some magic."

Maia swallowed hard as she followed the Goblin queen into an octagonal room that hummed like someone had settled the floor over a large beehive.

"Wow."

"Can you feel it?" Tricia paused in the center of the room and raised an eyebrow.

Maia nodded. "What is it?"

"This is our safe room for newbie magic wielders. Once I close the wards around it, nothing's getting in or out." She waved her hands around the room. "The wards absorb errant magic to keep the palace safe and to recharge themselves, like a battery."

"A what?" Maia frowned.

"A battery…" Tricia cocked her head. "You don't know what a battery is?"

Maia shook her head and let her gaze slide around the rough-hewn rock walls.

"Uh, hm. I don't know if I can explain it." Tricia rubbed her chin with a frown. "Think of it as an energy reservoir. You can fill it with excess energy for use later."

"That sounds like a wise idea, especially if you have someone who doesn't know what they're doing." Maia noted the scars and scorch marks on the walls.

"Uh, yeah, I mean, yes. I suggested it to Jakran after we had some near-misses." Tricia grimaced and ran a hand over her twisted horns. "Anyway, we constructed this safe room so anyone could practice without damaging anything." She brought her hands together as if closing an imaginary set of doors and something clicked in Maia's head. "There. Wards set. We're ready to begin."

The room didn't look any different, but the hum had changed to something more subtle and steady. Tricia nodded with satisfaction and fixed her gaze on Maia.

"All right. What we need to do is start with the basics. The first step to controlling and directing magic comes from the ability to see it." Tricia gestured at the floor. "This floor has ley lines in it. These you'll be able to tap into without causing damage. But I need to know if you can see them. Take a look."

Maia nodded and inhaled deeply before she opened her senses. The room changed from a dull, gray stone with torch sconces to a kaleidoscope of colors pulsing in time to some unknown heartbeat. The floor held a spider's web of glowing golden lines that continued up the walls and into a nearly matching web on the ceiling. The shadowed spaces between them shifted in color as if each pulse of the lines cast off a different light. When she dragged her gaze back to Tricia, the Goblin queen blazed incandescent white and Maia covered her eyes.

"Yes," she mumbled through her hands. "I can see the ley lines."

Tricia laughed. "Yes, I'd guess you can from that reaction. That makes our job easier." She stood in one of the shadowed areas between the lines. "Here's where things get interesting. I want you to 'grab' one of the lines with your hands."

Maia stilled, but left her eyes covered. "Grab one?"

"Yes. You're going to need your eyes." Tricia's voice held amusement. "Can't grasp what you can't see."

Maia snorted. "I might not be able to grasp it anyway."

"Now, now, no need to be negative. You managed to find your center and keep it when I threw all sorts of things at you."

"Some of which hit me." Maia dropped her hands and glared at the queen.

"I am sorry about that. Think of it this way. Once you learn to grab a ley line, no one will be able to hit you with anything again."

Maia raised an eyebrow. "Oh?"

"Oh yeah. I'll teach you how to use your power for defense, and even better, offense." Tricia smirked. "So, let's get to it, shall we?"

Maia sighed, but focused her attention onto the lines in the floor. She reached out with her senses blazing and made to grab one. She could feel the pulse of the energy the closer she got to it, but when she closed her hand around it, it squipped out of her grip like it had been slicked with grease.

"Try again."

The next time she made a grab for a line, it scurried out of reach like a pet trying to escape a bath. She scurried after it and ended up resembling a woman desperately chasing chickens.

"Again."

That became her mantra. Over the next week, grabbing magic seemed to be an exercise in futility. She managed to grasp a line or two a few times, but they'd either die as if she had a black thumb or flare in her hand before burning out. Just when she thought she'd gotten an understanding of how to hold magic like a rope, it would snap back at her like a whip. Once it smacked her across the ass and she swore she heard it chuckling.

"Again."

Maia found she could tie the lines together so they wouldn't snap and whip her, but sometimes the connections wouldn't stay tied. They'd explode apart like hay bales released from their twine and she'd have to start again.

"I'm never going to get this." Maia rubbed her hands over her eyes, exhausted from wrestling with the lines of energy. The skin on her hands felt raw and burned, though she hadn't touched anything physical in days.

"Let's take a break. Drink some water and just sit. I think we're over-thinking this." Tricia gestured to break the wards and they left the training room.

Maia followed after the Goblin queen, wondering if

she was really meant to be the Keeper of the Key. *Not if I can't master magic.* So far she'd smacked herself in the ass and burned her hands, but she hadn't managed to connect to the lines the way Tricia did. They sat down on a bench beside a window that looked out on the forest around the palace and Tricia handed her a glass of something fruity and tart.

"What's this?"

"Lemonade. I finally convinced the cooks to try it here. They thought I was crazy."

"It's refreshing." Maia sipped her drink as she let her gaze drift outside. The trees swayed in the rhythm of the winds rippling through their spires. If she let her senses come to play, she could see the energy of the wind flow like waves, splashing up against rock cliffs and eddying in the valleys.

"I think we're going at this the wrong way." Tricia ran her finger around the rim of her glass.

"The wrong way?" Maia snorted. "I'm not sure there is a right way."

Tricia frowned and nodded. "You have natural ability and you can already do more than I could, but you're not connecting the ability with the instruction."

"Are you suggesting I'm unable to learn?"

"No, that would be supremely arrogant." Tricia shook her head with a rueful smile. "No, I think it's because I'm teaching you wrong."

Maia blinked. "Teaching me wrong? I don't understand...which seems to be my constant way of being."

The Goblin queen nodded. "I've been teaching you the way I was taught. Push through your obstacles, blast ahead, and grab the prize. But I can't teach you to be me. I have to teach you to be you."

Maia groaned. "That doesn't make sense at all." She rubbed her eyes with the heels of her hands. "I'm never going to get any of this."

"I don't think that's true, but why don't we take a break today? You've been pushing pretty hard and I think we're burnt out." Tricia gave her a smirk. "Why don't you go hang out with that handsome bodyguard of yours? I'm sure he's been missing you. He looks downright dour when you're not around."

Maia snorted. "He's always dour." But that wasn't quite true. At least, not for a while now. "So should we resume tomorrow morning?"

"Yes. That'll give me some time to figure out how to change my approach." Tricia gave her a lop-sided smile. "And I've missed spending time with my husband."

Maia returned the smile, but it felt forced. "Of course." She nodded sharply. "I'll see you in the morning, then."

"Good. I should have an idea of what to do by then. Have a good afternoon and night."

Tricia stood and sauntered out of the room. Maia watched her go, envious for the first time in decades. Tricia had mastery over her gifts, a handsome husband to find solace with, and the confidence about her place in the world. Maia had none of those things and it hurt. Hell, all she had was an old book she couldn't read and pieces of some magical jewelry she couldn't use.

She sighed and rubbed her eyes again. She didn't often fail at things, but it had been centuries since she'd had to make an effort. *And Tricia makes it look so effortless.* Maia let her gaze rest on the landscape outside. She had to master these skills or her sisters' lives would be forfeit. She couldn't fail, and they were running out of time.

I'm sorry, Mama. I don't know how to do this. It tasted remarkably like failure and Maia allowed herself to cry bitter tears. *I don't know if I can save them.* That admission hurt most of all. How could she be a hero in her own life if she couldn't even master the most important task of her quest?

****

Quinn spent most of his time while Maia trained exploring the palace and grounds. To keep from getting bored, he exercised, practiced his archery and knife-throwing skills, and engaged in a little hand-to-hand against shadow opponents. He told himself he did it to keep from growing soft, but in reality, he did it to keep his mind from missing Maia's company.

The Goblin king caught him practicing and offered to spar against him. At first, Quinn declined, not willing to be on the receiving end of the guards' suspicions. But the king insisted and soon they had weekly workout routines. Quinn liked the king overall, but he suspected the man held something back given all the speculative glances he received.

Four weeks into their stay with the goblins, Quinn received a note to attend the King in the library. Maia had already started training for the day and Quinn had nothing planned beyond another foray into the grounds of the palace. The last time he'd poked around, he'd damn near been caught by the servants as he snooped around the secret passages of the palace. And there were a lot of them.

Following the directions in the note, Quinn came to the library to find a set of fierce guards standing on either side of the doorway. The guards watched him as he knocked on the door and he understood their veiled hostility. He'd made it clear what he did for a living and letting a known assassin in with their king ranked right up there with cleaning a latrine. The King called for him to enter and he slipped through the door.

"Ah, good. Quinn. I've been waiting for you. I have something I need to share with you." Jakran waved him over to the desk against a large bank of windows. Bookshelves and comfortable chairs filled the spacious room and Quinn wondered if the King had read them all.

"Share with me, Your Majesty?" Quinn perched on a simple wooden chair facing the desk. "What about?"

"Curiously enough, family."

Quinn snorted. "I don't have any family."

"Not alive, perhaps, but this definitely concerns your family." Jakran leaned back in his chair and narrowed his eyes. "I saw the resemblance when you first had supper with us, but your attention to detail in everything you do confirmed it. That, and your devotion to Maia."

"Resemblance to whom?" Quinn raised his eyebrows, not impressed with the king's attempt at suspense.

"To Druid Reuben."

Quinn barked a laugh. "What? What would make you think I'm related to him? He died centuries ago."

"He did, you're right. But here's the thing." Jakran tilted his head with a half-smile. "He said he had only one regret and that was leaving his brother's family without the knowledge of where he'd gone. He'd dropped his surname when he became the Queen's protector. But one night after the Queen was gone, he confided that he'd been part of an honorable family with the name Tarlen and he had a brother with nephews, whom he missed."

Quinn narrowed his eyes. "Are you saying Druid Reuben, the man responsible for the imprisonment of Maia and her sisters, and the so-called protector of Maia's mother, was my father's brother?"

Jakran nodded. "Yes."

Quinn shook his head. "Can't be. My uncle disappeared long before I was born. The King hadn't married yet."

Jakran shrugged as he pulled a book from beneath the pile on his desk. "If I've learned nothing about the way time works between the strictly human world and this one, the one thing I know is it doesn't flow the same in either of them. Decades pass here in only days there. Only rarely do the two worlds match up." He opened the book and slid it toward Quinn. "But take a look and tell me what you see."

Quinn peered at the pages. A pencil drawing portrait of a man dressed in friar's robes with intricate symbols embroidered along the lapels lay beside a family tree. Below the drawing, written in the same hand he'd seen in Maia's book, was a name and a birthdate. *Druid Reuben Tarlen, Protector of Queen Ashlynn and Friend to King Jakran.*

The tree was that of Reuben's family, including his brother and nephews. Quinn bent closer to see the miniscule cursive writing.

"Quinn Mathias Tarlen."

"That's you, isn't it?"

Quinn studied the pencil drawing. He had to admit it was life-like, and Reuben shared many of the traits Quinn saw in the mirror each time he looked. *But there's no way he could be my paternal uncle. Could he?*

"That's my name. But surely there could be more than one Quinn Mathias Tarlen."

Jakran shrugged. "Not likely, at least not in this world. But your family isn't from this world, so the coincidence gets more strained." He sat back in his chair again. "I suspect the same man I knew three centuries ago as Druid Reuben, was your paternal uncle. And here's another thing that makes it more likely. Humans aren't common in this world at all. Most of the peoples here have never seen one. You're myths. To see two with similar names and countenances…? Damn near impossible."

Quinn shook his head. "That would explain a lot. My father was extremely disappointed in my younger brother Sean when he volunteered to figure out the mystery of the Twelve Dancing Princesses. He kept saying things like the Crown had already taken enough from his family. I just assumed it was because of taxes or because the aristocracy always wanted dresses last minute and my mother hand to work her fingers to the bone for them."

Quinn rested his gaze on the pencil drawing, the image like looking at a younger version of his father. "But if it was because his brother had gone to the Queen and then disappeared, that's a better and more likely explanation of his frustration. He kept losing family members to the Crown." Quinn sighed. "He was devastated with Sean's execution."

Jakran's face fell. "Your brother was executed?"

Quinn nodded. "Yeah. When the princesses didn't return, Sean was put to death because he didn't find out where they'd gone, and therefore the King couldn't send anyone to search for them."

Jakran frowned. "Surely he knew how to get to his wife's world. Why wouldn't he search there?"

Quinn shook his head. "I don't know. Maybe the way to this world was closed, either in the usual spot or to him specifically. From what the dryads told us, they were so infuriated with the Key's loss and the princesses' collusion, they forbade the connection to Ashlynn's whole family. Maybe that prevented the King and his guards to come search."

"But you made it to this world, so there must still be a way across."

"And I've encountered men in this world." When Jakran raised his eyebrows, Quinn nodded. "Yes, it's how I fell in with the dryads. I had a contract to kill the leader of this brigand gang of men. I did my job, but came close to getting caught after a dog boy spotted me. They chased me to the dryads' lands. Perhaps the King did get a few guards across and they're what's left of them."

"How did you make it into this world, Quinn?" Jakran rubbed his chin. "We have a portal here in the palace, but it's only attuned to the ruling Goblin family. If all the members of the family die out and the crown passes to another family, special servants have the ability to connect the portal to their bloodline." He narrowed his eyes and raised his chin. "But there aren't very many portals that I know of. How did you get here?"

Quinn frowned and rubbed his chin. "I went looking for the serving woman who was the last to see Sean alive. She said she knew where the princesses had gone, but not what became of them. She snuck me into the palace and helped me through the portal. That's how I met the dryads, or at least saw them, first. I stumbled across an assassin from the Guild who took me with her on her escape from the dryads. Since I had nothing and no one, she brought me to the guild and I signed a ten year contract. Thus here I am."

Jakran raised his eyebrows. "How much time is lift on your contract?"

"None. It ended fifteen years ago. I'm under no obligation to them except to complete any unfinished assassination contracts."

Jakran nodded. "And how many unfinished contracts do you have?"

Quinn smiled. "None. The last one brought me full circle back to the dryads."

Jakran snorted. "That's convenient."

"I didn't think so at the time, but now I'm reconsidering." He shot a look out the King's window. "I find myself less interested in being an assassin and more interested in being a bodyguard."

Jakran barked a laugh. "I'd wager you'd like to do more than guard Maia's body, but that's a worthy thought." He reached into his desk and pulled out parchment and a pencil. "I just happen to have a contact in the Assassin's Guild and I'd be happy to send a missive to them about your whereabouts, your choice of ending your association with them, and your gratitude for their training. If you're serious about guarding Maia's body, that is."

Quinn raised his own eyebrows as he took the paper and writing implement. "Why would the King of the

Goblins have a contact in the Assassin's Guild?"

A half smile curled Jakran's lips. "Back in my father's time, the Goblin tribes were much less civilized and often had assassins on retainer, just in case they had a rival they needed to dispatch. It was a brutal way to rule, but fairly effective for exposing the most ruthless of us. I inherited my father's contacts and found it a useful connection to keep open. I haven't chosen to use it, yet, but you never know when something like that could come in handy." The smile evolved into a full smirk. "It seems to be handy for this transaction."

Quinn snorted as he bent to write his letter of resignation. He made sure to be clear that he was under no duress and he'd made the choice after careful consideration. He read it over three times, making corrections to his wording until it was perfect before signing.

Do I know what the hell I'm doing?

No, not remotely, but he'd never turned away from a challenge before. Hell, he'd crossed into this world, learned to be an assassin of mythical beasts, and taken on a quest with a woman he thought he hated. *I shouldn't start trying to be sane now.*

One thing he did know for sure. He loved Maia, and he needed to be with her and see this quest to the end. He couldn't accept any other assassination contracts until he'd helped her regain her sisters' lives, and he had no idea how long that would take.

And I don't ever want to leave her.

Before he sealed the letter, he withdrew a coin with the Assassin's Guild crest on both sides and slipped it into the envelope along with the missive. Each assassin was given one upon completion of their training, and should they be killed, the coin had a spell that would return it to the Guild. If they survived, the coin could only be sent back upon retirement. *It's definitely time for me to retire from the trade.*

He sealed the letter and allowed the King to add a blob of wax to the parchment before stamping it with his official signet. The King handed it back to him.

"Thank you, Your Majesty."

"You're welcome, Quinn. I personally think you're making a wise choice." Jakran rose and gestured for Quinn to follow. "Come. You can send it with one of our messenger birds so you know it's on its way. Then maybe we can have dinner with the ladies tonight if we can convince them to stop training for a moment."

Quinn hoped so. He missed Maia and he wanted to talk to her about his decision to retire. He nodded and followed the King out. Today was the first day of his new life.

CHAPTER SIXTEEN

Quinn found Maia in their rooms, staring out at the mauve evening sky. A dust storm had swept through earlier that day and filled the air with so much grit, it sparkled in the sunlight. Now the evening sunset painted rosy colors on the sky's bowl. Despite the beauty outside, Maia's expression held sadness and fatigue, and Quinn's heart squeezed.

"Good evening, Maia. How was your training today?"

"It went as well as a centaur using a jump rope."

Quinn laughed. "That's a hell of an image." When Maia didn't crack a smile, he sobered. "What happened?"

"Nothing. Nothing happened." She gripped a cup of something in her hand as if debating the merits of throwing it against the wall. "Nothing's ever going to happen."

"Whoa, whoa, slow down." He settled beside her on the window seat and took the cup before it flew across the room. "Start at the beginning. What happened to put you in this mood?"

"I can't do it, Quinn." Tears glittered in her eyes as she turned them on him. "I can't grab the magic. I can see it, it's right there in front of me, but I can't grab it or manipulate it or anything. What's the use of being able to see it but not use it? And if I can't harness it, I won't be able to save my sisters."

"Okay, I hear you. Deep breaths. We'll figure this out." He nodded and felt like he was looking at himself over twenty years earlier. "What did Queen Tricia say about it?"

"Nothing. She told me to take a break for the day and said she was going to try to figure out a way to teach me because the way she was taught isn't working." Maia clenched her fists. "I'm so damn useless. Even Tricia has to give up for the day."

"Hey. Let's not go borrowing trouble. She didn't say you were useless, did she?"

"No, she didn't have to."

"Stop." Anger curled under his voice and he used it now to get her attention. "One setback does not a failure make. You can't do things like everyone else. That's not your style, Maia." He pursed his lips and tilted his head. "Let me tell you about when I first came here."

"Came here?"

"Yes, to this world where all the myths and beasties were real and we were the mythical beasts."

"That must have been a shock for you."

Quinn barked a short laugh. "You have no idea. But when I first arrived and was granted the acceptance to the Assassin's Guild's training, I didn't have much ability at all. Not in fighting, not in stealth, not in tracking or listening or even standing still. I think all the instructors decided I represented the most useless species for assassination they'd ever seen."

He shook his head with a rueful smile, recalling Master Hellspell, a gryphon assassin who could shapeshift into a man's shape or a gryphon depending on the situation. "They all pointed out I had no claws, wretched hearing, sight, scenting, or grip. I was weak, not meant for running or flying or grappling, and I didn't even have the necessary claws for climbing or hand-to-hand. Basically, I was the worst assassin candidate they'd ever trained. I represented a helluva failure."

Maia blinked. "Yes, that sounds like a recipe for failure for sure."

He nodded. "Exactly. But one Master, a gorgon who could freeze someone into stone with one look, taught me a secret. She said I had to learn what I was good at, what no one else could do, and capitalize on it. I was human, someone most of the peoples who lived in this world had never seen, and therefore I could do things they couldn't. I didn't have claws or wings or thumbs on my feet or the ability to change my skin to match my surroundings. I had to figure out what I could do that no one else could, and become a master at that."

"What could you do that no one else could?" Maia wiped her eyes and sat up a little straighter.

"I could read body language and perception better than anyone else." He smirked, remembering the fight he'd had with a goblin opponent. "I didn't have to be as strong as everyone because I could read what they were going to do before they did it by paying attention. I watched how they moved and how they punched, and I used that knowledge against them. I figured out their tells, I learned how to anticipate where they would punch and how they would move so I could either counter their blows or not be where they impacted."

Maia sniffed and shook her head. "That's good for hand-to-hand, but how does that translate to this?"

He nodded without a smile, but squeezed her hands. "You have to figure out what your best strength and ability is. You have the ability to see the magic. Maybe grabbing it isn't your thing. Maybe you have to connect to it in another way. This isn't an insurmountable obstacle, this is a new way of being for you. A new way of understanding yourself that no one can duplicate. You have to learn to be the best you there is, not copy someone else."

Maia grunted. "That's what Tricia said. She said she had to teach me to be me rather than be her."

"Exactly." Quinn nodded. "So, what can you do better than anyone else? And how can you apply that to connecting and interacting with magic?"

****

Maia sat in the octagonal room and stared at the floor, watching the ley lines pulse through the cracks in the flagstone. *I can do this. I can see them better than anyone else in this world.* Or at least anyone else she knew. Now she just had to figure out how she could use that ability to allow her to access those ley lines. It didn't really matter if other people could or did access them. It only mattered how she could.

Okay, so I can see them. Now what?

Quinn's voice rang in her inner ear. *Find that strength that is yours alone and use it to the best of your ability to get things done.* He hadn't told her how he'd mastered his ability to read people, but she understood the meaning behind the story. *I have to be the best me I can and no one is a better me than myself.* It sounded silly when she said it aloud so she kept her mouth shut, but the truth sat right in front of her.

She opened her senses and the lines shone brightly along the floor and walls. She still couldn't close the wards herself, but she could see them. *So how can I manipulate them?* She reached out her hands to grab the lines the way Tricia had described, but as before, they squipped out of her grip and wriggled away.

Maia growled and pulled her hands back. *Okay, so they don't like to be grabbed.* To be honest, she didn't like it either. She preferred people to gesture or ask her to move with their voices rather than physical coercion. *Maybe that's where I need to focus.* Could she cajole or coax the magic into doing her bidding? She snorted.

That's the stupidest thing I've ever thought. Magic was inanimate and couldn't respond in a sentient manner. Could it?

Maia frowned. What could she lose by trying? Taking a deep breath, she opened her senses and looked at the lines in the room. They pulsed like a creature breathing. *Or a heartbeat.*

She watched them for several minutes, trying to find the pattern and sequence. Every twelfth pulse came a little slower and ran a little longer than the others. She counted three more sequences until she learned the pattern, then "spoke" to the magic. It was more like a whisper of her thoughts in the same cadence as the pulses, but she coaxed its "attention", with a rhythm and rhyme.

Time disappeared from her estimation. She had no idea how long it took to attract the magic, but eventually the pulses took on whichever cadence she gave it and she was able to reach out to touch the ley lines. She didn't try to grab them, only stroked like patting a favorite pet. The third time she stroked, the ley line arched up to her hand like a cat and her palm tingled with energy.

She stroked a few more times before she closed her fingers around it and lifted it out of its bed in the floor. She wrapped it around her hand so it couldn't wiggle free and held it, allowing the energy to sift through her. Strength, vitality, and excitement zinged through her and she let out a yip of glee.

Unfortunately, the magic "startled" and slipped free of her grasp. She gasped in dismay, but let it go before it slapped her in its hurry to escape.

"Well done! That's better than I've ever been able to do." Tricia's voice intruded and Maia dropped her senses to focus on the Goblin Queen. "How did you figure out how to do that?"

"Quinn helped me." She blushed and waved at the floor. "He basically said what you did about being the best me I could be." She shrugged. "I talked to it and it came to me."

"Talked to it? To the ley line?" Tricia raised her eyebrows.

"Yes…is that wrong?"

Tricia blinked and shook her head. "No, I just never thought to talk to the magic. How did you figure out that it would respond?"

Maia shrugged one shoulder with a frown. "I just thought about the times I've been grabbed or physically manipulated into doing something. It always infuriated me and made me more resistant to doing whatever it was. I thought if I coaxed or requested the magic to respond, the result would be better."

"Wow. That's really smart." Tricia smacked her forehead with the heel of her hand. "Think of how much easier it would've been for me to learn this magic manipulation stuff if I'd understood it could be talked to. Sheesh. Wake up and smell the coffee, Trish."

Maia laughed at her odd turn of phrase. "To be honest, I wouldn't have thought of it except for what you and Quinn said. He said humans are so few and far between here and there isn't anyone to teach us how to be the best at our human skills. He said I had to figure out what I did best and become a master at it." She waved at the room. "I think he was right."

Tricia nodded before she tilted her head. "You're bound to him."

Maia snorted. "Yes, because the dryads' Keeper put a spell on us to make sure he didn't kill me right out of the gate."

"No, well yes, I can see that spell, but this binding is deeper." Tricia's eyes unfocused and she appeared to look through Maia. "This connection is more like heart and soul connections. I can see thick strands of energy connecting the two of you through your...chakras. Do you know that word?"

Maia shook her head.

"They're energy centers in the body and they each have a different internal sound." She paused and grinned. "Let me see you talk to the magic again. I want to see if I can tell how you do it from outside looking in."

Maia nodded and settled herself before she opened her senses. The room glowed in the soft light of the ley lines and she counted the pulses until she got to twelve. *The pattern's the same.* Again she sang her own cadence to the beat and reached for the magic. This time the ley line arched to her hand much quicker and infused her body with its scintillating energy.

"Nice, hold it there for a moment, Maia." Tricia's voice intruded, but didn't throw her off her game. "Okay, the wards are set. Now let's see what you can ask it to do."

Maia wasn't sure she could get the magic to do anything but hang out with her, but Tricia gave her a series of instructions to make the magic act. She had Maia construct a box strong enough to hold things off the ground like a vase full of water and flowers. Fortunately the vase was wood and didn't break each time it fell through the box.

When she finally mastered the box, which blazed like a thousand candles in her sight, Tricia instructed her to compress the box into a shelf or tray and move the vase around the room. The vase sat empty to keep from drenching them both, but it still toppled and fell off the shelf of magic Maia had constructed.

By lunch, Maia ached with the effort to direct the magic, but she'd gotten good at making a solid box and shelf out of the energy. After they'd eaten, Tricia had her make the shelf move around and stop without jarring the vase. Her focus started to fray as they closed in on the evening. When Tricia told her to fling it like a knife, she lost control and the shelf pinged off the sides of the wards, making them duck.

"Whoa!" Tricia dove to the floor and laughed. "Okay, I think that's enough for one day. Rein it in there, girl and we'll go to dinner."

Maia put the magic to bed with a whisper and slumped against the wall. "I'm tried."

"Yeah, you look it. Me too. Tonight, you need to eat and drink really well." Tricia opened the wards and fixed Maia with a sharp look. "Working with magic like this is draining. Your body is basically a conduit and the energy flows through you. You need to make sure you refuel with food and water or juice for electrolytes."

"Elec-what?"

"Electrolytes. Oh, uh, salts in the water to make sure your body is fully recharged." Tricia shook her head. "I keep forgetting you haven't been in the world we both came from for a long time. In any case, eat, drink, and rest. We're gonna kick some magical ass tomorrow."

Maia nodded with a tired smile and helped Tricia clean up the water and scattered flowers. She'd made huge strides toward using magic, but she still had control issues and could easily hurt someone that way. *What did Quinn say? Practice, practice, practice.* And master the skill no one else had. *Right.*

Easier said than done, but she couldn't argue with the veracity of his words. By the time she made it back to the rooms she shared with Quinn, she could barely keep her eyes open. She wanted to lay down and sleep for a week, but she headed for the pitcher of water before she collapsed. Her hands shook as she poured and she drenched the tray as much as her cup, but at last she had enough to suck down.

I'll just take a little nap before dinner and be refreshed.

She retreated to her bed and was asleep before her head hit the pillow.

****

Quinn stared down at his sleeping beauty and debated waking her for the evening meal. Tricia had mentioned she might fall asleep and she needed to eat to replenish her magical reserves, but Maia slept hard, her mouth open and her body relaxed.

So beautiful.

That was an understatement. Maia could be many things—annoying, snarky, pointed, strong, impatient, and sultry—but she'd always been beautiful in his eyes. He wanted to wake her up with teasing touches and bring her to rapturous pleasure, but he understood how hard she trained and how much it took out of her. She wouldn't thank him for disturbing her.

He sighed and shook his head. *Best leave her and talk to the King and Queen about where we'll be going next.*

He headed out of their rooms, sure to lock the door behind him. He didn't want anyone to disturb Maia until he returned. His thoughts turned to his decision to leave the Assassin's Guild and become a full-time bodyguard to the Keeper of the Key. He nodded to the few courtiers and servants he passed, automatically scanning them for threats, but his main focus remained inward.

To be brutally honest, he wanted to be more than just a bodyguard. *Unless by bodyguard I get to spend time pleasuring her sexy body.* He wanted more from Maia than professional relationship. He needed her to remind him of his humanity and to bring color back into his black and white world. She made him see and feel more than he'd ever felt in his whole adult life, and he found himself addicted to it.

Quinn paused at the doors to the dining chamber and

waited for the butler to announce him to the King and Queen. If they'd both remained in their original world, Maia would've become a queen or at least a duchess of some region. And Quinn? *I would've been a tailor like my father.*

That didn't ring true, but it was all moot anyway. Now he was a master assassin who guarded the lovely body of the Keeper of the Key to the Twelve Worlds.

"Good evening, Quinn. Will Maia be joining us?" Jakran looked up from his seat at the intimate table the royal couple shared.

"No, I don't think so. She's completely out." He sat down at one of the open seats.

"Uh-oh, that's not good. She's going to need fuel or she won't be able to do anything tomorrow." Tricia's brow creased. "Should we wake her?"

Jakran shook his head. "Let her sleep for a short time. We'll make sure Quinn takes food to her after supper. He can wake her and make sure she eats then."

"Okay." Tricia bit her bottom lip.

"Don't worry, *solara.* She'll be fine with Quinn to look after her."

It wasn't long ago where that wasn't true. But Quinn nodded and served himself some food from the fragrant dishes arranged on the table.

"If it's not too much of a bother, can you tell me how long you think the training will take?" Quinn met Tricia's raised eyebrows with a grimace. "We have one more station to visit for the last portion of the Key and we only have until mid-summer to reach it and get back to the dryad's forest to rescue her sisters."

"Hmm, I don't really know what to tell you." Tricia picked at the food on her plate. "Maia has figured out how to access the magic in the ley lines and she can make constructions like boxes or boards, but she only figured that out today. The next few days will give me an idea of how easily she'll master her skills. Or build them." She shot a look out the window at the starry night. "It's February, or rather the second month after the Solstice, so you still have about four months or about a hundred and forty days until the summer Solstice. That should give them enough time, right, Jakran?"

The Goblin King nodded. "I believe so. But they do have a long path from here. They need to get to Cedarfell. That's where the last hiding place is."

Quinn frowned. "Cedarfell? I'm not familiar with that location."

"It's an old temple to the Goddess that was abandoned about two centuries ago. Druid Reuben left the last portion of the Key there with the monks, but a disease swept through them and the temple had to be abandoned. I haven't heard if it's been resettled at all."

"If it's been abandoned, how will we recover the Key?" Quinn stopped to gape at them. *Sweet Lady Death, has this all been for nothing?*

"Druid Reuben visited the temple after the monks left and he secured the Key with a magical lock left on it. All you need to do is get into the building and recite the incantation, and it'll be revealed."

"Which incantation?"

"The same one you learned in Reuben's book. Speak it in a voice of command, and the location will appear." Jakran rubbed his chin. "At least, that's what he said to me. Magic doesn't usually go bad over time, but it can lose some of its potency if not renewed."

"And you don't know if anyone has moved into the area?" Tricia shot her husband a surprised look. "I thought you knew everything happening on this continent."

Jakran snorted. "I have many connections, but I've been concerned with the Goblin demesne recently. It leaves other things to take care of themselves." He returned his gaze to Quinn's. "I don't know if anyone has taken up residency near the old temple, but you should be aware that Reuben did encounter Nightmare boars there the last time he visited."

"Nightmare boars?" Quinn raised his eyebrows.

"Yes, great horned pigs about the height of a centaur's equine back. Big, odiferous, and more ornery than a usual wild boar."

"Lovely."

"Plus they generally damage anything and everything they live around, digging holes for roots."

"Fantastic. What do we do if someone has moved into the area despite the boars?" Quinn had to know what he'd be facing, although if Maia got a handle on her magical abilities, that could be used for defense as well.

Jakran rubbed his chin. "I guess that depends on who it is and whether or not they'd be willing to let you visit the temple. You could always have Maia disable them with magic."

"Or you could just ask nicely." Tricia rolled her eyes. "You catch more flies with honey than you do with vinegar, my mother used to say. Who knows, they might be reasonable and willing to treat with you like civilized folks."

Jakran shot him a dry look, but said nothing. Quinn tended to take the King's perspective, but Tricia had a point. They'd just have to see what was there before making a decision about using force as opposed to negotiation. *Goddess of all, I just hope anyone we meet is willing to talk instead of attack.* Putting Maia in unnecessary danger didn't sit well with Quinn.

CHAPTER SEVENTEEN

It took Maia another four weeks with Tricia to learn how to use her magic for both offense and defensive moves. By then, she could easily create shapes and boxes of physical magic to move around the room. She could make a shield and thin, nearly-invisible blades to use like a real sword in hand-to-hand. Those were the easy parts.

The harder skills she worked on allowed her to dismantle old and protective spells, contain runaway magic in an energy bubble, and create illusions. Tricia called them glamours used by the Fae, but the general idea was to encourage the minds of anyone she met to slide away without registering their presences.

"Well done. I didn't even see you that time and I'm pretty sure neither did the servants." Tricia laughed when Maia appeared after they'd walked down the corridors of the palace under a glamour. She'd allowed Maia to work out of the warded room once she'd gotten her magic under mastered control.

"I can be taught." Maia grinned. *Thank the Goddess.*

"Yes, you can. Now, let's get some lunch and we'll work on your hand-to-hand combat."

Maia raised her eyebrows. "Physical fighting and grappling?"

"Yup."

"Why?"

Tricia snorted as they headed for the dining area. "Just because you can use magic doesn't mean you should let your body get weak. Magic is as much a skill as the physical martial arts. It's not the only one you have and you shouldn't depend on it alone. Plus, sometimes you don't have to use that kind of draining energy to get what you want or need."

"But I've built up endurance. It doesn't drain me now."

"It doesn't drain you as much, but it still drains you." Tricia passed her a plate as they hit the buffet set out by the servants. "You'll find you're just as hungry as ever, but you're not as tired."

"Ugh."

Tricia laughed. "That's exactly what I said when I was doing this."

Quinn and the King didn't join them for their meal, but it was a good thing because thoughts of Quinn almost always distracted Maia from her training. The man was too sexy by half and when he touched her, she lost all control. The words "wanton wench" entered her mind, but she shoved them away. Neither she nor Quinn was beholden to anyone else and if she wanted to take pleasure in his attentions, she damn well would.

She looked forward to seeing him each evening when she was done with training and missed him at lunch when he couldn't be there. She wondered what he did while she trained and if he enjoyed his time cooling his heels until she was ready to move on. *Goddess, I hope he's not bored.*

She kept looking for him in hopes he'd show up in time for lunch, but eventually she had to join Tricia in the courtyard for more physical exercises. They strapped on thick padded jerkins to protect their midsections and picked up long staffs. Maia shoved her disappointment back and focused on not getting her ass handed to her when Tricia came at her with a furious barrage.

But I want to see him. I bet he could teach me hand-to-hand techniques.

If she could keep her mind on them and not stripping him down and touching his sexy body. Just the idea of him naked totally derailed her thinking and Tricia whacked her hard in the ribs.

"Ow!"

"Pay attention. You're daydreaming and I'm going to kick your butt if you don't watch out." Tricia shook her head with a frown. "Where were you just then?"

"Nowhere. Let's go again." Maia blew the hair that had escaped her braid from her eyes and took a better grip on her staff.

"I bet I know what you were thinking about." Tricia smirked as she thrust her staff at Maia's midsection. "I bet some hot guy has your innermost thoughts. I bet you're mooning over your bodyguard."

Embarrassment and anger curled through Maia and she made a couple of clumsy strikes at the Goblin Queen.

"That's it, isn't it?" Tricia easily deflected and her smirk grew. "What were you thinking of? His broad shoulders? His narrow waist? Those hard thighs and strong hands? Oooh, I could see why they'd be very distracting."

Maia snarled and redoubled her efforts, but Tricia blocked and smacked her on the butt hard enough to sting. When she whirled to try again, the Goblin Queen grabbed her jerkin and pulled her nose to nose.

"Focus, Maia. Your physical opponents won't hesitate to use what you love or what you fear against you to make you angry and therefore clumsy. That's a good way to die." Tricia let her go and stood back, letting them both catch their breaths. "I'm serious. You can't let anyone taunt you into fury. Love whom you love, worry for them, but don't let your opponents see they're getting to you because they'll use it to make you careless and abandon your training. Love isn't a weakness no matter what men like to tell you, but it can be used as leverage. You have to outsmart and out-stoic your opponents. Or out-infuriate them."

"How do I do that if I know nothing about them?" Maia panted, releasing some of her anger. She'd deal with her strange feelings for Quinn later.

"Easy." Tricia winked. "Men have egos, big ones, when it comes to fighting, and they particularly have issues with being beaten, physically, by women. Don't ask me why they're so convinced we're weaker or inexperienced or unskilled. It's a continual failing on the part of the male guards here. So much so, that the female guards often beat them." Tricia rolled her eyes and shook her head. "Dumbasses."

Maia laughed. "I can see them getting a bit irritated with a woman beating them."

"Oh, yeah. You should've seen when I kicked the daylights out of Corlith, Jakran's brother. He was all overconfident and arrogant, and I taught him not to underestimate his opponent no matter how small and fragile she looks." She waved the thought away with a laugh. "But my point is, if you start taunting them with, 'is that the best you can do?' and 'you say you're the best at this?', it usually gets them to make a bad mistake and you can disable or kill them."

Maia swallowed hard. "Kill?"

Tricia lost her smile. "Yeah. They won't give you the chance to give up. Most of the people you'll be meeting in hand-to-hand won't stop when you submit. They'll be aiming for your death. Keep that in mind when you're outside of the training circle."

Right. No thinking about my sexy lover or actually loving him until I'm done fighting.

Loving him?

The thought distracted her enough that Tricia got in a few good blows, but Maia yanked her wandering attention back to the fore and focused. She wasn't nearly as experienced with the long staff as the Goblin Queen, but she didn't do too badly. *If you don't count the bruises and the aches in my muscles.*

"Okay, that's enough." Tricia put her staff down and Maia slumped in relief. "You've learned pretty fast. Don't worry, it'll get easier as we go along."

"That is not what I'm worried about." Maia groaned as she set her staff on the rack. "I'm three hundred years old and I'm feeling every bit of it."

Tricia raised her eyebrows. "Three hundred?"

"Yes." Maia stretched her aching arm muscles. "Druid Reuben knew my elder sister Inge and he absconded with the Key the night of the last party we attended with the dryads. Three hundred years ago."

Tricia rubbed her chin. "I didn't think humans lived that long."

"We don't." Maia straightened her clothes after removing the padded jerkin. "Not unless we're turned into a magical inanimate object and posted as a warning to others not to defy the dryads." She raised her gaze. "My other ten sisters are still there in that state."

"Ten sisters? Dear Goddess, how many of you are there?"

"There were twelve. Now there are just eleven of us." She allowed a humorless smile to curl her lips. "The dryads killed my eldest sister when Druid Reuben left with the key. They turned the rest of us into lamps with pretty stained glass shades. To keep the rain off, they said."

"Holy shit." Tricia shook her head with a scowl. "I still think that's sickening."

Maia shrugged. She couldn't change it and fury had gotten her nowhere beyond exhausted.

"Oh, we're definitely going to teach you how to use your magic so you can get that shit changed." Tricia's brows lowered. "We're going to work on your hand-to-hand, but then we'll combine it with your mastery over your magic. We'll make you a double threat."

Maia snorted, but a smile curled her lips. "Double threat?"

"A knife-wielding ninja with magery." An odd expression flooded Tricia's face. "Hey, we'll make you a real-life D&D character." She grinned.

"A what?" Maia frowned.

"Never mind, it's a human world thing. The point is you'll be ready to face the dryads and save your sisters when I'm through with you."

Maia hoped Tricia was right, but she wasn't entirely sure she'd make it through the training alive. "How about we just focus on the training and worry about the dryads later. That's not too much to ask, is it?"

"Done." Tricia winked. "But I really wish I could be there when you roll a twenty and smite their asses."

"You say some of the strangest things." Maia shook her head.

Tricia laughed and led her back into the palace for the evening meal.

****

Quinn faced off with the king again and watched to see which way the bigger man moved. Jakran feinted left and swung his wooden sword at Quinn's midsection from the right. Quinn grasped his wrist, and turned into the reach of Jakran's arms as he swept the man's feet out from under him. Jakran grabbed Quinn's shoulder, but Quinn wriggled out of his grip and let the man topple to the ground of the practice yard.

The assembled guards didn't make a sound or appear

to have noticed the king on the ground and Quinn gave a small prayer of thanks. Until he wondered why.

"Are your guards always this inattentive?" He held his hand out to the king as Jakran rolled to his knees.

"No, not usually." Jakran took the hand and stood, brushing himself off. "Usually they'd have been swarming us." He frowned. "What the hellfire are they looking at?"

They put up their wooden weapons and headed to the back of the crowd surrounding another portion of the practice yard. Beyond the helmed heads of the guards he caught sight of two women, one with gnarled horns and one without, whaling on each other with wooden staves. The Goblin Queen drove her staff toward Maia's feet, but the princess jumped and slashed down with her own. The crack of wood against wood echoed in the yard and the guards gave a murmur of appreciation. But they gasped as Maia threw up a wall of sparkling energy like a shield and stood behind it, sizing up her opponent.

Holy shit, that's magic.

The two women faced off, sweat slicking their hair back from their faces and their chests heaving. While Quinn enjoyed that sexy view, he was more turned on by the calculation and concentration in Maia's expression.

"Damn, she's so sexy." The king's voice penetrated his focus and Quinn blinked.

He's not talking about Maia, is he?

Quinn shot a look at Jakran, but the King's attention was fixed on his wife, her ringing blows against Maia's defense deafening. Quinn had to admit the queen was very good with physical fighting, but Maia seemed like grace in motion. When the queen's staff swung at her shoulder, she bent in half backward and used her staff to push the blow past her. She followed the move with a ball of magic to tangle the other woman's feet.

Tricia whooped as she went down and the crowd roared as it surged forward. But before Quinn could do more than dart toward them, the entire mass stopped as if held at the edge of a large bubble around the women. *Sweet Lady Death, what the hell is that?*

Maia held the fingers of one hand spread as if she palmed a large ball as she shot a look at Tricia. "Are you well, Your Majesty?"

Tricia shook her head and laughed as she climbed to her feet. "Damn, girl, you handily kicked my ass. I'd say you're ready."

"Ready?" Maia returned her gaze to the mass of goblin guards pressed against her invisible magic bubble. "Ready for what?"

"To graduate. Congratulations! You've mastered magic and hand-to-hand combat." Tricia turned her gaze to the men plastered against the bubble. "Uh, what's wrong with them?"

"I think they thought I was trying to kill you and now they're coming for me." Maia grimaced. "Only my shield is keeping them at bay at the moment."

Tricia raised her eyebrows and nodded. "Nice. You're stronger than I thought you'd be if you can hold off all of them." She scanned the crowd and her gaze lit on the king. "Hey, darlin', do you think you could call off the guards long enough to let Maia take a break?"

Jakran bellowed something in his own language and the guards paused and backed off. Quinn let them flow past him, but he remained at the edge of her energy bubble and he couldn't contain the hard-on straining his pants. Damn, the woman got sexier every day. He'd already liked so many things about her, but watching her battle the Goblin Queen and hold off a hoard of guards made pride and something like excitement surge in his chest.

Maia twisted her hand and snapped her fingers. The bubble of energy popped and he moved forward with the king to where the queen brushed herself off with a grin.

"That was impressive." Jakran brushed a hand over

Tricia's ass and tugged on her tail. "Are you all right?"

"Yeah, I'm fine. Maia's become a formidable warrior and mage. She's gonna give the dryads hell." Tricia grinned.

Maia snorted and shook her head. "We'll see. They have known about and used their abilities since day one. I'm just figuring this out right now."

"Aw, you're a natural. Heck, Jakran had a worse time teaching me how to use magic. Of course, I thought I was human back then." Tricia shook her head. "But now I want a bath and a glass of wine to celebrate your accomplishment. Let's break out the good stuff."

Maia smiled, but she shook her head. "Thanks, but I'm going back to my rooms to take a bath and rest. I'm tired."

"Don't forget to eat well tonight." Tricia shook her finger at Maia. "You need to replenish that energy."

"Yes, mama."

"Oh, you don't want me to go all Goblin-mama on your ass. It ain't pretty."

Maia snorted and nodded while the King and Queen headed for the palace. Quinn waited for Maia to finish putting away her gear before he approached and slid his hands around her waist from behind.

"How are you feeling? Your display was pretty impressive." Despite his better judgement, his cock stiffened against her ass as the scent of her hair flooded his nose. *Holy hell, the woman turns me on just by smelling her.*

She shook her head and grimaced. "It was impressive when no one's really trying to kill me or resist." She frowned as she met his gaze over her shoulder. "I don't feel complete, like I'm missing something that'll help me focus my abilities."

Quinn released her and turned her to face him. "Do you think this has to do with you being the Keeper of the Key?"

She tilted her head. "You mean, since the Key isn't complete, I'm not feeling complete?"

"Something like that. Or another way to look at it is once the Key is in one piece, you'll feel more in control with a focal point." He walked beside her as they returned to the palace, catching some of the looks from the guards. "You know, we might consider heading to the next location soon. I think we make the guards here nervous."

She shot a look around as they continued their path toward their suite. "Yes, I noticed that when we arrived. They are concerned about you and your skills."

"And now they have something to worry about with you and your skills." Quinn snorted as he let them into their suite. "You might be more scary than me."

She snorted with a smirk. "No one's more scary than you."

"I think that's debatable given I'm not the one who can hold off an entire garrison of guards at once with just a pretty light show." He laughed as she swatted him with the flat of her hand. "What? It's true."

"That 'light show' as you call it, wore my butt out, and now I want a bath and a meal." She slowly gathered up her toiletries and towel before she hesitated and met his gaze. "But I think you're right."

"About what specifically?"

"About needing to leave, probably as early as tomorrow. We're running out of time to get back to the dryads before they kill my sisters." She winked. "And you might be right about my connection to the Key as a focal point."

She headed into the bathing room before he could comment or offer to help her with her bath.

CHAPTER EIGHTEEN

Taking leave of the King and Queen of the Goblins was more emotional than Maia expected. She'd enjoyed her time in the palace and liked Tricia despite all her odd sayings and quirks. *And who doesn't have quirks?* The Goblin Queen had been sorry to see her go, but made her promise to keep in touch by pigeon.

"It's not as fast as phone call or email, but it's rather nice to get real written letters."

"Phone call or email?" Maia had shaken her head. "You're so strange."

"Heh, you don't know the half of it. Here." Tricia had handed her a little silk bag filled with a silver charm bracelet. The charms were in the shapes of horseshoes and little egg-shaped balls with groves cut in regular lines. "This was a gift from my brother Mack. It's always brought me luck and I want to send it with you. Don't worry about being perfect, because like in the game of horseshoes or when using hand grenades, getting close is good enough."

"I'll remember that."

Tricia had grinned and hugged Maia before the company of guards escorted them outside the palace environs. She suspected the guards were just as eager to get rid of them as they were to leave their glowering company. Fortunately, once they were on their way, Maia and Quinn fell into their old pattern of travel from before their stay. This time, however, most of their winter gear remained packed.

The journey to Cedarfell could be best described as hot, sweaty, and violent. Though the violence came from Quinn's constant insistence on practicing her hand-to-hand combat skills, both with and without magic. Maia wasn't sure what ached more. Her shoulders from carrying her pack, full of her winter gear, or her limbs from all the blows she sustained from Quinn's training. The man was sexy as hell, but he was also relentless and despite her ability to move quickly, always saw her attack before she made it. When she complained, his only response was, "Learn to hide your thoughts better."

They didn't meet many bandits on their journey north from the desert, but Maia made sure to keep their camps concealed with deflection magic. Tricia had described such a practice as energy to make the mind deflect off the truth. They weren't truly invisible, but the magic helped keep marauders and bandits from scouting their location. There were a couple of times the brigands marched right past their camp without a look in their direction.

It took them roughly a fortnight's worth of days to reach the rise above Cedarfell and by then, Maia was ready to stop for longer than a night. The weather had been remarkably mild, though they'd had to dig out some of their gear as the nights in the north remained cold. Quinn donned his sexy coat and despite her fatigue, she'd insisted he fuck her a few times while wearing it. He'd shot her an amused look when she requested, but never turned her down.

The sun rose high in the sky as they crested the rise and they stopped at the well-worn road ahead of them.

"Well, I guess the temple's not abandoned anymore."

Maia shook her head. "Where did all the centaurs come from?"

Instead of an empty valley with the ruins of a temple beside the river, they found a thriving village of centaurs surrounding a refurbished shrine with glass windows and fine thatched roof.

"Do you think they found the Key?"

Quinn shrugged. "I don't know, but I bet we'll get the chance to find out. Heads-up, here come the guards."

Maia squared her shoulders and raised her chin as a company of well-armed and armored horse-men approached at a canter. She wondered how they managed to keep their balance with having so much body located at the front of the horse portion, but they managed to do just fine as they thundered to a stop around her and Quinn.

She wanted to give them each a snarky look and remark, "What, did you forget the wagon part of welcome wagon?" But she thought it would be wiser to remain civil and professional. She recalled from somewhere that centaurs had very little sense of humor and tended to shoot first and ask questions later.

"Who are you and what are you doing here?" The big appaloosa guard thrust a spear at them and Maia took a few deep breaths to calm herself before she answered.

"I'm Princess Maia Silvercloak and this is my bodyguard Quinn Tarlen. We've come on a pilgrimage to visit the Temple of the Goddess and had no idea this area had been settled." She tried to keep her voice light, but the long spear not far from her nose made her nervous. "Would we be able to visit the temple?"

The guard eyed her with suspicion. "Pilgrims you say? Strange to have a Master Assassin from the Assassin's Guild with you as guard for merely being pilgrims."

Maia hadn't counted on Quinn's profession being recognized, but she smiled and nodded. "We all have our pasts, don't we, sir?" She gestured ahead of them. "Perhaps you could escort us to the Stallion and Lead Mare of your village so we might confer with them?"

The guards shared a look over their heads while Quinn shifted closer to Maia. She suspected he prepared to do something drastic, but she didn't want to cause trouble. Centaurs were known to be tough, both to negotiate with and to kill, and she didn't need more obstacles in completing their quest.

"Very well, we'll bring you to Captain Yarren and Lead Mare Sonja." The gruff guard eyed them as if checking for visible weapons.

Good thing my abilities aren't particularly visible.

"Thank you." Maia inclined her head before she waved at Quinn to stand down. He didn't so much as blink or nod, but some of the tension across his shoulders released.

The centaurs herded them down the road into the village and Maia hoped they'd be able to find a place to stay and rest. While she wasn't looking forward to negotiating the ability to visit the temple, having a place to sleep indoors brought some relief. She shot a look at the oncoming buildings and hoped one might be a bath.

They'd almost reached the center of the village when a woman with golden-brown hair pulled back into a ponytail stepped out of the building beside the temple. Maia's steps faltered as she took in the other woman's appearance.

There are more humans here?

The woman shared the same surprised expression as the centaur guards ushered Maia and Quinn into a barn-like enclosure with a wide arena and odd half-stalls stationed facing the arena at one end. Two of the stalls were filled with a male and female centaur. The mare had white blond hair pulled up into a tight braid that hung down her back and a long-sleeved tunic to help protect her from the spring chill. The stallion stood a few inches taller than her with reddish brown hair and a matching coat. He crossed his arms over his chest and waited for them to approach.

"What's the meaning of this, Corporal Ronin?" The male centaur raised his chin. "Who are these people?"

Corporal Ronin shook his head. "They claim to be pilgrims to the temple, Captain. The mare is called Princess Maia Silvercloak and the stal is Master Assassin Quinn Tarlen."

So much for being simple pilgrims.

"Master Assassin?" If the captain had possessed horse's ears, they would've been laid back along his skull. "What brings a Master Assassin to our village?"

"I'm merely escorting my sister-by-law on her pilgrimage around the kingdoms." Quinn's voice remained calm and measured, even when she shot him a look of surprise.

Sister-by-law? *That's stretching any relationship between Sean and Sorsia pretty damn far.* But she didn't correct him. Better to be seen as family than whatever they were now. *Although, to be honest, I'd rather be known as his lover or wife.*

The idea shocked her so much she almost missed the rest of the conversation.

"And why have you come to Cedarfell?"

"It is the last stop on my pilgrimage before I return home. To be honest, we had no idea it had been settled." Maia stepped forward and nodded to the ruling pair. "We have journeyed from the Goblin kingdoms to the south and as far as they knew this place remained abandoned. We are just as surprised to see you as you are to see us."

A side door opened and the woman she'd seen in the village strode in with a man by her side. Both were human as far as she could tell, but the man was every inch a soldier. She didn't recognize their clothing from her own memories of her father's world, but she could sense their energies. *Though she's not quite as human as he is.*

"Ah, Master Healer Bethany. We could use your guidance."

"Oh yes?" The woman approached the half stalls. "What's goin' on?"

"These travelers claim to be pilgrims to visit the temple." The Lead Mare gestured at Maia and Quinn. "Since you keep the temple now, perhaps you'd like to vet them."

The Master Healer shot a look at the human soldier before she nodded. "All right." She strode straight up to Maia and held out her hand. "Good afternoon. My name's Bethany McMacken, Master Healer to the Cedarfell Herd. Who might you be?"

Maia took her arm, grasping it behind the wrist. "I'm Princess Maia Silvercloak and my companion is my bodyguard, Quinn Tarlen, retired Master Assassin with the Assassin's Guild."

"Nice to meet you. What brought you to Cedarfell?"

"The temple. We're visiting holy places around the region and this was the last one we had planned to visit before returning home." The lie tasted sour on her tongue, but she didn't know how these people would react to her wanting a magical artifact from "their" temple.

Bethany's eyes narrowed, but she nodded. "Uh-huh. You said you were a princess?"

Maia shrugged. "My father was a king, so I was born a princess, but to be honest, I haven't been one for a long time."

"Heh, I know that feeling. So glad you've come to Cedarfell." Bethany turned to face the Stallion and Lead Mare. "I think we should bid these folks welcome and give them a place to stay. We can learn more about them and I'd be happy to escort them to the temple tomorrow."

Maia held her breath. She didn't know what the centaurs would do, but she suspected they'd have a harder time getting into the temple without their okay. She also suspected Bethany didn't quite believe her story, but was too savvy to call her out on it in a public forum.

"Very well, Master Healer. Perhaps you could give them a place to stay since they appear to be similar to your species and would find your accommodations more comfortable." Captain Yarren nodded but his lips tightened. "However, given that Mare Maia's companion is a Master Assassin, though retired, there will be a guard placed outside your dwelling to keep watch for the village's safety."

Maia shot a look at Quinn. His expression didn't change, but she thought she caught a quirk of one corner of his mouth. She hid her own amusement. *At least they acknowledged his ability to cause damage.* He could probably slip out without them noticing, with or without a guard, but she hoped he'd stay to protect her against the others. She didn't trust any of them, but she'd go with the Master Healer and find out more before they made any additional moves. *And I always have my magic.*

"Sounds good to me." Bethany smiled. "Come with me. I'll show you to the clinic and our home. And I'm sure your companion could talk tactics with my husband, Mack. He was SpecOps in the human world."

Maia blinked. "SpecOps?"

"Yeah..." Bethany frowned as she led them through the door she'd entered. The soldier fell into step behind them, quieter than Maia expected. "You don't know what SpecOps is?"

"No, Master Healer. That's an unfamiliar term."

Bethany nodded slowly. "Huh, well, that just means we have lots to talk about. How about some tea and a meal?"

"That would be lovely." Maia suspected the Master Healer didn't believe their story and wanted to know more but had the ability to be patient. "Thank you for your hospitality."

Bethany smiled and nodded as she led them across the main road to a smaller building resembling more of an estate house than a barn. It sat in between the ruined temple and a large long building reminiscent of a clinic or hospital.

"Welcome to our home. We'll show you where you can stay."

"If we choose to do so." Quinn's voice came out of the silence and Bethany raised her eyebrows.

"You won't be staying?"

"It all depends on whether we'll be able to visit the temple or not." Maia shot a look at him and he settled into his stoic assassin's mask. "That was our goal. Once we've made our visit, we can leave you all in peace."

Maia caught the look Bethany shared with the soldier and wondered what it meant. She sensed the energy around the portion of the Key in the temple, but there was something more.

"Yeah, let's talk about that." Bethany moved into the kitchen space and set the kettle on the fire. She nodded to her husband who positioned himself against a convenient wall with his arms crossed over his chest. "Now that we're not in the earshot of the centaurs, you want to tell me the real reason you're here to visit the temple?"

And the other shoe drops.

Maia paused and met Bethany's gaze, aware of the other woman's intelligence and perspicacity. She didn't trust these people, but she needed to get into the temple. Maia met Quinn's gaze, but the man was as transparent as mud. *Just means I have to figure out how to negotiate on my own.*

"To be honest, I don't. We came expecting the temple to be abandoned and nothing beyond nightmare boars to impede our quest to visit. Instead we find people here, controlling a temple that used to be open for anyone to visit, and becoming suspicious of us as if we were there to do you harm. You, who have only recently settled here." Maia raised her chin, but kept her arms at her sides. "Our quest here had nothing to do with you or your village. And we don't want to harm anyone. We merely want to spend some time in the temple and we'll be on our way. We aren't trying to take anything from you."

Bethany nodded, but her expression remained implacable. "What could be so important in an abandoned temple to make you come all this way? And don't try to tell me a pilgrimage. Your clothes don't support that assertion."

She met Quinn's gaze again and the man gave a one-shouldered shrug. *Oh yeah, easy for you to say.* The assassin would probably wait until the cover of darkness, slip into the temple, and take what he wanted. *But he doesn't know where the last piece of the Key is, and it's not him who has to recite the incantation.*

Maia dropped her chin with a sigh. "We've come in search of an artifact left here for me by my mother through her druid protector."

"An artifact?"

"You're too late. The temple was completely empty of anything of value when we arrived." The soldier spoke up, his voice measured and calm, but she sensed the curiosity under it.

Maia nodded. "Be that as it may, I would like the chance to visit and look for it."

"We can't allow that." The soldier shook his head.

Frustration welled up, but Maia pushed it back and met Bethany's gaze. "Why not? What could be so important in an abandoned temple to make you guard it as if it held something precious?"

Bethany snorted and a smirk curled her lips. "Nice. Well played." She took the kettle off the fire and poured hot water into four cups before she addressed Maia's question. "You just said it does hold something precious."

"Which you didn't know about until I said something. What are you guarding?"

When Bethany said nothing, Maia turned her head and let her senses fill the space. Colors changed and energy fluctuations became clear. Bethany blazed like a summer sunset, reds, golds, oranges, pinks, with a hint of purple. *She's a guardian to a rift.* Maia shifted her gaze to Mack and found similar colors muted behind an overlay of strong red. *Warrior guardian.* And if a pair of guardians were here, then a rift probably existed too. *The temple.*

It was the last clue to the puzzle of why Druid Reuben had hidden the piece of the Key here. This place housed a rift gate and would always be guarded. *Except when it wasn't.* He'd laid the enchantment over the hiding place so no one would notice it, including any new guardians who came into possession of the rift.

"A rift."

"What?" Bethany's gaze sharpened.

"What?" Quinn straightened as he met Maia's gaze.

"You're guarding a rift between worlds." Maia nodded. "You're the guardians to keep people from passing through willy-nilly."

Bethany narrowed her eyes. "How would you know that?"

Give a little, get a little.

"My mother, Queen Ashlynn, was such a guardian. She guarded the doorway in the dryad's forest some distance east of here before she died." Maia gestured to Quinn. "My protector and I have been traveling from place to place seeking the artifacts left by my mother and her protector so I might take my place as another guardian of the rifts." She didn't include her added task of guarding the hub.

Bethany tilted her head. "You know of the rifts. Which world are you from?"

"Both the human world and this one as it turns out. My mother was a dryad and my father was human."

"And you think there's an artifact in the temple that's hidden there for you?"

"According to the notes and clues left by my mother

and her protector, yes." Maia nodded. "I have no intention of stepping across your rift, Master Healer. I have things to do in this world, including returning to my own rift to guard."

"You sure do sound convincin' and all, but we don't know you all that well and we aren't into trusting folks just because they show up all friendly-like."

Bethany gave her a lazy smile and her accent thickened, but Maia wasn't buying the good-ole-girl act. She settled her pack onto the floor with a sigh to buy her some time as she gathered her magic around her from the ley lines running along the ground toward the rift. While they weren't as strong as the ones in the Goblins' palace, they had enough power to make things interesting.

She stretched her back and shook out her arms as she took a breath to speak. The charm bracelet Tricia had given her fell out of her sleeve and rattled around her wrist. A hiss was the only warning before Mack moved and reached for her wrist. Maia pivoted and pulled her body out of the way as Quinn stepped up beside her, his hands full of blades.

"You will not touch her." She'd never heard Quinn sound so deadly, but a chill ran up her spine and her hair stood on end.

"Where did you get that?" Mack pointed at the bracelet, his face white.

"It was a gift." Maia stood in front of Quinn to keep him from doing something violent. The cold anger seeping off him made her shiver. "Tell you what, I propose a trade."

"A trade?" Bethany raised an eyebrow. "What kind of trade?"

"I shall tell you all you want to know about this bracelet and where I got it if you allow me and Quinn ten minutes inside the temple." Maia raised her eyebrows in question. "Fair?"

"A bracelet and its origin story for ten minutes?"

Bethany snorted. "There's a lot of damage you could do in ten minutes."

"The choice is yours. I give you my word as a Princess and a guardian of the rifts that I will honor my promise, tell you all I know about this bracelet, and not walk through the rift in exchange for ten minutes alone in the temple with Quinn. Deal?"

Bethany shot a look at Mack but the man stared at Maia's wrist with his jaw clenched so tight Maia suspected his molars strained. Bethany narrowed her eyes, but nodded slowly.

"Deal. Shake on it, please." She held out her hand.

Maia stepped to the side and held out her hand without the bracelet. The other woman grasped her palm and met her gaze.

"Ten minutes once you cross the threshold."

"Agreed."

"Great." Bethany released her with a wide smile. "Let me show you our temple."

****

Maia paused beside Bethany at the archway of the temple. A new door had been installed of rough cedar planks held together with iron bolts. Bethany gazed at the door for a few moments before turning to Maia.

"We've got a deal. Ten minutes alone in the temple in exchange for the information about that bracelet. And you promise not to step across the rift."

"Yes, Master Healer. We are agreed."

Bethany nodded. "Okay. Ten minutes it is."

"Please close the door behind us." Maia waited to see what they would do with that request as Quinn entered the temple in front of her.

"Close the door?" Mack's brows lowered.

"Yes. What we have to do is private, but we will honor

our agreement to only do what we came to do and no more." She met his gaze. "You must take us at our word. Besides, I suspect the Master Healer is attuned to the rift. She'll know if we cross or not, and you can easily catch us."

"You're right. Ten minutes and that's it."

"Thank you, Master Healer." Maia inclined her head and stepped into the temple, closing the door behind her. She leaned against it and took a deep breath, letting out a long sigh. "We have ten minutes."

"Then we shouldn't waste it." Quinn glanced over his shoulder as he stood in the middle of the small dodecahedral room.

Grooves between the flagstones radiated from the central stone that sat directly beneath a twelve-sided hole in the ceiling. She wondered if it had once had a roof, but now a piece of glass sat in the opening, allowing light to shine down into the room. Archways holding small hexagonal windows marked each short wall and an alter sat directly opposite the door. Two of the archways showed alcoves, one to a small back room which must have been a supply closet for the temple, and a second which seemed to go nowhere beyond the darkness.

Maia nodded to the second alcove. "That's the rift between worlds."

"Really? You can see it?" Quinn shot a look at the space, but stayed where he was.

"Yes, it has the same colors as the Master Healer. She's attuned to it."

"Good to know. Shall we get started? We don't have much time." His voice sounded uncharacteristically tight.

"Are you nervous, Quinn?"

He dropped his chin and looked at her from under his brows. "Are you jesting? There's a man and several centaurs just outside who'd easily do damage to both of us if we slip up. I much prefer to get this done and leave them to their temple."

"Fair enough." Tension crawled up her back and she shivered to relieve it as she took a deep breath. "Keep your eyes open. I'll recite the incantation and you look for any changes."

"Right."

Maia straightened her back and flattened her hands to feel the energy in the space. The whole place vibrated with the presence of the rift, but she hoped to distinguish the energy of the Key from it.

"Sun and the Moon to light the realms. Wind and the Rain to nourish them. Fire to cleanse and prepare the way. And Earth to give place to flourish in." A new vibration rumbled through the stones of the temple. "The Keeper will hold the Key to keep the Twelve Realms free."

A loud squeal of protest between stones echoed in the air and Quinn gave a shout of surprise as the central twelve-sided stone rose up a few inches and twisted as if unscrewing itself open. He tumbled off into an awkward roll and ended up crouched beside the altar.

"So much for the graceful assassin. I can't take you anywhere." Maia grinned to show she teased as Quinn growled.

"I'd like to see you try to stay upright when the floor moves." Quinn rose and approached the stone. "There appears to be a latch and a hinge cut out of the stone. Look."

She skirted the stone to his side and found the clever latch he spoke of. She gave him a long look. "Ready?"

He grinned. "Not remotely. Let's do this."

She laughed and pressed the little release button. The latch scraped and complained, but popped open and the top of the stone rose on its hinge. Inside, nestled in what looked like goose down rested a large forest-green silk bag. She bit her lip and reached for the treasure. A tingle of energy filled her palm as she grasped the bag, and recognition filled her awareness.

This is mine to guard and protect.

"It's the last piece of the Key." She whispered the words, not sure why she needed to be so quiet. Then she frowned. "And there's something else in the bag with it."

"Bring it out and let's close the stone. Time is fleeting and I'd rather this space remain hidden." Again, Quinn sounded tense.

She nodded and closed the clever latch, before pushing down on the stone. It didn't budge.

"Uh, Quinn? What do I do if it doesn't return to the floor?"

"Push harder and turn?"

"Thanks for the help." Maia shook her head and did as he suggested. But the stone remained stubbornly still. "No luck. Maybe it requires magic to put it back the way it was?"

Quinn shot a look at the door. "Maybe. But whatever you do, you need to do it soon."

"Yes, I know. Thanks for the update." Maia closed her eyes and took a deep breath before she opened her senses to look for the ley lines.

The room blazed with sunset-colored light, just like the Master Healer. Most of it emanated from the rift, but a the twelve-sided center stone gave off a green marbled light matching the silk pouch. Reaching out, she whispered a request to the stone, coaxing it to return to its former place in the temple floor.

Without hesitation, the stone rotated counter-clockwise, screwing itself back down until it rested level with the others around it. Maia nodded and whispered her thanks before she turned her gaze back to Quinn. A small smile curled one side of his mouth and he nodded.

"You're amazing."

His compliment warmed her more than she expected. "Thank you. Will you help me put the necklace together?"

"Yes." He shot another look at the door, his tension plain, but he took the connected necklace she handed him and waited for her to withdraw the last piece. "What else is in the bag?"

"It feels like a scroll."

"Should we read it before we put the pieces together?"

Trepidation hit her gut. "I don't know. What do you think will happen when we connect all three?"

He shook his head. "I don't know, princess, but I'm pretty sure you're meant to find out. We don't have a lot of time left, but if you want to read it first..."

"No, I don't think we have the time. I'm just...nervous."

He closed his hand around hers and met her gaze. "It's going to be fine. You're meant to do this, Maia. And I'll be with you the whole way."

She swallowed hard and nodded. "Okay."

She took the connected necklace from him and straightened her shoulders before she pushed the new pieces together. The same subtle *pop* sounded like the first time they'd connected pieces of the Key together and another invisible wave of energy rolled across the room from their location. Power, strength, vitality, and clarity surged through Maia and she gasped, closing her eyes. *I know who I am and what I have to do. I'm the Keeper of the Key to the Twelve Realms and the guardian of Chamber of Rifts.*

"Wow."

"You can say that again." Quinn sounded as breathless as her.

"Do you want me to?" She raised an eyebrow at him and he shook his head.

She looked down at the necklace in her hands. It matched the image she'd seen in her book back at Windbreak Keep, right down to the gleaming ornate metal and eleven drops of opal hanging from the lattice of the loop. The large opal in the center sparkled with electric blue and purple fire, and it radiated heat in her hand.

"Can you put this on me, please? I think I need to be wearing it from now on."

"Right." He took the ends of the necklace and looped them around her neck before moving behind her to clip it together. "There." His fingers brushed the back of her neck and another shift in the energy flashed through her. "Oh, holy Lady Death, Maia, you're beautiful."

He wrapped her up in his arms from behind and held her against his chest. She fell into his embrace, but had the presence of mind to tuck the scroll into the folds of her coat before she grasped his arms and closed her eyes. This was the man she wanted, more than any other, to stay around her, stand with her, and help defend her.

"I love you, Quinn."

He took a breath to respond, but the door to the temple opened and light flooded in. They stood where they were and waited for the Master Healer to enter with her husband. Bethany's gaze scanned the alcove holding the rift before switching back to Maia and Quinn.

"Did you find what you needed?"

"Yes, Master Healer. Thank you for the opportunity." Maia inclined her head.

"Great. Come back to the house and we can talk about that bracelet you're wearing." Again, the woman scanned the room as if trying to find anything out of place.

Maia nodded and stepped out of Quinn's embrace. She missed his warmth immediately, but the necklace resting on her chest hummed with power and heat she often associated with him. *I think he's bound to it as much as I am.* She shot a quick look at him before she stepped out from beneath the arched doorway.

The sun had come out and chased away a little of the chill in the air. *Summer approaches.* Which meant she had to get back to the dryad's forest soon. And the dryads wouldn't be getting what they expected. The idea made her raise her chin and smile.

CHAPTER NINETEEN

Quinn stepped out of the temple with Maia and kept an eye on both McMacken and the centaurs arrayed before them. All of them scowled. *I knew centaurs were a suspicious people, but the human's scowl is new.* To be honest, he'd feel the same if someone like Maia showed up, but Quinn suspected McMacken's unease came from the bracelet she wore.

Neither of them said a word to their gathered hosts as they returned to the McMacken household. The Master Healer closed the door of the temple behind her and followed them, her expression curious. She didn't appear nearly as unhappy as her husband.

Once they settled into the house, Bethany reheated the water on the fire and poured tea before she had them sit down at her rough-hewn kitchen table. She handed out the mugs of tea before she sat beside her husband and fixed them both with her direct stare.

"So, you got what you came for and didn't go through the rift." Bethany nodded, acknowledging the completion of their promise. "Now, tell us about your unusual charm bracelet."

Maia set down her mug and unclipped the bracelet

from her wrist. "This bracelet was a gift from the Goblin Queen. She said it had brought her luck and she wanted me to have the same." She raised her gaze to meet McMacken's.

"That's the bracelet I gave to my sister, Princess. Where the hell did you get it?" His eyes blazed.

"I told you. The Goblin Queen gave it to me." Maia paused as her eyes widened and she raised her chin. "Oh good glory, I didn't make the connection until now." She handed him the bracelet. "Queen Tricia told me she was given the bracelet from her brother Mack. That would be you, correct?"

Instead of relief and hope, fury rippled across the other man's face. "Don't fucking play games with me, Princess. My sister's been missing for years. How the hell did you get this?"

"Mack." Bethany laid a hand on his arm. "I think she's telling you she got it from your sister. I think your sister is the Goblin Queen." She switched her gaze to Maia's. "You said the queen's name is Tricia?"

"Yes, Master Healer. I spent the last several weeks with her training to use my gifts. She lives with her husband, King Jakran."

"Sonuvaprick!" Mack roared as he rose to his feet. "Are you telling me my sister has been in this fucking world all this time and I didn't know it?"

"Mack, calm down."

"Calm down? I've been searching for her for over a decade and you want me to calm down?"

"Perhaps you can send her a message by pigeon." Quinn spoke up before he hauled Maia out of harm's way.

"What the fuck are you talking about?" Mack rounded on him.

Maia shrugged. "Not as fast as a phone call or email, but she rather likes to get real letters."

Silence filled the kitchen for a few heartbeats until

Bethany barked a laugh. "That sounds like something you'd say, Mack."

"What?"

"I bet Yarren knows how to get in touch with the Goblins. You could easily send a message to the King and Queen. I'm sure Her Majesty would love to hear from her younger brother."

"As for us, we should be on our way." Quinn finished his tea and stood. Maia blinked and finished her own as she scrambled to her feet.

"What? But you just arrived." Bethany rose as well.

"We only came to visit the temple. We've done what we needed to do." Quinn nodded, but didn't smile. Something in the way Mack stared at Maia made him uneasy. *We need to go.* "It's fairly obvious the centaurs aren't used to having more humans about and we wouldn't want to make things uncomfortable for anyone. Besides, we have to get back to the dryads' forest by mid-summer and we don't know how long it will take us from here."

"It's a little over a day's ride east from here." Bethany frowned. "Are you sure you won't stay? Even for just one night?"

"Thank you. Your invitation is kind, but we're equipped for long travel and we knew this would be a short stop." Quinn helped Maia gather up her pack and sling it over her shoulders before grabbing his own. "We'll get out of your way so you can sort out your family obligations."

The look Maia shot him conveyed her surprise, but Quinn didn't have time to argue. McMacken glared at them as if they'd been the ones to hide his sister from him all this time. *Yeah, I got my own missing sibling to worry about.* Except Sean was dead rather than just missing. *Maybe that's easier. I don't have to go looking for him.*

"Thank you again for the time in the temple. I wish you luck and fair weather in your efforts to reconnect with your sister." Maia nodded as Quinn guided her to the door, watching her back should the soldier try to stop her progress.

"We don't mean to chase you out." Bethany tried to catch up to them and shot a narrowed gaze at her husband, but Quinn didn't pause. "Please, don't leave on our account."

"Thank you, but we'd only planned on visiting the temple and moving on." It wasn't true, but Quinn didn't correct Maia. They needed to leave before they weren't allowed to do so. She waved a hand at him. "Quinn and I are used to it."

"We will try to make it as far east as we can by nightfall so we'll be out of the centaurs' patrol range." He gave a perfunctory smile and bowed before he escorted Maia back up the road.

"Many thanks for the tea, Master Healer." Maia called it back over her shoulder as she hurried her steps to keep up with him. He momentarily felt bad for making her rush, but his gut told him they needed to move as centaurs emerged from the barns along the road.

"Quinn, slow down. What is the need for all the hurry?" She sounded out of breath.

"Just a feeling I have. Something tells me if they can keep us here, they will and we'll miss our deadline while they figure out if we're dangerous or not." He watched everyone around them, but kept moving toward the exit of the village.

Maia snorted. "We are dangerous."

"Exactly, but I'd rather not show our hand if we don't have to."

"Stay close. If it gets difficult, I'm can put a shield around us and make us disappear so we have a chance to get away."

"Can you now? That's a useful little trick."

"Do you really think they'll come after us?" She hurried her steps to keep up with his longer strides.

"Yes, I think if they see us as a threat or a powerful tool, they'll seek to hold us." He loosened the snaps on his hatchet as they headed up the hill from the river valley.

"The Goblins were less threatened by us." Maia's grumble made him smile.

"The Goblins had nothing to gain. They were simply holding the artifact for the Keeper. These people came across an abandoned temple and moved in." Quinn kept moving but his neck and back prickled with the centaurs' attention. "They could see us as thieves if they perceive the temple and all it contained as theirs."

"But Reuben left it for me." Her brows came down as they reached the top of the hill. "And they've been here a relatively short time. It wasn't theirs to keep."

Quinn nodded, understanding her frustration. "They don't know us and they know nothing of Reuben. From their perspective, we could've made up the tale to steal something from them."

"But they didn't even know it was there and we didn't come for the rift gate. We didn't know that was here."

"I know, Maia." He shot a look over his shoulder at the village. The centaurs gathered together and the appaloosa gestured toward them. *Oh hell, they aren't going to let us go.* "When we get over the hump of the hill, we need to get off the road and I want you to do your invisibility thing."

"What? Why?" Maia turned to look, but Quinn caught her elbow.

"Keep going and don't look back. I think they're headed our way to collect us." He shook his head and growled. "Ever the control freaks, centaurs." He spared a moment to look again and caught movement just before he lost sight of the village. "All right, let's go. Quickly. We need to get off the road and head into the surrounding fields. Will the invisibility keep working while we move?"

"I think so, and it isn't really invisibility, more of a camouflage spell to deflect the mind and convince the observer that what they see isn't important." She scowled. "They're really coming after us?"

"Yes, I'm pretty sure they are."

"Sweet glory." Anger threaded under her voice. "Very well. Tell me when you're ready and I'll set up the spell."

"Don't wait." He dragged her off the road so they wouldn't leave any footprints. "Do it now because centaurs are fast and refuse to change their minds." He just hoped the spell would disguise them long enough to get away.

****

Maia took a deep breath before she opened her senses to see the world of energy. To her surprise, the vision came easily and fast, far faster than ever before. A large ley line ran under the road straight for the temple. A few meters away, another less-powerful line converged on the larger one. She reached out to the less powerful line and asked it to give her the camouflage, to make her and Quinn look like part of the landscape. She imagined they'd resemble the breeze rippling through the new spring grasses growing in the fields along the road.

The magical energy leapt to her command and swirled around them, settling over their bodies like a shimmering cloak. Quinn didn't disappear to her sight, but he wore an iridescent sheen that muted the edges of his form. It made him appear nearly transparent. She tilted her head. *Not transparent. More like reflective.* She hoped it would be enough.

They kept their strides quick and purposeful as the sounds of hoofbeats thundered behind them. Maia couldn't help looking over her shoulder toward the road. A large group of centaurs galloped over the ridge of the hill and her gut sank. *Sweet glory and light, please don't let them see us.* They wore scowls of intent and their sharp gazes swung over the world around them.

"Keep moving, don't stop, Maia." Quinn's whispered command brought her back to herself.

She nodded and kept her focus on the spell as they turned their backs to the sun and headed in the direction their shadows pointed. The centaurs kept going along the road, but the appaloosa corporal shot looks in their direction. Quinn pushed them at a steady, fast pace over the next two hills, but paused at the top of the second and flattened himself against the ground.

"Maia, get down."

She settled into the grass beside him. Their view overlooked the road as it looped back around and the centaurs appeared, trotting now as they scanned the area.

"Is your invisibility spell still intact?" Quinn whispered the words in case the wind carried it down to the road.

"Yes." Maia nodded. "It works better when we hold still. Hard to see what's not moving."

"Let's hope you're right." He pointed at the troupe below.

"I am right." *I better be right. I better be right.*

The clouds had gathered as the sun headed for the horizon and the wind kicked up, bringing the smell of rain. She didn't look forward to being out in the elements when a storm blew in, but she'd rather be wet and free than warm and captive.

The centaurs stopped and the corporal gestured to them to fan out on either side of the road. They searched the ground for any marks and some even came close to where they hid among the dry grass. Maia held her breath and watched them saunter just below the crest of the hill.

"Anything?" The corporal called from below.

"Nothing, sir. No sign of them."

"Dammit! We must have missed them somewhere on the road. They couldn't have gotten very far on two feet." The corporal scowled. "Get back into formation. We'll backtrack and find where they left the road."

The soldiers returned to their cohort and they all set off back down the road at a gallop. Neither Maia nor Quinn moved until the last tail disappeared, but when she would've gotten up, he held her arm.

"Wait."

"What for?"

He pointed toward the road. "Outrider."

Sure enough, a lone centaur dressed in tans and browns much like the surrounding grasses emerged and brought up the rear. He scanned the landscape, looking for movement, but Maia and Quinn held their position. He continued his patrol at a fast walk until he finally disappeared after his cohort. Maia released the breath she hadn't known she'd held and shot a look at Quinn.

"Okay, now we can go. But keep up your invisibility spell."

"Right."

They rose and scrambled down the hill toward the road. Maia thought her heart might leap out of her chest, but no other centaurs appeared as they reached the muddied track.

"Try not to step in the mud. Our footprints are distinct from theirs." Quinn waved at the muddy road.

"Really? You don't wear boots shaped like horseshoes? I'm stunned." Maia shook her head as she picked her way over the dirt road. There were a few places dry enough to step, but only big enough to hold the toes of her boots.

"They're in my summer gear."

She smothered a laugh with her sleeve as she glanced at him. He grinned and danced across the road without leaving tracks. *Bloody assassin.* She tried to follow his moves, but she felt like a wobbly colt beside him.

"How long do you think we have until they discover our path where we left the road?" She panted as they upped their pace up the next hill.

He shook his head. "Not long. We should try to get a few hills between us and the road before nightfall. We might not be able to stop for a while."

"Marvelous."

She saved her breath for their rapid travel. As the sun dipped below the rolling hills behind them, the temperature dropped. They kept going and Maia listened hard for the sounds of hoofbeats heading their way. All she heard was her own breathing and her pounding heart.

"Quinn. Please, we have to stop." Maia hoped he heard her, but she was out of breath and exhausted. "I need to rest."

The assassin paused and looked back over his shoulder. His face remained shadowed by his hood, though his breath plumed out in front of him to show his breathing. Though the night remained clear and cold, the moon hadn't risen yet and they had relative darkness. He looked mysterious and dangerous, and sexy as hell.

"Please, Quinn. Do you think we can make camp? I know we can't have a fire, but we need to stop. I'm pretty sure we're close to where we camped last night." She hoped that was true. To be honest, all the plains looked the same to her, especially in the spring when the new growth hadn't taken over the old dead grasses.

He sighed and his breath billowed out in a steamy cloud. "We need to keep moving. We're still inside the centaurs' borders."

Maia groaned. "How do you know that? They didn't notice us until we crested the hill above their village this morning."

"They weren't actively looking for us then."

"How determined do you think they'd be? Are we worth a night search?" She shot a look over the dark plains behind them, worried the centaurs would appear at any moment.

"We're talking about centaurs. They're more stubborn

than most mules." Quinn scanned the horizon around them. "But I don't know how determined they'll be with regard to us." He returned his gaze to hers. At least she thought he did. She couldn't see them under the hood. "Let's crest one more hill and camp in the valley. We'll need to fill our water skins anyway. Hopefully there's a stream. I think I can smell the water, but that might be a storm coming."

Maia's heart sank. *Another hill and a storm?* She raised her gaze to the twinkling stars in the sky. "What storm?"

Quinn started to walk again and she had no choice but to follow. "You can't smell it?"

She shook her head, too tired to argue.

"I'm hoping it's a stream, but if it's rain, we'll use a bowl to catch some of it."

Marvelous. She nodded and gestured for him to lead them. She didn't have the energy to keep an eye on the uneven ground and behind them for their pursuers in addition to keeping up her illusion. She trudged up the hill behind Quinn, hoping they'd reach the top and still have the energy to come back down the other side.

She made it to the crest and they looked down into the swale.

"I think that's a stream."

"Wonderful." She couldn't help the sarcasm.

"We'll camp there for the night." Quinn started down.

"What if the centaurs come?" She didn't bother to look up. She kept her gaze on her feet to keep from falling down the decline.

"We should be fine if you can keep up your illusion all night."

He said it so blasé, so easily as if the magic could be turned on with a flip of a switch. Anger kindled and beat back some of her fatigue.

"I can't." She raised her gaze from her toes and glared at him. "It doesn't work that way. I have to be awake and I need to sleep, Quinn. I'm not some magical gadget you can turn on or off with a flick of your hand. There's no cover down there and I can't stay awake all night. I've been walking since early this morning and I'm exhausted. So what do you propose to do if the centaurs come?"

"We'll deal with that when it occurs. No use in borrowing trouble."

"You really don't care, do you? Just push, push, push, sure that my newfound abilities will save us." She shook her head. "You have no idea how much this takes out of me." She knew she was whining, but her exhaustion and fear had gotten the better of her.

He must have heard something in her voice because he stopped and turned to face her. She couldn't stop nearly as fast and collided with his chest. She tried to avoid him, but her legs felt weighted with stones. She attempted to push away from him with a mumbled apology, but his arms tightened around her and he held her close.

"Maia, I know how much it takes out of you. I've seen it. And I'm just as concerned about the centaurs." His breath warmed her face even when she couldn't see his eyes. "But I also have faith in our abilities to remain disguised and get away should we need to." He ran one thumb over her cheek. "I know you're tired. Let's get down to the stream and use our blankets to cover us. Hopefully in the dark we'll appear to be a boulder." He leaned forward and kissed her forehead. "We'll get through this, I promise."

"How can you be so certain?"

"Because I know you and your strength." He snorted. "And I know me."

She chuckled at the arrogant comment, but she couldn't argue. She'd seen him fight. "Yes, you know you very well."

"See? It'll all work out." He stepped back, but kept a grip on her arm. "Let's make a camp and settle in. We're almost there."

He helped her down the rest of the hill until they reached the stream. She cast her gaze around in hopes they'd find some sort of cover, but the rolling plains offered nothing but grass to disguise them. *We will stand out like a beacon.* It couldn't be helped. She'd run out of energy and needed to rest. They'd just have to hope the centaurs had given up for the night. Their one saving grace was a moonless sky.

"Sit here and rest while I fill up the water skins. Can you get the blankets and bedding out?" Quinn knelt in front of her as she settled into the dry grass.

"Yes, I think so. I can't hold the illusion for much longer."

"Let it go. We'll use old fashioned disguise techniques for tonight." He nodded and took her water skin. "I'll fill these."

Maia closed her eyes and released the magic. It fluttered away and settled into the nearest ley line like a bird coming to rest and Maia sighed with relief. It had drained her, but the boost she'd gotten in the temple had helped sustain it. *Maybe the more I use it the longer I'll be able to hold it.* She hoped she could build up some stamina. *I'll need it to rescue my sisters.*

She slumped onto her back and settled into the beckoning silence of sleep, but Quinn returned and jostled her awake.

"Oh no, not yet, princess. Drink some water while I get out the blankets. Just hold on there a little longer." He thrust the water skin into her hands as he removed her pack and rifled through to the bedding.

She dutifully drank and the water slid down her throat, making her shiver at its frigidity. Despite the cold, she sank deeper into her exhaustion and only roused when Quinn insisted she lay down on something soft. He said something about keeping watch and making sure her head was covered, but she lost track of the conversation and let the darkness take her into its silent depths.

****

Quinn settled himself beside Maia as her breathing evened out. He took the water skin out of her hand and made sure it wouldn't leak before tucking her under their shared blankets. He understood the magic took a lot of her energy, but he hoped they'd gained enough of lead on the centaurs to continue their journey without hindrance.

They'd completed the quest to retrieve the Key to the Twelve Realms, but they still needed to return to the dryads' forest and make a case for the release of Maia's sisters. He frowned into the darkness, listening for anything beyond the sounds of the stream. He didn't believe Maia would give up the Key, but he didn't know if she could free her sisters with her power alone.

No use borrowing trouble.

He glanced down at the woman asleep beside him hidden under the blankets, and sorrow etched a line in his heart. *The quest is done.* They'd finish their respective tasks and be free to go their own ways. Even if the dryads refused to lift the bonding spell, he suspected Maia could find a way to extricate them from it. She had the capability if not the skill.

But as the night sounds returned after their passage to the stream, he found he didn't want her to break the spell. He'd already given up being an assassin and sent a letter of resignation. But he'd done that when he believed he would be with her and she'd need him. Now he wasn't so sure.

Quinn took a deep breath and settled his body into a comfortable position to keep watch all night. He didn't want to be caught unawares. *Too late.* His heart crumpled at the thought of walking away from Maia. He'd grown to love her. The way she never gave up even when everyone seemed leveled against her. The way she laughed. The smell of her hair and the way she fought hand-to-hand. The woman was perfect, and yet not. To be brutally honest, it was her quirks he loved most about her.

She could be as regal as a queen and yet she didn't seem to take herself too seriously.

Thank the Goddess for that. She'd be insufferable if she did.

But he liked her and liked being with her. And he liked himself around her. She wasn't hard, unforgiving, or self-centered, all the things he'd accused her of being when he first met her. Maia cared enough to do this on the urgings of a lost queen, a dead druid, and the belief that her sisters deserved freedom. She could rule in her mother's stead if she put her mind to it, but it wasn't what she wanted.

But would she want a retired assassin from a world she'd forgotten who'd only gone on the quest with her because he was required to do so?

When put like that, he wouldn't want such a person either.

Quinn sighed and listened for sounds of hoof beats. So far the night had been quiet and cold. The only sounds reaching his ears belonged to the wind in the grass and the burbling of the stream. It was too early in the year for crickets and most of the nocturnal mammals had probably fled at their arrival. He'd just have to sleep lightly and hope he'd be fast enough to defend Maia while she rested.

No matter what the next few days would bring, he'd see her safe and sound before she sent him on his way. They'd rescue her sisters and return to the Windbreak Keep. The Aerys people would watch over her and she'd be safe. He could live with that.

At least, that was what he told himself as he settled down to sleep. But his heart protested and slumber was a long time in coming.

CHAPTER TWENTY

Maia woke to find the world full of sunshine, chuckling water, and heat. She lay against a warm and breathing body with her head cradled in his lap. The scent of heated wool and leather offered comfort and familiarity and she had the odd urge to have this every morning.

But memories of their flight the night before wiped away the relaxation and comfort, and she pulled the blanket away from her face. Blue sky and dried grass met her gaze, but no horse legs or heavy spears. She dared to sit up and cast her gaze in a wider arc. She and Quinn sat alone beside a stream cutting through the grasses. Somehow, he'd managed to find tall reeds in which to settle and disguise them. *Thank the Goddess.*

She stretched and something crackled against her chest. She paused and reached into her coat. She pulled out a flattened scroll tied with a leather thong and grimaced. She could just hear her father's archivist gasping in shocked dismay. She shook her head with a rueful smile. The man was long dead and couldn't reprimand her now. Still she carefully untied the thong and spread out the scroll.

Elegant handwriting matching the one from Rueben in

her book from Windbreak Keep flowed across the parchment. She ran her fingers over it, opening her senses to detect anything unusual, but it was ordinary paper and ink. She returned her sight to normal and read the letter.

Congratulations. You've found a piece of the Key to the Twelve Realms, and you must be the Keeper of the Key because this box cannot be revealed except to the one with whom the Key connects.

The most recent Keeper of the Key was Queen Ashlynn Silvercloak, dryad healer and mother to twelve daughters. Each woman was meant to be a Keeper in her own right to one of the Twelve Realms. Ashlynn also had eleven siblings, born from the roots of each realm, but over time, she received word that these guardians have slowly disappeared or died. No one in this realm is quite certain the hows or whys of this situation, but Ashlynn was the last to succumb to death and had me, Reuben Tarlen, pass this information along to you.

You now have a piece of the Key. I can only hope this is the final piece and you have the means to control it. When we began the journal describing the reason behind its dismantled state, we had no idea that the loss of the Keepers would be something you'd have to face. But when the Keys from each world appeared one after another at the Chamber of Rifts in the Windbreak Keep of the Aerys people, I realized Ashlynn's death had been orchestrated by some nefarious group or force. I suspect Ashlynn knew on some level and that's why she gave birth to so many children in such a short time.

When you visit the Windbreak Keep of the Aerys people, a people sworn to protect the Keeper to the Key of the Twelve Realms, they will show you the vault where I've stored the Keys that arrived from the abandoned realms. I have no idea what happened to their respective Keepers, or why the Keys came here, or what the new Keepers will find

*in those abandoned realms. But I do know that you, as the
new Keeper to this realm, must help your sister Keepers
find their places and restore them to their positions.*

*I hope, much like I was left here to help you, such that
I can, there are those in the other realms waiting to help
these new Keepers. I wish I had more to tell you about the
individual or group or force that has decimated these
guardians, but except for the slow poisoning of your mother
by the dryads' Archdruid, I know nothing of use. The
Archdruid is gone, I made certain of that, but beware the
stories told among the dryads. There is no love in them for
me or your eldest sister Inge, who from all reports was put
to death after my departure. As I understand it, she was the
Keeper for your father's world. Her loss is heartbreaking.*

*But you, Princess, are here and your true education is
about to begin. I hope I'm there for it, for you. But if I'm
not, I pray there's another to take my place, and I know the
guardians to whom I've entrusted the pieces of your Key
will be willing to help. All are long-lived peoples and will
remember. Blessings of the Goddess be with you.*

Sincerely, Druid Reuben Tarlen

Maia blinked at the signature. *Does that say Reuben
Tarlen?* She read it again. Quinn had the surname of Tarlen.
Is he related to Reuben? She shot a look over her shoulder
and met his curious gaze.

"What?" He raised an eyebrow.

"Good morning. Thank you for being my pillow."

A slow, sultry smile curled his lips and pleasure
tightened her gut. "My pleasure, Maia. In truth, you kept
me warm."

"You stayed awake all night?" She lost her smile.

"Not all night. I slept lightly, but I did sleep a little."

"Did he centaurs come near us?" She swung her gaze
away to scan the grounds around the stream for hoofprints.

"No, we escaped their notice so far."

"So far?" She returned her gaze to him. "Should we get going?"

Quinn tilted his head. "Yes, soon. What were you reading?" He nodded to the scroll.

"Oh, it's the letter that came with the Key piece. It..." She bit her bottom lip. "How common is the Tarlen surname?"

He lost his smile and retreated behind his assassin's mask, though he didn't look away. *Damn near as good as doing so.* She waited for him to say something, but the silence grew. *Can I outwait an assassin?* Fortunately, she didn't have to as he nodded and turned his head, scanning their surroundings for enemies.

"In this world? Not very." He met her gaze again. "What did it say?"

"It said that mine is not the only Key. There are eleven others that were meant to go to my sisters and they're all at the Windbreak Keep." Maia handed him the scroll. "You can read it if you'd like."

He said nothing, but turned his gaze to the creased paper in his hands. Maia loved his hands and how they made her body feel. Long, strong fingers with callused tips electrified her skin each time he touched her. *But when he finds out his family has been associated with mine longer than forever, what will he do?* She didn't know why she feared his reaction, but she didn't want him to leave her after their quest concluded.

She couldn't watch him read the scroll. Instead, she listened to her stomach and dug into her pack for some of the travel bread the goblins had sent along with her. The sleeping had done her a world of good, but she needed to eat to maintain the magic illusion hiding them from discovery.

"So now you know he's related to me." Quinn's voice dropped into the silence between them.

"What?" She returned her gaze to him. "You already

knew? For how long?"

He shrugged and handed the scroll back to her. "Since our stay with the goblins. Jakran brought me into his office and showed me a family tree leading to me and Reuben. Reuben was my father's younger brother." He grimaced. "My father had a sore spot for your family. I always thought it was only because of my brother's death, but it turns out he lost his brother to the Silvercloaks long before he lost a son."

Chagrin swelled in her gut and the bread stuck in her throat. She coughed a little and reached for her water skin.

"I'm sorry, Quinn."

He shook his head as he pulled the stopper off the skin. "Don't be. My uncle believed in something so much, he left his family and his world to serve something greater. Something my father, and I suspect your father, knew nothing about."

She raised her eyebrows. "You don't think my father knew my mother's role as a Realm Keeper?"

"No, I don't." He shook his head again. "Otherwise, he wouldn't have sent young men in after you and he wouldn't have executed my brother."

She opened her mouth to say something, but Quinn's head jerked and he held his hand up to stall her words. Unease slid through her and she held her breath, listening hard. The wind shifted direction and carried voices with it along with hoofbeats.

"Shit." She'd never heard Quinn swear aloud. "Can you get your magic working? We have to get moving. I figure we are only a few miles from the edge of the centaur patrol limits, but we still move slower than they do."

Maia scrambled to her feet and scanned the ridge of the hill above the stream. Nothing showed yet, but the voices on the wind grew louder. She swallowed her fear and took a deep breath, letting her senses open. She caught sight of the ley lines and coaxed the magic into painting her like a reflective mirror. She extended the bubble to include Quinn, but the magic bulked.

Frowning, she tried again with the same result. *What could be wrong?* She'd never had the problem before. Again she asked the magic, but this time it showed her a lovely spreading willow tree growing at the edge of the stream. *Willow?* The moment she thought it, the illusion of a great spreading willow took over her and Quinn, covering their tracks, their gear, and their forms.

The illusion solidified just as a group of centaurs crested the hill and looked down on their small camp. Quinn sucked in a breath of warning, but Maia waved her hand at him to be silent and still. He froze, his gaze locked on the oncoming troupe. She hoped they were still and quiet enough to be mistaken for a tree. *Please, Goddess, let us appear as part of your living landscape.*

The centaurs flowed down the hillside, their sharp gazes scanning the whole stream. Maia bit her lips together as they came close to where she stood. Her heart thundered in her chest, but she held still and tried to remember to breathe.

"Their tracks lead to the stream and die out, Corporal." One centaur pointed at the ground.

"Any beyond the tree?" The corporal paused on the opposite shore from Maia.

"No, sir. Looks like they changed direction."

"Hellwinds. They must have followed the stream to hide their tracks. The question is which way?" The corporal scowled as he turned his head to look up and down the stream. "Dammit, we need to catch them before they get beyond our borders. Captain Yarren wants them brought in for questioning."

Maia shot a look at Quinn and raised her eyebrows. *Questioning for what?* Quinn shook his head and kept his gaze on the group of horsemen.

"Cantrell."

"Yes sir?"

"Take your patrol south. I'll take the rest north and we'll meet back at the village at midday. They can't have gone far on only two legs."

"Yes, sir."

The corporal waved to his men and the split in two groups, each following the stream at a gallop. Maia waited until they'd disappeared from sight in either direction before she dared turn her gaze to Quinn.

"What do we do now?" Her whisper still made her nervous.

"Is there a way to keep this tree illusion up after we've gone?" He packed up their gear in near-silent movements.

"I don't know. I've never tried a long-term spell like that. Why?"

"It would maintain our distraction by having a tree here, but if not, we'll be gone by the time they come looking." He rose to his feet and handed her pack to her before turning and looking around. "If I bundle a bunch of reeds together, could you settle an illusion over them to seem like the tree?"

She thought about all she'd learned at Tricia's hands. "Maybe. Do we have time?"

"I think the more time we give them to get ahead the better off we'll be." He used his hatchet to break off the reeds and used some of the grasses to tie them together. "Remember their village is to the west of us and we're heading east. Hopefully, they won't be back this direction for a while. But just in case…"

He set the reeds upright and piled more grasses around them so they'd remain upright even when the wind blew. When he'd anchored them well enough, he stepped back and nodded to Maia, shouldering his pack.

She opened her sight and asked the magic to take her lovely illusion and fasten it to the reeds, keeping the tree for a few hours. She didn't know if the magic understood the concept of time, but even if it only stayed long enough for them to make it over the next hill, it would be enough. When she was sure it would stay, she opened her eyes and stepped back.

"Is it still there?"

Quinn looked at her and nodded. "Yes. Still there. But we don't have a lot of time. Let's get moving." He held out his hand to her.

"What's that?"

"What?"

"That." She pointed at his hand.

"It's my hand." He smirked and wiggled his fingers.

"I know it's your hand. What are you doing with it?" She shrugged her shoulders until her pack rested more comfortably.

"Offering it to you?"

"Why?" He'd never done that before in all their travels together.

"Because I want to continue our connection from this morning before the centaurs rudely interrupted us." He gave her a sexy half-smile.

"All right." She placed her hand in his and a sense of belonging ran through her again.

I don't want him to leave when this is over. But how could she make him stay? Tricia had said they were bound, but Maia wasn't convinced it was more than the dryads' spell. Yes, they'd shared some physical loving, but he'd never admitted his love or promised to stay when the quest was finished.

Quinn shot a look in either direction along the streambed before he pulled her in fast strides. She kept up with him, enjoying the breadth of his shoulders in his black coat despite their hurried passage. Memories of making love with that coat on the man had her pussy lips wet before she knew it. Too bad they hadn't had more time together that morning.

They traveled in silence until midday and the smudge of a forest sat on the horizon to the east. Despite their fast pace, she didn't feel as exhausted as she had the day before, but she was glad when Quinn stopped.

"Do you think we're far enough ahead of the centaurs?" She turned to look over her shoulder, but the grasslands remained empty.

Quinn nodded. "At least that herd. We'll have to watch for the Forest Edge herd, but I think we're far enough ahead to avoid them. They won't have time to send a messenger to catch us before we reach the dryads."

"What about pigeons?"

He blinked. "I hadn't thought of that."

"Great." She scrubbed her face with her hands. "Do you think we'll have enough time to have a meal before we head for the tree line?"

He rubbed his chin. "No. But let's eat on the go. We'll reach the edge of the forest in early afternoon and have the luxury of rest to plan for our encounter with the dryads."

"I really hate to eat and run." She dug in her pack and pulled out the dry bread when she heard a snort of humor.

"Are you handing me a snide comment, princess?" Quinn dug out his own food.

"What?" She threw her pack over her shoulders again and frowned. "Oh. No." She laughed. "But it might be a good idea with the threat of another centaur herd finding us. And I need fuel to keep up the magic."

Quinn nodded. "Then eat and run it is." He grinned. "After you. I'll watch our backs."

She had to hand it to traveling with an assassin. She didn't feel nearly as exposed or vulnerable. *Now if I could just make sure he's willing to stay with me.* She pondered about how with each step she took toward the distant forest.

****

Quinn kept his ears and eyes trained on the plains around them, but despite the concerns of pursuit, they made it to the edge of the forest by late afternoon. The weather had been mild with few clouds. Patches of snow remained in the swales of the rolling hills, but the rest of the grasslands sat dry. The weather had cooperated with their journey and a balmy breeze dogged their steps. Birdsong came and went as the season advanced, but Quinn kept an eye on the sky, hoping none of the flitting silhouettes were messenger pigeons.

Maia stopped short and grimaced. "I'm not ready to go in there yet."

Quinn paused to let his gaze slide over the landscape. Nothing moved beyond wind and birds. The heat of the late spring sunshine beat down on his shoulders, his black coat absorbing the warmth as he wiped the sweat off his forehead.

"Do you think they know we're here yet?" He returned his gaze to her.

She reached out with one hand and her eyes unfocused. *Or maybe they focus more than mine do.* She swung her outstretched hand from one side to the other before she shook her head.

"No, their borders are still locked down from when we left. Good for keeping unwanted visitors out, but not so good for seeing what's coming." She refocused on him. "They can't really see us unless they physically look."

"Good, then let's find a place to make camp and take advantage of the calm." He nodded and turned his feet toward a small rock outcrop with old, weathered tree roots. "Let's use this for shelter and cover, and we'll tackle the dryads in the morning."

Maia followed him to the outcropping and settled her pack on the ground against the stones with a sigh. "That sounds wonderful. Do you think we could have a fire?"

He shook his head. "No. The dryads and centaurs

would be sure to see that. But I know something else that would keep us warm." He waggled his eyebrows to make her smile.

She gave him a laugh. "I like the way you think."

While he wanted the pleasure of a sexual release with her, what he truly desired was one more night of intimacy before they went their separate ways. On the morrow, she would win her sisters' freedom and then they'd be done with their quest for real. *And she'll be done with me.*

The thought pulled the edges of his mouth down and he turned his back to her to hide his grimace. She didn't need his sudden attachment to her. *She's a princess and the Keeper of the Key, for Death's sake.* He was just her bodyguard. Despite that, he needed this time with her if only to make memories he could hold up and look at when he found himself cold and alone.

"Let's set up camp at least and eat before we do anything else. I want to scout around this pile to make sure nothing like a basilisk or wyvern has set up its territory here."

And it would give him a chance to compose himself. For some reason, the sorrow seemed sharper now than they stood within a day of the conclusion of their quest. Maia didn't seem to notice his distress as she sighed and dropped her pack. Quinn turned his attention to scanning the rocks for sign of residency, but his mind kept returning to on thought.

Tomorrow I'm going to lose her.

CHAPTER TWENTY-ONE

Something had changed. Maia dug out the last of their rations as she puzzled over the sense of impending doom approaching. They had nearly come full circle to where this adventure started, and soon it would end.

The bread turned to dust in her mouth. *I don't want it to end.* That wasn't completely true. She didn't want to constantly move from place to place, dodging hostile people as they traveled. But she wanted to stay with Quinn. He'd become important to her, and not just because he could easily defend her.

I love him.

She didn't want to say goodbye, and send him on his way. She wanted him to stay with her.

But what would he do? He couldn't be her lackey or cabana boy. He was neither clueless nor unskilled. She could offer him a position as captain of the guard when she officially became Keeper of the Key, but she didn't want him to just be a guard. She wanted more.

Maia unpacked the food and laid out their bedrolls while she waited for Quinn to return. She wanted to show him how she felt and at least say goodbye in a way that would allow her to remember the good times with him. *I could seduce him.* Could she? Would he allow it? *If he doesn't want it, he'll tell me.* Goddess, that would be embarrassing after all they'd shared. *I'll just have to take the chance.*

She considered her tactics as Quinn reappeared around the pile of rocks. The sun painted his white coat into shades of peach and gold, and she couldn't remember a time she found him more beautiful.

"You look like a hero from the old tales." She had no idea where the statement came from, but as an opening gambit it wasn't bad.

Quinn snorted as he settled beside her. "Not much of a hero when clearing out the rocks of bugaboos."

"'Bugaboos?' Who says that anymore?" She grinned as she handed him the travel bread.

"What would you call them?" He raised his eyebrows.

"Gremlins?"

He laughed. "Not sure that would work. I've met gremlins and they prefer warmer environments than a pile of rocks."

She lost her smile. "You've met gremlins."

"Yup. As a team, they're incredibly useful for distraction and causing chaos so you can get in and out without being noticed."

"You mean for doing your job of killing." She lost more of her humor.

He sighed. "Yes. But I gave that life up, Maia. I'm done with contract killing."

She nodded, trying to push back the unease about Quinn's past. *He gave it up, he won't be going back.* Unless she screwed it up and he had nothing better to do.

"I know."

He shrugged. "The good news is we have a pretty sheltered place to rest before we face the dryads tomorrow." He waved at the sun setting over the shoulders of their rockpile. "In the dark no one will get a clear look at us unless they inspect the outcrop. I don't anticipate too many problems tonight."

"Not 'too many?'" She snorted. "Only a few then."

He flashed her a grin. "Yes, only a few."

She nodded and brushed the crumbs of her meal off her lap. "Then in the meantime perhaps we should take advantage of the relative calm."

"Oh, and do what?" He took a bite of his bread and chewed, his dark eyes trained on her face.

"Make love with me, Quinn, before we have to fight the dryads." She crawled up in front of him until they sat almost nose-to-nose. "Let me thank you for choosing to let go of that other life."

Quinn swallowed hard as if the bread stuck in his throat. "You want me to make love with you here, now?"

"Yes. Here, now, and I want to wear your coat." She loved his coat. It smelled like him and reminded her of how damn sexy he looked wearing it.

"You want to wear my coat?" He raised his chin. "You don't want me to wear it?"

"No, this time I want you to surround me while I make love with you." She licked her lips and he swallowed again. "I want to wear nothing but your coat." She leaned in and brushed her lips over his, and he moaned. "Will you let me wear your coat while we make love?"

"Yes." His response prefaced his action of setting her back from him and shrugging out of his coat. "But I want you to wear the black side out. Less visible at night."

She let a smirk curl her lips. "All right."

He divested the coat of weapons before he handed it to her and she smiled as she sat back to watch him undress. He paused and raised his eyebrows again.

"Will you undress?"

"Oh, yes, but I wanted to watch you."

"Do you?" He smirked back. "I'll make you a deal, then. I'll strip for you if you let me undress you myself."

Pleasure and lust skittered down her spine to settle in her gut. "That sounds fine to me."

He held out his hand. "Shake on it."

She blinked, but extended her arm to take his. He grasped her hand and pulled it to his lips before running his tongue over her knuckles. Hot, slick pleasure zipped up her arm and she whimpered a little. The smirk on his face widened and he unfolded her hand to kiss the palm. She shivered as he released her and shrugged out of his coat.

"Hold this for me, won't you?"

Maia took the coat and licked her lips as he pulled his shirt off his body. She'd never get tired of seeing him naked. His copper-colored oval nipples grew taut in the cool evening air and she ached to run her hands over them. The scars on his body outlined the lovely muscles, badges of experience and courage. She bit her tongue to hold back the urge to lick them.

"If you keep looking at me like that, this won't last long." Quinn rose and stripped out of his pants. His cock bobbed in front of her and her mouth watered.

I want to taste him. She'd loved it the first time he'd allowed her to wrap her lips around his shaft, but he'd stopped her before she could do more.

"You're beautiful, Quinn."

He raised his eyebrows. "This body? With all its scars?"

"This body." She rose to stand in front of his naked glory. "I like everything about it." She lifted her hands to his shoulders and ran them down his muscular arms. "From your shoulders, to your arms, to your flat tummy." She stroked his rippled abdomen until she rested her hand against his straining cock. "And this. May I taste you tonight?"

His brows came down. "I don't think that's a good idea."

"Why not?" She squeezed his shaft as she slid her hand

up and down its length.

"Oh, gods above, because I don't have any control around you." He hissed through his teeth as she stroked him harder.

"But Quinn, I want to suck on you until you release." She dropped to her knees and gaze up his body. "Please? This will give me pleasure, I promise."

He held her gaze for several heartbeats, one hand cupping her cheek as he considered. "I'll grant you this pleasure. But first, you must be undressed." He lifted her up and stepped behind her. "I want to feel your skin against mine."

He skimmed his hands down her sides until he could grasp the hem of her shirt to lift it over her head. The cool air touched her breasts and hardened her nipples, but his warm hands returned to the taut peaks and soothed them. She arched her back to press the tips into his palms, but he dropped his hands to her waist to remove her light-weight pants. To her delight, he pushed them off her hips, but his hands lingered, sliding along the creases between her groin and thighs.

"You're so responsive, Maia." He speared his fingers through the curls on her mound. "I love the way you rub your pussy against my hand."

She wanted to do more than rub his hand, but she remembered her earlier goal and pushed out of his arms.

"As much as I'm enjoying your touches, I want to pleasure you." She crouched in front of him and grasped his straining shaft. "I think this needs attention."

"Uhh…"

Anything he meant to say ended in a drawn-out moan as she closed her lips around the flared tip of his cock. He hissed his pleasure as he locked his knees, and she smiled around him. *I'm going to bring him to his knees.*

She ran her tongue along the underside of his shaft while she slid her hand down to cup his balls. Quinn shivered and groaned. She sealed her lips around his cock behind the head and sucked harder.

"Sweet Lady Death. All right, stop. Please."

She whimpered as he pulled his cock from her mouth. "Why?"

"Because I'm going to fall. Let me lie down."

A grin pulled her lips wide. "I think that's a wise idea."

He snorted but settled into their sleeping blankets. She watched his body move with sinuous grace and her mouth watered with the need to kiss every muscled inch. She rolled forward to her hands and knees, and settled herself between his legs, inhaling his musky scent.

"You smell so good, Quinn." She rubbed her nose against his scrotum and the skin grew taut. "I'm going to inhale you."

"Oh? And how are you—Ohhhhh."

She sucked him deep into her mouth as far as she could take him and swallowed. His cock stiffened in her mouth as she ran her fingers over his balls. She pulled back off his cock and trailed her tongue around the ridge of the head.

"Goddess have mercy, you're killing me, Maia."

That's the idea. She grinned around his shaft as she sank back down on it before closing her lips as far down as she could. Tangy pre-cum hit her tongue and she moaned with her delight. *He tastes wonderful.* She slid off and dropped her lips to his scrotum. She nibbled at the soft skin before suckling on it and his cock flexed, weeping more pre-cum.

Quinn moaned and arched his hips into her caresses. She sucked harder with his urging then rose to take his cock back into her mouth.

"Oh, yes, Maia. Suck me. Suck me hard." He fisted the blankets beneath him and thrust into her mouth.

She grasped his shaft and tightened her hand as she scrubbed the edges of his head with her tongue. She hummed as she bobbed her head, enjoying the slide of his hot shaft in her mouth. The sounds of his pleasure ramped up hers and she tightened her lips, sucking hard as he'd instructed.

"Aw fuck, I'm going to come, Maia. Holy Lady Death!"

The tangy cum shot into her mouth and she swallowed it down as she kept licking and sucking his hard shaft. His back bowed and he groaned, his hands clutching her hair as he thrust into her mouth. Maia licked and sucked his cock until he relaxed into the blankets.

She licked her lips as she pulled off him and smiled. *I love making him moan.* Seeing Quinn bonelessly satisfied warmed a place in her heart she hadn't thought was cold. Despite the warmth, she shivered and looked around for her clothes.

"Are you cold, Maia?"

Leave it to Quinn to notice that little detail even when riding the wave of euphoria.

"Yes, I think I'll get dressed."

He slowly shook his head. "Put on my coat and snuggle against me." He winked. "You're sexy in my coat."

Maia blinked. "You do?"

"Yes, and it will keep you warm. Come on." He handed her his coat and she shrugged into the white-side of the coat. The hood settled over her head and she immediately warmed. "There. Now snuggle against me and I'll keep you warm."

She settled up beside him, his warm body cushioning hers, and sighed with satisfaction. His masculine scent surrounded her, and she realized this is what she wanted from now on. *But how do I tell him?* He hadn't declared his feelings for her, though his body seemed to appreciate her attention. But somehow, she'd gone and fallen in love with him somewhere along their journey.

She laid her cheek against his chest and listened to his heartbeat slowing as he came down from his pleasure.

She'd told him she loved him and her feelings hadn't changed, but he'd never said it back to her. *To be honest, he didn't really have time.* They'd rushed out of Cedarfell and hadn't had enough quiet moments. *It's now or never.*

But she had no idea how to broach the subject.

"Why are you so warm? I'm never this warm." She snuggled up closer to him.

His chuckle rumbled through her. "This from the woman wearing my coat?" But he tightened his arm around her. "I'll do my best to warm you up once I've caught my breath."

"Oh? Did I wear you out?"

He snorted. "Continually." His face smoothed into a smile. "It's been worth every moment." He tilted her head up so he could kiss her lips.

"You're not just saying that because the dryads magically bound you to me, are you?"

Quinn paused and met her gaze, his expression growing serious. "No."

She waited for him to say more, but he remained stubbornly silent. "All right, I'll take you at your word." She dropped her head to his chest again and tried to push aside her disappointment at his reticence.

****

Quinn cursed himself for a fool, but blamed his addled brain on the overwhelming pleasure Maia had given him. Not only the blowjob, but also her interest in cuddling up next to him while wearing his coat. He'd never considered clothing to be erotic, but seeing Maia in his coat made his heart flutter with excitement.

"Maia?"

"Yes, Quinn?" She didn't turn her head, but at least she was listening.

"What do you think will happen after tomorrow?"

She drew circles on his chest with one finger. It tickled and soothed him at the same time.

"I don't know. I don't know how it will go with the dryads." She buried her face against his chest. "What am I going to do? I can't give them the Key and I need to save my sisters. But if I don't give them the Key, they'll probably try to hunt me down." Maia stared at the trees turning gold in the evening sunshine.

He stroked her hair. "Use your magic."

She snorted softly over his nipple. "How?"

He allowed a half smile to curl his lips. "Renegotiate the deal."

She shook her head. "I have nothing to renegotiate with. I won't give up the key."

"You don't have to." He ran his fingers over the necklace on her chest. "Tell them you have the key, but you want all your sisters returned to you for such a valuable object."

"But I'm not going to give it to them." Maia frowned.

"No, but you can give them something that might resemble the key and make them think they have it long enough for us to get away."

"Like what?" She pushed herself up on one elbow to look down at him.

Her beauty with her golden skin and her dusky nipples distracted him and he ran his fingers over the soft tips. Her dark hair turned a rich copper gold where the light touched it and he was struck dumb. *I want to keep her with me forever.*

"Don't keep me waiting, now. What could I give them that would make them think they have the Key?"

Quinn blinked. "It could be anything, although something that resembles the necklace would probably wisest."

She slid one hand down his body to tickle his belly and his cock twitched with awareness. "I suppose I could make something. But how will it work?"

"Spell it to look like the key, either as a necklace or a tiara. Most of them don't know what it looks like or they would've found it themselves." His half smile shifted into a smirk. "And I suggest in addition to the illusion spell, you add a spell that releases a memory wipe. Should they try to invoke the power of the "Key", it makes every dryad in the forest forget about the real one, Druid Reuben, your sisters, your mother, and you."

"You mean, coupled with the illusion is a spell that takes the memory of anyone within a specific area?"

Quinn nodded. "I saw an assassin mage do that once. To keep anyone around their target from remembering her job, the assassin mage created a spell that wiped out the memory of her presence to everyone within the town where she'd been working."

"And it worked?"

"Ever heard of the assassination of the High Chancellor of Carabeth?"

"No."

"Neither has anyone else." Quinn winked and she rolled her eyes. "Yes, it worked, and the magic takes the memory and either dismantles it or substitutes a more plausible explanation for the event."

Maia lapsed into a thoughtful silence, still stroking his belly and his cock grew with each caress. Something about this woman turned him on, even while she lay naked beside him doing nothing more than innocent touches. *Or not so innocent.* Her hand slid down to wrap around his shaft and squeeze. He loved her sensual nature and how secure she was with showing him pleasure.

He couldn't lose her.

The irony of wanting her when he started out believing she represented the worst of the world didn't escape him. But she'd shown her resilience and determination throughout the time he'd been with her, and he'd fallen for her strength of character. He'd never met a woman like her. She made him feel something other than anger for the first time in decades.

And tomorrow I might have to say goodbye.

His heart contracted at the thought and before he realized what he was doing, he'd pulled Maia's face up and brushed her lips with his. Her taste exploded across his awareness and he moaned, needing her more than he'd never needed anyone, including his brother.

"Stay with me, Maia." He had no idea where the words came from, but they felt wrenched from his soul.

"I am with you, Quinn."

"No, not just now. I mean after tomorrow." He tipped her head up to meet her eyes. "Let me stay with you when you take your place as Keeper of the Key in the Windbreak Keep. Let me guard your back while on duty, pleasure your body while in bed, and hold you in my arms. Please, Maia."

"You really want to stay with me?"

"I do. For as long as you'll have me." He shifted her on top of him, her legs straddling his hips as his cock rose with the proximity of her pussy. "Let me stay with you, protect you." He met her gaze and hoped his sincerity came though his eyes. "Love you."

Her eyes widened as she looked down at him from under his hood. "You love me?"

He almost frowned, but looking up into her coffee-colored eyes he realized he'd never said the words aloud.

"I love you, Maia."

She bit her bottom lip. "Are you sure?"

He laughed and ground his hardening cock against her clit. "Yes, I'm sure."

"Sex doesn't equate love, Quinn. My sister Sorsia loved your brother and they never had sex." She squirmed on his cock and he had to fight past the stars in his vision.

"No, it doesn't, but I've shared more than sex with you, and I'd like to continue."

"With my company or with sex?"

"Both." He smirked as he wiggled his hips, but quickly sobered. "I want us to face everything from now on together. I've been alone for so long I don't want to lose the gift of your company and conversation." He arched his back. "And your body."

She snorted. "Of course." But her fingers followed the lines on his face around his lips and he turned his head to kiss them. "I love you, Quinn. I meant what I said in the temple at Cedarfell, and I mean it now. But if this is just a reaction to the lovemaking we've done, I need to know that."

She was offering him an out, pulling away to protect her heart even while her naked body lay atop his. *I can't lose her.* Yet, he didn't know the words to express how he felt. He'd never needed them before and now he scrambled to come up with a way to show her his heart.

"I'm not as good with words so I don't always say the right things, but I meant what I said. I love you, Maia, and I want to be with you always." He grimaced as he cupped her cheeks with his hands. "Let me show you how I feel. My body speaks more eloquently than I can."

He pulled her head down to meet his lips and kissed her with infinite gentleness. He wanted her to know his heart and he hoped she'd feel his love through his actions. "Please, Maia."

She tilted her head and smiled. "Regale me with your love, Quinn." She reached between their bodies and grasped his cock, stroking the tip with her thumb.

"Oh glory, Maia. Ride me." He helped lift her as she positioned his cock at the entrance of her sweet sheath and at her nod, let her settle her hot pussy around his shaft. He moaned his pleasure at her tight heat. "Sweet Lady Death, you're so tight."

Her inner muscles squeezed his cock and she smiled at his groan. "And you're so hard."

"I'll always be hard for you. You inspire arousal."

She laughed and it reverberated straight to his cock. "Do I? Good to know."

He rocked his hips slowly, gritting his teeth as he held back the rising pleasure. He'd be damned before he failed to give her pleasure first. She gasped and ground her pussy harder on his shaft, but he kept their movements slow and measured. He wanted her to fall apart in his arms. *The way she's made me fall apart in hers.*

She sat up and braced her hands on his shoulders as he rocked her. He couldn't resist touching her full breasts and used one hand to thumb a dusky nipple playing peekaboo with the sun's golden light. She looked like a goddess, a mistress of death in his black coat, and his love swelled in his chest. *By all the gods, I love her so much.*

"Oh glory, Quinn, that feels so good."

He had no idea if she meant him strumming her nipple or rocking her slow and deep on his shaft, but he agreed with her completely.

"That's it, Maia. Ride me slow and deep and take your pleasure. Let me show you how much I love you."

She whimpered and her inner muscles tightened more as he slid in and out of her hot sheath. His own orgasm built up in his balls and he gritted his teeth to hold it at bay. He'd see her fall into the abyss of ecstasy before he succumbed to it again.

"Oh glory. I'm going to come, Quinn. I can't hold it…"

"Don't hold back, by sweet goddess. Come for me. Come hard."

She wailed her pleasure as she clenched tight on his cock and sank her fingers into his shoulders. Her breasts trembled with her release, teasing him with her hard nipples. Quinn tried to hold back, but the beauty of his woman coming apart deteriorated his control and his release blazed through him, shooting him into the stars behind his eyes.

He wanted to drift there in that perfect moment with her heat encasing him and their releases mixing over his balls, but a series of sounds intruded into his bliss. His eyes snapped open—when had he closed them—and he jerked Maia down on top of him.

"What—"

"Shhh." He gestured with one finger to the west where a little light remained in the sky from the sunset. "I heard something."

She closed her mouth and held her breath while they both listened hard. After a few moments, heavy footfalls and dark shapes moved past their camping spot. Maia settled down tighter to his body and pressed her face against his chest as a patrol of centaurs armed with long spears marched no more than a few feet from them. Quinn swallowed hard and followed their progress with his gaze, but he kept himself still.

"Remind me why we're out here tonight, sir?" One of the burly horsemen asked the leader as they paused to scan the rocks. Quinn tightened his arms around Maia under the coat and hoped it would disguise them well enough.

"I told you. General Warrick received a message from Cedarfell to be on the lookout for some fugitives."

"You got a good description, sir?"

"Said to be a man and a woman, human-like, and armed to the teeth."

"More humans?" The burly horseman snorted. "They might be creepy, but they should be easy to catch. They only have two legs after all."

The leader scowled. "They might only have two legs, sergeant, but they're crafty and quick. Don't get too overconfident with your bulk. A human could hamstring you before you have the time to turn." He shook his head. "Move out. I want to get back to the village before shift-change."

He waited for his men to move past him, his gaze seemingly fixed on Quinn and Maia's position within the cradle of the rocks. Quinn swallowed hard and hoped he would have to do anything drastic. *Yeah, like a naked man poses a huge threat.* He'd killed in the nude before, but it wasn't particularly comfortable.

But the centaur must not have seen anything to alarm him and he soon trotted after his men into the gathering darkness. Maia and Quinn remained still for a few more minutes, waiting and listening to determine if the patrol would return.

Maia let out a blast of air and melted onto him. It would've been sexy if the centaurs hadn't come by. "I think they're gone."

"Yes."

"That was so damn close." She lifted her head and look down on him. "Do you think they'll be back this way?"

He shook his head. "I don't know, but perhaps we should disguise ourselves for a little while."

She raised an eyebrow and smirked. "You mean as something other than sexual partners dressed in a coat?"

He grinned and rubbed his hands over the globes of her ass. "It would probably be wise as much as I hate to have you cover this lovely body up."

She wriggled and his cock started to stiffen, but he released her as she rolled off him. "It's getting cold anyway." But she admired his wayward anatomy and licked her lips. "But I want more when we're safe again."

He caught her around the waist and tugged her close to his chest again. "Count on it."

CHAPTER TWENTY-TWO

Maia stared at the wall of the dryad's forest and took a deep breath. *I don't want to go in there.*

The morning sunlight painted the trees with an innocent brush, but she wasn't fooled. The spell they'd settled over their borders when she and Quinn had left in the winter remained and drained some of the vibrancy from the forest's appearance. But she knew how dangerous they could be.

The question is, how much more dangerous am I?

"Are you ready for this?" Quinn shrugged into his pack and shifted his shoulders to settle it. Despite his lack of sleep, he looked ready for anything.

The centaurs hadn't returned in the night, but Quinn insisted on keeping guard. Maia admitted she'd been grateful for his determination because their lovemaking had relaxed her beyond endurance.

"No." She glanced down at the flower crown she'd woven out of grasses and spring blooms to help release some of her nervousness. "I know what the plan is, but I still haven't worked out how we'll get away once we have all my sisters. They're not just going to let us walk out of there and the Grove is in the center of the forest."

He nodded. "What about opening a portal?"

Her jaw dropped. "Opening a portal? How? And to where?"

"You're the Keeper of the Key to the Twelve Realms. You have dryad magic and you'll be in their stronghold." He shrugged. "Use the Key to open a portal from there to the Windbreak Keep. You'll have plenty of magic to power it at your fingertips."

Maia bit her bottom lip. "I've never opened a portal. I don't even know how."

"I bet the Key does and if it's like other magical artifacts, I bet it responds to the wielder's needs and focus." He pointed at the flower garland in her hands. "You'll need to spell that and hide the real one before we do this."

"Oh, right."

She closed her eyes and focused on the magic around them. Energy swirled along the ground like wisps of mist as the plains came alive with the spring. A thicker cloud formed around the forest, but she refused to alert the dryads to her presence before she was ready. Instead, she drew on a latent ley line running west under her feet.

She asked the magic to make the grass and flower garland appear as a diadem of gold and jewels. She didn't want it to resemble the real Key, and many would expect her mother to have worn the Key as a crown. After the illusion settled around the garland, she asked for a memory charm and pictured the whole of the dryads' forest. The dryads would forget about the Key, Maia, her sisters, Druid Reuben, or Queen Ashlynn if they tried to activate the 'key' to open a portal anywhere. *And Quinn Tarlen.* He would never be their pawn again.

The magic swirled and leapt to her bidding, weaving a pulsing aura around the garland. When she opened her eyes, it looked the same to her. The mixture of grass and flowers caught the sunlight, but appeared no different than when she started. But Quinn grunted with surprised approval and nodded.

"Well done, Maia. That looks amazing."

"Does it?" She frowned and lifted the garland. "It looks the same to me."

"I suspect that's because you're the one who made the spell. To everyone else it appears to be a pretty necklace worthy of a King's ransom. Best put it in your bag before some thief thinks it's a prize worth taking." He grinned and she was struck at how youthful he appeared.

"You should smile more." She opened her pack and placed the garland on top. "I love your smile. It makes you so handsome."

Quinn blinked and a blush stained his cheeks. "Does it? When this is done, I'll try to do it more for you." He bent close to whisper in her ear. "You make it easy for me to smile, princess." One hand drifted over her breast in a soft caress before he stepped back and Maia couldn't hold back her own smirk.

"Right, well, let's start this charade." She raised her head and swung her pack onto her shoulders. "Time to let the dryads know we're here." She shot a look at him. "Ready?"

"Lead the way, princess."

Maia took a deep breath and approached the forest. She'd seen the magic swirling around the forest, but didn't know if the spell would hurt anyone trying to enter. She paused a few feet from the trees and studied them, wondering if guards had been posted after the centaurs' patrol.

One way to find out.

She bent and grasped an old dead limb left over from a storm, eyeing the distance to the trunks. Twisting, she tossed the branch with all her strength into the waiting trees. A shimmer of light rippled outward from where the branch hit the woods and sparks flew from the impact.

Glad I didn't try to walk through.

She didn't wait for anyone to appear. "I am Princess Maiasora Silvercloak and I seek an audience with the Keeper of the Grove."

"How long do you think they'll make us wait?" Quinn stood beside her with his arms crossed over his chest.

"I don't know. I guess it depends on how fast the message gets to the Keeper." She shifted her sight just in time to watch the shield around the forest disintegrate like a popped soap bubble. "The shield is down. They might let us enter."

"Let's wait for the escort." Quinn nodded toward the trees. "I'd rather not enter without their say-so. We're going to anger them enough when the time comes."

Maia snorted a laugh. "That's true."

They didn't have to wait long for the dryad guards to appear. Four tall men appeared at the edge of the forest holding long spears with barbed ends. Maia took a deep breath and rearranged her goblin scarf to make sure the necklace remained hidden before raising her chin.

"The Keeper of the Grove has granted you an audience, Princess Maiasora Silvercloak." One of the guards gestured toward a path between the trees with a disdainful scowl. "We will escort you."

"I'm happy to accompany you." Maia nodded. "However, I have some conditions before I enter the dryad domain. I require all ten of my sisters to be restored to their human forms and be present at the audience. I also require this meeting to take place somewhere close to the edge of the forest. That way my sisters, bodyguard, and I can be on our way quickly when the negotiation is complete without causing extra disturbance."

"You have no authority to dictate such terms, princes."

She raised her chin. "On the contrary, I have the item for which you've been searching three centuries and for which my family has been imprisoned. Without these conditions being met, we are at an impasse. It's mutually beneficial to come to an agreement."

She met the guard's gaze and held it, hoping he couldn't see or sense her pounding heart. She couldn't let them know that she'd do damn near anything to save her sisters. *Anything except give them the Key.* She remembered watching her father's court and learning the art of negotiation. More than half were won or lost by the ability of the negotiator to convince the other side of their willingness to walk away.

Please don't make me walk away.

Maia stood her ground and hoped her expression gave nothing away.

The guard's scowl deepened, but after a few moments, he nodded. "The Keeper has granted your conditions. There is a protected glade along our northern border. Your sisters will be there with the Keeper."

Maia nodded. "We shall follow you outside your borders until we reach the easiest access point on your northern edge."

The guard froze. "We're instructed to take you through the forest."

"No." Quinn spoke for the first time. "If this glade is near your northern border we will be able to follow you on the outside more easily and there will be less likelihood of foul play. Our honor requires us to uphold our commitments, but we will do so outside of your borders."

Again, the guard scowled and Maia clenched her jaw to keep from smiling at his frustration. She suspected the Keeper wanted them within the forest so they could direct their movements wherever they chose without Maia or Quinn being the wiser. *They're dishonest enough to do that.* Fortunately, Maia knew how their magic worked, and it wouldn't be successful, but once among the trees, it would be harder to circumvent their influence.

"This is not acceptable." The guard shook his head.

"Then we shall be on our way." Quinn's voice held a

note of disinterested finality and Maia's heart contracted, but she held her face still. "Come, princess."

She turned with him to retreat toward the west and shot a look of unease at him. He gave a quick shake of his head beneath his hood and she swallowed hard. Had she lost her sisters forever?

"Wait."

Quinn turned toward her with a smirk that disappeared as soon as he faced the guards. Maia shifted with him and raised her eyebrows.

"We accept your terms." The guard wore an expression of a man who'd stepped in some sort of fecal matter. "We will lead you to the glade where your sisters will be waiting. You may follow along outside our borders."

"We have an accord." Maia inclined her head. "Lead on. We shall follow." She didn't add that she'd be watching through her magical sight to make sure they didn't shift the borders enough to ensnare them while they traveled.

The guards nodded and melted into the trees, but their passage remained visible enough to human sight. Maia nodded to Quinn and they shifted their progress to follow.

"Will they keep to their word?" Quinn's voice was only loud enough for her to hear.

She shrugged. "In so far to get us into the glade, yes. After that, all bets are off."

He snorted. "I figured as much."

"Also, follow my lead. If they can trick us into the forest before we reach the intended entry, they will be able to take the upper hand with the negotiation."

"You think they'll try to do that?"

"I wouldn't put it past them." She grimaced. The dryads had been less than truthful since the beginning and she was done taking their word.

They lapsed into silence as they traveled along the line of the forest northward. The dryads remained within sight, but Maia kept a sharp lookout for where the trees bowed outward to keep from stepping beneath their boughs.

For a while, everything remained straight-forward and easy, but after about an hour, something seemed off. The dryads became harder to track and Maia almost shifted closer to the forest to get a clearer view. But she stopped and stretched her back, closing her eyes before opening them to use her magical sight.

Ahead of them, an arm of the forest stretched out into the plains several meters to their left. If they'd continued on their current path, they would've walked straight into it. *Crafty bastards.*

"Quinn, we need to move to our left or we'll walk into the forest before it's time."

Quinn scowled. "So they did try it. I can't see anything but plains ahead of us."

She nodded. "It's an illusion to disorient us into a disadvantage."

"I'll follow you."

She shot him a smile. "I like knowing that."

Despite the seriousness of their situation, his laugh rang out in the clear morning air. She took a distinct left from their position and marched away from the offending arm of the forest. Calls of dismay and frustration sounded behind them as they skirted the trees to avoid the trap, and she allowed herself a little smile of triumph. The ground rose in the form of rocky hills and the forest stopped half-way up their slopes. Maia and Quinn hiked around the other side of the tree line and followed a wildlife path higher into the hills.

As they paused to rest and drink some water, Maia took in the view. The line of hills marched away to west with sparse pine trees and rocky outcrops of glittering boulders. It reminded her of the country she'd seen around the Windbreak Keep.

"Quinn, do you suppose this is the same range of hills we encountered this winter?"

He paused and followed her line of sight, the silence broken only by the wind in the trees to the south. He swallowed more water before he spoke.

"Very likely. I'd have to look at a map to be sure." He stoppered his water flask and turned his attention to something behind her.

She studied his expression to assess any danger and slowly turned around. The dryad guards had reappeared with matching scowls and she raised her eyebrows at their obvious displeasure.

"Why did you move so far away from the border?" One of the gestured at her with his spear.

Maia shrugged. "I felt the need for a little extra exercise. It's always good to have the high ground." She stoppered her flask, refusing to admit to their deception. "Have we arrived at the location for the meeting?"

"Nearly. The entrance to the glade is just past those rock pillars there." He pointed at two weathered hoodoos no more than a couple of meters apart. "The path will lead you to the glade where we shall conclude negotiations."

Maia nodded and shot a look at Quinn. He gave her a short jerk with his chin and she took a deep breath before meeting the dryad guard's gaze.

"Very well. Lead on." She gestured to the guards and they waited for her at the pillars.

Here we go. The game has begun.

They set off between the hoodoos and the forest's gloom immediately covered them. The temperature dropped and she stifled a shiver. She'd be glad when she was done with the dryads for good. *Let's just hope the spell of forgetfulness works.*

True to their word, the dryad guards delivered them to a glad just a few meters within their border. The open space sat surrounded by trees on three sides and at the fourth stood a solid granite wall. The sun had risen high enough to drop light onto the grassy floor. It would've been beautiful if not for the shapes standing just out of the light.

All of Maia's sisters stood in their shabby party dresses along one of the wooded sides, their expressions a mixture of anger and confusion. Maia understood their apprehension. She doubted the dryads had bothered to tell them why they were awakened and brought to this place.

The Keeper of the Grove stepped forward wearing robes of mottled greens, colors Maia recognized from new leaves and soft pine needles. She wore a serene and wise expression, but her eyes showed cagey intelligence and avarice.

"Be welcome to our forest once again, Princess Maiasora Silvercloak. Has your journey been a profitable one?" The Keeper gave a wise smile.

Yeah, not fooling me, bitch.

Maia nodded graciously. "It was."

"That is good news. And you've brought the artifact we require?"

"Yes, I have." She felt more than saw Quinn move to cover her back.

"May we see this treasure?" The Keeper barely keep from making grabbing motions with her hands.

"You may." Maia shrugged out of her pack and set it at her feet. "However, before we do this, I must ask to renegotiate the deal."

The Keeper's eyes narrowed, though her smile remained in place. "Renegotiate how?"

"Before I hand over the Key to the Twelve Realms, I must insist that all my sisters of the Silvercloak family be released from their imprisonment."

The Keeper lost her smile. "You ask much, Princess."

Maia shook her head. "No, I ask for commensurate value. This magical artifact is very powerful. Mayhap the most powerful artifact in our world. I think the lives of my whole family are more than compensated for by the return of this item."

The Keeper shifted into the stillness of a wood statue.

"Think of it this way. Once I've returned the Key to you, my family will be gone from your keeping forever and shall never return. You have my word."

"Your word?" The Keeper snorted with disdain. "Why should that mean anything?"

"Because I've done what I said I would. I searched out the Key, I've returned here to your forest, and arrived before the deadline. You have no reason to doubt my word." Maia met the Keeper's gaze without flinching. *Play the part even while lying through my teeth.*

"Very well. Give me the artifact and your sisters shall go free." The Keeper gestured imperiously.

"No, first my sisters come to stand by me and my bodyguard, then I shall hand over the Key. We both know my word is good." She left of saying the Keeper's word was questionable, but suspected the woman understood.

"I will give you the two sisters you were promised in our deal."

"You will release them all. Once you have the Key back, you have no need to keep my family. You've already executed the one member responsible for this theft." Maia kept her gaze on the Keeper, but her sisters reacted to her words with expressions of shock and anger. "The others had no idea what she planned and should not be held responsible for actions done three centuries ago. The Key is here and I will return it for the freedom of myself and them."

Irritation flashed across the Keeper's expression, but Maia waited for her to make her response. She didn't want to use her magic and show her hand just yet, but she would to make sure her family survived.

"You're standing within our forest, Princess. You don't have the power to enforce any demands."

"You have no idea what I'm capable of, Keeper." Maia kept her voice even. "I've been gone for months. It was quite a journey in more ways than one. But I don't wish violence or dissention. I only wish for my family, my bodyguard, and I to go free in exchange for the Key. That's it."

Silence descended over the glade as Maia waited for the Keeper's answer. Her sisters exchanged looks, but said nothing. Maia wished she could fill them in, but until they escaped the forest, she had to play the game close to her chest. Minutes ticked by intense anticipation, only the sound of the wind in the trees marking the time.

At last the Keeper sighed and inclined her head. "Very well, Princess. I'll grant you, your bodyguard, and your sisters their freedom in exchange for the Key."

"And we'll be free to leave your domain and forest?"

"Yes." A tight smile curled the Keeper's lips and Maia didn't believe her for a moment. "As long as you promise never to return to the dryad's forest."

"I promise we'll leave and never return." Maia nodded as well. She switched her gaze to the women waiting beside the silent trunks. "Ladies, if you would please step over here, we can finish this exchange and be on our way."

Maia's sisters blinked a few times, trading looks between them, but Nara and Nora took the lead and marched over to stand behind Maia. The others followed more slowly, her youngest sisters Isabella and Elisabet skittering across the open space like spooked deer.

"Very well. Now the artifact." The Keeper held out her hand.

Moment of truth.

Maia opened the pack at her feet and withdrew the flower garland, hoping it still looked like a diadem. She lifted it out and held it carefully in her hands as if the gold and jewels she'd envisioned were real. *Please, Goddess, let the illusion hold long enough for us to get away.*

She walked the few steps to stand before the Keeper and handed her the spelled diadem. The Keeper's expression filled with avarice as she grasped the 'Key' and Maia released it, stepping back to the protection of her sisters and Quinn.

"The exchange is made. Are we free to go?" Maia swung her pack onto her back and held her breath. Would the Keeper keep her word?

"The exchange is made. You may leave our forest." The Keeper waved her hands in dismissal, her attention on the diadem.

Maia didn't wait to see if the woman put it on her head. "Let's go. Now. Explanations can wait." She shot Nara and Nora quelling looks as the younger women opened their mouths.

She and Quinn herded them up the path toward the hoodoos, hoping to make the edge of the forest before the Keeper changed her mind. Maia shifted into her magical sight and kept an eye on the path. She didn't trust the Keeper to hold to the deal. The hoodoos loomed ahead, but the path suddenly veered to the left of them and Maia paused.

Something's not right.

"What's wrong, Maia? Why are you stopping?" Quinn's whisper brushed her ear.

"They're trying to divert us deeper into the woods. If we get lost, we'll never escape, and we'll lose our memory if she invokes the Key." Maia swallowed hard. She'd forget him, her sisters, her mother, and the dryads would keep the Key after all.

Quinn's expression hardened. "Make a portal. Now. Take us out of here."

She swallowed hard. Could she really do it, use her gift and the Key's magic to take them to safety? *Won't know till you try.* Or die in the attempt. She shook her head. *Not great odds.*

Maia took a deep breath and focused on the magic, coaxing it to form a doorway between the hoodoos. She used them to frame the edges of a portal and give it an anchor in space. Then she pictured the doorway to the sepulcher in the mountain entrance of the Windbreak Keep with its macabre bone décor.

A swirling vortex of green and golden light filled the space between the hoodoos, opening wider and wider like iris in a cat's eye. Through the widening gap the gray and dusty flagstones surrounded with bones could be seen. *Oh sweet glory, I did it.*

"Quinn, lead them through. The Aerys will know you and allow them in. Please."

Quinn shot her a look of incredulity. "I can't leave you, Princess."

"You have to. I can't go through first. I need to keep the portal open, but the Aerys might not recognize my sisters. Please."

Quinn scowled and swallowed hard, but he gave a quick nod and headed for the open vortex. "Ladies, please follow me. We're taking you all to safety."

"And just who are you?" Karissa crossed her arms over her ample breasts and scowled.

"Quinn Tarlen, Princess Maia's bodyguard and the man who's getting you out of here."

"I know no such person—"

"Karissa, please." Sorsia put her hand on her elder sister's arm. "You can trust him. I knew his brother. Let's follow him. It will be all right."

Maia met her younger sister's gaze and gave her a grateful smile. "Thank you, Sorsia."

"See you on the other side, Maia." Sorsia nodded to her and Quinn, then followed him as he strode for the portal.

The others shot looks between Quinn and Maia, but hurried after Karissa and Sorsia. *Oh glory, please hurry.* Holding the portal open took focus and energy, and she'd already begun to tire. In addition, she suspected the dryads wouldn't remain quiescent for long.

"Let's go. I'll follow you." Maia gestured to Nara and Nora, the twins waiting for her.

"When did you become this crazy magic wielder, Maia?" Nara raised an inquisitive eyebrow.

"Yes, do tell." Nora nodded her head, her golden braids still plaited after all these years.

"I'll tell you that story when we're safe." Maia watched Quinn lead the others through the portal. "Come on, we have to keep up. We don't have much time."

She damn near pushed her sisters through the vortex as she paused and looked back. The dryad guards had regrouped and headed her direction, their faces full of surprise and anger. She wanted to flick her chin at them, but instead she gave them a sweet smile, stepped across the threshold of her portal, and closed the energy behind her with a flourish of her hand. The last thing she heard as the energy fizzled into nothingness was a roar of fury from the guards.

CHAPTER TWENTY-THREE

Quinn's gut seized as the last of the princesses came through the portal. *But not Maia.* Where the hell was she? He waited, but when nothing happened, he pushed through the women to get closer to the door. *Where's Maia?*

Panic clawed its way up his throat as he took a deep breath and prepared to step back through the swirling opening. The last thing he wanted was to be trapped just outside the dryads' domain, but he couldn't leave Maia there alone.

Before he could do more than straighten his shoulders, Maia stepped through the portal, shot a sweet smile back at the advancing dryads, and waved the vortex closed. A subtle *pop* sounded somewhere low in his ear canal and the magic swirled away like sparks from a fire. Maia turned with a satisfied smile and a sharp nod.

Relief crashed through Quinn and he jerked her into his embrace, tightening his arms around her. "Thank the Goddess you made it across safely."

She laughed and squeezed him back. "I'm fine, Quinn. And we're safe."

"I was so afraid you'd be stuck there and I couldn't leave you. I was coming back for you." He cupped her face with his hands, meeting her gaze.

"You know if you came back for me and the Keeper invoked the Key, we would've forgotten everything." Maia grimaced. "I didn't specify the spell to only work on dryads. It would've been better for you to wait to come for me."

"Never. I'll always have your back." He pressed his forehead to hers. "I love you, Maia."

She sighed and a smile curled her lips. "I love you, too, Quinn."

Squeals of delight erupted around them and they looked up. He'd completely forgotten their companions in his relief at her safety. Most of Maia's sisters cheered and clapped their joy, though a couple eyed him with reserve and suspicion.

"What's this about, Maia? Who is this man and why are you so familiar with him?" Karissa eyed Quinn with implacable intensity, but he refused to let Maia go.

She turned herself in his arms to rest her back against his chest and laid her hands on his arms around her waist. "A lot has happened since we were imprisoned as lamps, Karissa. I know you have a lot of questions, and I'll be happy to answer them all after you've all had a chance to get some food and take baths."

Many sighs echoed throughout the room and Maia laughed.

"I'm sure you're looking forward to that. The Aerys people are the caretakers here in the Windbreak Keep and they'll show you to your quarters and bring you food. Please treat them with the utmost respect."

"The man, Maia?" Karissa wouldn't budge.

"Quinn Tarlen is my bodyguard and lover. You may treat him with the same courtesy you expect for yourself." Maia lifted her chin. "You may be the eldest of us now, Karissa, but you're still out of your depth here. Go get something to eat and a bath, and I'll explain everything.

Right now, I'm tired and want to revel in my victory."

"This isn't over, Maia." Karissa scowled, but turned for the hallway leading into the keep.

Maia snorted. "Oh, you have no idea."

Her other sisters went with much less fuss, though many of them shot Quinn speculative looks. The last set of twins commented on the creepy bone room and how they could each eat an entire horse, but they went until only Sorsia remained, staring at Quinn with a light frown.

"You're Sean's elder brother, aren't you?" She tilted her head as she studied him.

"Yes. He was the last man to try to decipher where you went each night." The sorrow still stung, but not as sharply as it had before he met Maia. "When you didn't return, your father the King had him executed."

Sorsia's frown deepened. "Executed?"

"Yes, a few days after you went missing."

Maia squeezed him tighter. "I'm sorry, Quinn. I never wished anyone dead."

"Oh, Sean's not dead." Sorsia shot them a secret smile. "Or he wasn't the last time the dryads allowed me to wake."

"What?" Maia gaped. "What do you mean he's not dead?"

"I received a message from Sean through Gretchen." Sorsia withdrew a piece of parchment from the pocket of her tattered dress. "I have it here and kept it secret from the dryads. Gretchen said when the time was right, we'd be reunited. All I had to do was take my place as a Keeper in our home world and we'd have our chance at love."

"Sean's alive?" Quinn gaped, hope and disbelief warring inside his chest. "How? Where?"

Sorsia shook her head. "Gretchen didn't say anything other than I'd learn how to find him when I returned to take my place as the Keeper of the Key. Do you know what that means?"

Maia and Quinn shared a look, before she smiled at Sorsia. "Yes, and I'll tell you all about it later. But at the moment, I'd like to get settled in and eat before I do anything."

"And I imagine you want some intimate time with your bodyguard and lover, yes?" Sorsia winked. To his surprise, Maia blushed and grinned while Sorsia nodded sagely. "Oh, I remember how you were, Maia. Lusty even in your fantasies. I'm glad you found a man upon whom you can bestow that appetite."

"Sorsia!"

Maia's younger sister only laughed as she sauntered out of the sepulcher, leaving Maia blushing in Quinn's arms.

"Lusty appetite?" Quinn squeezed her as she turned around to face him. "You've always been lusty? How did I not know this?"

"Oh, stop. You knew it the moment you got me into bed." Her blush faded away as her smile morphed into a smirk. "But if you're so surprised, I can take you into our suite and enlighten you." She reached between them to run her palm over his groin. His cock rose with enthusiasm.

He rocked his hips against her hand. "I am yours to command, Keeper. And I live to serve."

"Okay, I'm not buying that, but I'm interested in some specific services only you can provide." She drew him down the corridor toward the suite they'd shared when they first arrived at the Windbreak Keep.

"Oh?" He followed her, his heart filling with laughter. His brother was alive and his lover wanted him to pleasure her. "Which ones?"

She pushed open the door to their suite with a coy look over her shoulder. "Lip service and then a nice ride."

Quinn laughed as his cock stood up to salute. "I'm yours to command, princess." He caught her around the waist as he kicked the door shut behind him. "I love you,

Maia."

She grinned and kissed him. "I love you, too. Now, help me take care of my lusty appetites."

He growled and grinned. "With pleasure."

THE END

TAKE THE REINS
RIFTS, BOOK 1
SNEEK PEEK

Social change is normal for a senator's daughter, but affecting gender politics in centaurs wasn't on Bethany's agenda.

All Bethany Stanton needed was time away to think. She never imagined a walk with her horse might lead her so far from home. When she steps through a rift between worlds at an old archaeological site, she realizes she has bigger problems than marriage to the man of her nightmares. Like a herd of centaurs with distressing views on gender equality and "mythical" humans.

As part of the Supernatural Anomalies Investigative Field Unit, Major Stephen "Mack" McMacken has seen and done more weird stuff than written in a science fiction novel. When called in to track down a U.S. Senator's missing daughter, Mack figures it's more a case of runaway rich girl than supernatural mystery. Until his team finds the portal and he's nearly torched by a dying phoenix.

In a world ruled by mythical beasts, Mack and Bethany find themselves on trial for endangering the centaur village. With the only escape route they know gone, working together to establish their innocence might prove easier than avoiding seductive Sirens and ravenous native beasts.

And then there's the not-so-simple matter of finding a way back home…

ORDER OF THE DRAGON
WARBLER PENINSULA, BOOK 1
SNEEK PEEK

Drake MacGregor always adhered to the adage 'let sleeping dragons lie', until he slept with one.

In an effort to make up for his past as Vlad the Impaler, Drake has been living a small, quiet life in Three Lakes. As the town's archivist, his knowledge of history and his place in it weigh on him. Drake has one desire—to rectify the atrocities committed in the name of his knightly order. Too bad he can't keep his hands, or his fangs, off the local doctor, especially when he discovers she's an actual dragon.

Aliandra Cantora del Viento is old enough and wise enough to ignore her attraction to the handsome historian, especially when her heart suggests he might be something more than he appears. Drake stokes her fires and curls her tail, and after a hot night in her clinic, the game is on. But he avoids her and nothing she tries breaks through his reserve, despite his obvious interest. He turns her on then apologizes for it, repeatedly. Not exactly the kind of relationship she'd hoped for yet she can't walk away.

When a mysterious researcher arrives with his son, Drake becomes more edgy and irritable, and Aliandra must decide if she's willing to fight for him. Especially when he might be her True Mate.

OTHER BOOKS BY SIOBHAN MUIR

Her Devoted Vampire (from Three Lakes Books)
Queen Bitch of the Callowwood Pack (from Siren Publishing)
Not a Dragon's Standard Virgin (from Siren Publishing)
Second Chance Succubus (from Three Lakes Books)
Darwin's Evolution (from Amazon)

Cloudburst Colorado Series
A Hell Hound's Fire (from Three Lakes Books)
The Beltane Witch (from Three Lakes Books)
Christmas I.C.E. Magic (from Three Lakes Books)
Cloudburst Ice Magic (from Three Lakes Books)

Rifts Series
Take the Reins (from Three Lakes Books)
A Centaur's Solstice Wish (from Three Lakes Books)
In Death's Shadow (from Three Lakes Books)

Bad Boys of Beta Squad Series
Bronco's Rough Ride (from Three Lakes Books)
The Navy's Ghost (from Three Lakes Books)
Rimshot's Hard Target (from Amazon)
Bam-Bam's Inked Hart (from Three Lakes Books)

The Ivory Road
A Walk in the Sand (from Three Lakes Books)
Outback Dreams (from Three Lakes Books)

Triple Star Ranch Series
Rope a Falling Star (from Three Lakes Books
Star Light, Star Bright (from Three Lakes Books)

Warbler Peninsula Series
Order of the Dragon (from Three Lakes Books)
The Valkyrie's Sword (from Three Lakes Books)

Coming Soon
Deli's Take Out (Bad Boys of Beta Squad #4)
Wildfire's Heart (Elemental Hearts #1)
Loch'd Hearts (Elemental Hearts #2)

ABOUT THE AUTHOR

Siobhan Muir lives in Cheyenne, Wyoming, with her husband, two daughters, and a vegetarian cat she swears is a shape-shifter, though he's never shifted when she can see him. When not writing, she can be found looking down a microscope at fossil fox teeth, pursuing her other love, paleontology. An avid reader of science fiction/fantasy, her husband gave her a paranormal romance for Christmas one year, and she was hooked for good.

In previous lives, Siobhan has been an actor at the Colorado Renaissance Festival, a field geologist in the Aleutian Islands, and restored inter-planetary imagery at the USGS. She's hiked to the top of Mount St. Helens and to the bottom of Meteor Crater.

Siobhan writes kick-ass adventure with hot sex for men and women to enjoy. She believes in happily ever after, redemption, and communication, all of which you will find in her paranormal romance stories.

Connect with Siobhan online at:

http://siobhanmuir.com

http://www.facebook.com/siobhan.muir.35

http://twitter.com/SiobhanMuir

http://siobhanmuir.com/siobhans-blog

http://pinterest.com/siobhanmuir.35